R[illegible]EAD

TH[illegible]AN'S

GL[illegible]OST

[illegible]NYTHING BUT

DIANA

CW01650240

A DIKHED CREATION IX III

Londinium Press
Limited

RICHARD HEAD

THE WORKING MAN'S GUIDE TO ALMOST ANYTHING BUT

DIANA

"British is Best" you may all scream, but I am not quite so sure. Personally, I think that this over exposure of royal breasts is starting to cheapen them to such an extent that very soon they will be worth nothing at all - and then where will these big breasted royals be? I could be entirely wrong because what do I know about the real value of big royal breasts anyway?

Truth is only believable when one lies for conviction.

All this unforeseen panic at Buck House has been caused by your one and only - Dick Head, the world famous author. This again proves that all our well laid plans of total take-over are starting to work perfectly according to Plan B. Plan A was just a diversionary tactic that the Labour Party fell for hook, line and sinker, and still believes to be true. Maybe they know something that I don't know about the author and what his real motives are. An even worse scenario is that maybe they don't even read my books, or possibly they're just....................

THE WORKING MAN'S GUIDE TO ALMOST ANYTHING BUT

DIANA

First published in 1993 in Great Britain
by Londinium Press Limited, Rochester.

Copyright © Richard Head 1993
All rights reserved

The right of Richard Head to be identified as the author
of this work has been asserted by him in accordance with
the Copyright, Designs and Patents Act 1988.

Cover design by Tony Waterhouse,
Waterhouse Graphic Design and Visual Communications, Warwick

Printed in Great Britain by
Staples Printers Rochester Limited, Rochester.

British Library Cataloguing Data
Head, Richard
The Working Man's Guide To Almost Anything But Diana
I. Title
823 [F]
ISBN 0-906264-12-x

All rights reserved
No part of this publication may be reproduced, stored in a retrieval system
transmitted, in any form, or by any means,
electronic, mechanical, photocopying, recording or
otherwise, without the prior permission of the publisher

**All quotations used throughout this publication
(excluding those in chapter one by Confucius) have been created
by Richard Head and are therefore subject to
Copyright restrictions**

**Londinium Press Limited, P.O. Box 102,
Rochester, Kent, ME1 1NS**

THE WORKING MAN'S GUIDE TO ALMOST ANYTHING BUT
DIANA

Publisher's Note

The Working Man's Guide To Almost Anything But Diana is the second book in the 61 Working Man's Guide series. It is a work of inspiration - Richard Head is as expected, outrageous, funny and occasionally sad.

The narrative is fiction and no reference is intended to anyone, living or dead, except for those historical figures, past, present or future, who are addressed solely to project the Author's views.

Our New Generation

This book is dedicated to a young man by the name of Jack Edward Henry Bennett who recently joined us in this world and is soon to be a member of the Manchester United Army.

Up the Reds!

INDEX OF CONTENTS

Chapter 1 From Luckygate to The Royal Bugger 1
(What it's NOT all about?)

Chapter 2 Hello again Freedom fighters 13

Chapter 3 From Experts to Wenches 33

Chapter 4 From KYXZANTYN to Charity 51

Chapter 5 From Roads to DIK 1 83

Chapter 6 From Harpoons to Chat Lines 111

Chapter 7 From Getting Stuffed to A False Dawn.............155

Chapter 8 From Wally Bean to Very 'umble.....................175

Chapter 9 From Respect & Dignity to Up Me Bum! 195

Chapter 10 From Carnivores to Larry...............................231

Chapter 11 From big TITS to My Best Chinese Joss...........257

Chapter 12 From Waste Not to Want Not..........................277

Chapter 13 From Eternity to Diana Head 305

Chapter 14 Further Quotations from The Masters 321

Chapter 15 DikHed Masters Exam 337

Chapter 1

From Luckygate to The Royal Bugger (What it's NOT all about!)

How could one ever possibly serve one's prince alongside of such low-down creatures? Before they have got office, they think about nothing but how to get it; and when they have got it, all they care about is to avoid losing it. And so soon as they see themselves in the slightest danger of losing it, there is no length to which they will not go.

Confucius

On the first Sunday of each month, I always purchase my regular supply of toilet paper for ninety-nine pence per ten rolls from *Barney Birtwhistle's Stolen Goods* stall at Petticoat Lane Market in London. Barney also sells a wide range of Diana and Charles blow-up dolls and a wide range of stolen rubber goods. The Charles blow-up doll is supplied with a set of twenty different self-adhesive stick-on smiles and a plastic crown.

Due to the recent lack of public demand, Barney has been forced into rapidly reducing the price of the Diana dolls from the original price of fifteen pounds each to the bargain basement price of three for a pound. He tells me that he is expecting a new stock of the much larger Camilla dolls, complete with blow-up horses, next week and must clear the Diana ones before these arrive.

Because of the zero demand for the Charles dolls, he is giving one away free with every ten rolls of toilet paper purchased.

Each of these cheapo toilet rolls contains approximately one hundred sheets of tissue, thus giving you ten sheets of tissue for less than one penny. This seemingly irrelevant calculation illustrates that I am not a waster of the earth's resources and that my housekeeping budget is of great importance to me. Such controlled frugality gives me an extreme feeling of value for money when I am buying and using such disposable items.

It was not until the following morn after this month's purchase, that disaster struck in an unusual form. This was just before partaking of my usual breakfast of Kellogg's Bran Flakes and a really hot cup of Earl Grey tea. I had retired to read the Sunday Times in the tranquil environment of my fully tiled bathroom when this disaster erupted.

As a man having an eagle eye, I saw immediately that there was no toilet paper left in the toilet roll holder, so I delayed my reading pleasure temporarily whilst obtaining a replenishment roll. After unwrapping the wrapper, I was completely dumb-struck and fell back onto the lavatory seat in shock and horror. The toilet paper had been printed with the complete transcript of the Squidgy Tapes in bright pink ink!

Even this final bastion of male privacy in my bathroom had been invaded by the endless marketing of Princess Diana and the associated scandals. This became the final straw that finally broke this camel's back and something had to be done to protect the health and sanity of a complete generation.

My God! I'm unable to stomach any more media brainwashing associated with the so-called goodness and innocence of Princess Diana, that troublesome girl of arguably limited intelligence, whose calculated actions according to many, are in danger of destroying our monarchy. How can one single person even scratch the surface of a monarchy which has been responsible for so much good over the past centuries? Are we as a nation really that mentally deficient and short-sighted? If only Charles had learnt the lessons handed down by Henry VIII that you can screw around as much as you like but make sure that you chop off the wife's head off first. He still has plenty of time to rectify this error.

For those of you not yet introduced to the ***Working Man's Guide series of educational books***, I must explain that this series has been written explicitly to guide the working man to a better way of life. This is achieved by fighting against the everlasting Authority. Authority comes in various guises and we uncover them one by one, thus allowing all DikHed Graduates to succeed in life with a feeling of total satisfaction.

Following the huge success of ***The Working***

Man's Guide To The Galaxy, I had intended to entitle this book Pilgrims Progress Personified - until, that is, I read the pink Squidgy Story on my toilet paper and realised that the world had gone Diana mad.

Get the people to come through the door of the shop and the job of selling the goods is then made easy - this ploy is the standard policy of the modern day marketing men. Therefore, by using the same successful marketing methods, we decided to give this book a topical, albeit misleading, front cover to get you into the shop. However, this is definitely your luckyday, because instead of reading another book full of royal garbage, you are now being treated to the words of a literary master that will improve your quality of life forever.

You can thank me later, probably by the time Diana is working at MacDonald's and I'm a Knight of the Realm. Life can be so cruel in the shortest of possible time spans.

I have personally taken an oath not to watch any further television reports, read any more press garbage or hear any future radio reports about Princess Diana during breakfast, lunch, tea and supper, or at any other time during any day or night for the remainder of my living days - Amen. This is of course unless she's talking about me.

I suspect that there are millions of my fellow citizens out there having equal feelings of that awful debilitating disease ***Dianarrhoea***. I dedicate this latest blockbuster to you all, hoping that it allows you to forget for a few hours this weird Princess Diana plot that is being forced down our throats by the world's media.

This book is therefore concerned with discussing anything but Princess Diana and as from this moment her name will not be mentioned within these pages ever again. However, as I am renowned as being probably the fairest and most objective author on the world stage today, it is unfortunately necessary for me to refer occasionally to this fair royal lady of fame to make sure that all antagonisms are made known to all and sundry. How can this be achieved without saying her name?

After carrying out a referendum amongst my many jolly drinking friends at the Charlie was my Darling pub in Windsor to select a new name, we concluded that the new nickname for our princess of tape-recording fame would be ***Lucky***. This unusual name of Lucky was chosen by a majority of sixty-three, with only two voting against. The names chosen by the two drunks against were ***Lucky-Lucky*** and ***Lucky-Lucky-Lucky***, but anybody in the know would see that these other choices would be totally inappropriate for a lady of royalty.

For those ignorant and deprived people not in the know, all will be explained as we go along.

Despite my own feelings regarding the media, this book is not to be considered as an anti-Lucky publication because it is quite to the contrary. Not wishing to mention somebody in a book by name should simply be considered as the author taking a neutral stance only. Nothing more and nothing less should be construed from this. If I was an **anti-Lucky** author, I could have made horrible accusations relating to family values, the children come first, unfaithful wives, unfaithful husbands and so much more awful information that would do damage to the monarchy.

I have always been highly respected by the world's press, often being described as Dick Head the fairest author in the world; and you cannot be much fairer than that. Despite the satisfaction of receiving such high accolades from one's peers, one must constantly remain wary of attack from the unexpected. It is so easy to offend even the most strong hearted person once they start to believe that they are being personally criticised and their public image is in danger. This is particularly true when such criticism is coming from a real Dick Head.

To avoid any possible offence, I took the sensible precaution of sending a copy of my original manuscript of this book to Buckingham Palace, marked for the attention of *Her Royal Highness Lucky,* with the following letter:

Dear Royal Highness Lucky,

As it is on record that you are not deaf, blind or mute, it may have come to your notice that the world is totally infatuated with you and you are now the most photographed and recorded person in the world.

Your ability to pose for every camera angle is legendary and we are pleased that you do not charge for the privilege as we hear is the case with one of your close royal relations.

During a recent opinion poll, it was found that 21% of the population are sick to death of seeing and hearing about you during every moment of their rotten lives. The other 79% believe that you are a goddess from above and they just can't get enough of you. I am confident that if this majority waits just a few more months, or visits any good quality bookshop, then these shortcomings will be quickly rectified.

Despite being persistent at the palace gates, I could not interview His Royal Highness Prince Charles and are still awaiting a reply to my questionnaire, sent to him by Federal Express last week. I will willingly send you a copy of his reply together with any photographs or tapes he chooses to enclose with the completed questionnaire to prove his points.

I feel no animosity towards you Lucky, but do admit having considerable sympathy towards the 79% Lucky supporters that mistakenly believe in you. I must confirm that this book is specifically written for those other twelve million people (increasing by 23,987 per day) that are fed up to the back teeth with Lucky and all that you stand for.

Lucky, as an ex-future Queen of England, I am

requesting that you give me your comments regarding this book before its publication so that I can have your approval or otherwise. Such a quotation given direct from Lucky will be printed boldly on the front cover, thus guaranteeing the success of this literary masterpiece whilst increasing my royalties (excuse the pun) by a huge amount at the same time.

I can offer you a few suggestions for your royal comments on this book such as:

"Lucky is a Dick Head supporter!"

"Dick Head can phone Lucky at any time!"

"Don't call me Lucky, call me Lucky-Lucky!"

"Don't call me Lucky, call me Lucky-Lucky-Lucky!"

"I would like to be Mrs Diana Head!"

Please don't be shy to say whatever you feel is appropriate in your reply because even a rude and aggressive reply from Lucky is better than no reply at all.

You can visit me personally, if you wish to inform me of some dishy scandal not already printed in the media or in book form. You may wish to leak such visit times to the press well in advance so that maximum media coverage (ie: lots of photographs showing Lucky smiling in quaint ways) is guaranteed; but you probably know about this scheme already.

My mobile phone number is 00654 987654, should you prefer to call me direct, but I should point out that there is a danger of being overheard and having our conversations recorded. Lucky, I promise never to divulge such personal conversations or correspondence; even for millions and millions of pounds, or even at the threat of being beheaded, because I have just too much old fashioned honour within me for such underhand actions.

You can trust me. Your humble servant,

Richard Head Ph.D. (DikHed)

I received a reply from the palace three days later which simply said:

Dear Dick Head,

Her Royal Highness Lucky has gone away and we are not sure if she will be coming back another day.

Palace Doctor

I received no completed questionnaire from Prince Charles, or even any anonymous tapes. Life can become so difficult. There is nothing so dangerous as a Dick Head spurned.

I visited Highgrove, where I heard on good authority that Lucky was staying. I drove up to the main gate that was made from wrought iron and had a sign simply saying:

LuckyGate

Dick Head, Charles & Camilla

KEEP OUT!

I immediately went out and purchased an American QUESTECH telephone complete with voice change buttons. This black beast had a label on the base saying:

TRANSITION 2000TM, Digital Voice Changing Telephone, This equipment complies with Part 68 of FCC Rules, FCC Registration No. ISZHGK-18697-TE-E, (REN) 1.0, DATE MANUFACTURED: 5 April 1992, PASSED QC: 5A, Japanese high quality components.

In addition, there was another cheaper British label having a large red diamond printed across it with the wording of:

PROHIBITED from direct or indirect connection to any telecommunications system run by British Telecommunications. Action may be taken against anyone so connecting this apparatus.

For British Telecom's information, they can stop affixing such a restrictive label, because this telephone operates just as well for me in the UK as it does for everybody else in the world who is not prohibited from using it. No action has yet been taken against me for using this advanced instrument, but no doubt this is to be rectified as soon as one of British Telecom's executives read this book.

As a matter of interest, the voice change facility on this telephone is really fantastic and I have buttons pre-set for imitating each member of the Royal Family. They all sound very miserable and very authentic.

I deliberated for many weeks on how I could get Lucky to respond to my questions, but each new idea led up a blind alley and hence to nowhere. Then one Sunday night, I dreamt of the perfect answer to this quandary. My dream started with a picture of me depressing the right - Charlie - button on my special telephone before proceeding to call Highgrove with intent to succeed where I had previously failed. I can now give you the transcript of this DikDi tape-recorded conversation that seemed so real to me at the time:

Charlie: "Hello, Put me through to Lucky immediately."

Lucky: "Oh God! Not you again; what do you want this time?"

Charlie: "I've received an embarrassing questionnaire from a man named Dick Head. He's asking me all sorts of awkward questions about you and Camilla."

Lucky: "You fool, I hope you haven't answered these questions!"

Charlie: "Not yet, but I thought it would be a good idea to put my side of the story as I'm fed up hearing your fairy stories and tape recorded messages."

Lucky: "There is only one side of the story - and it's mine! If you say anything different then I'll leak more information about your father!"

Charlie: "Dear God! Lucky, what do you know about my father?"

Lucky: "That's for me to know and for you to find out. Now go away and stop bothering me! I need my beauty sleep for the cameras tomorrow."

Charlie: "If you want to be queen then you had better change your ways and be nicer to me!"

Lucky: "Sod off! By the way, I know who the royal bugger is."

Charlie: "My God, who's the royal bugger?"

Lucky: "We have two royal buggers; **KIWI** the Queen's shoe polisher and another person that remains my secret."

Charlie: "You don't mean! You can't mean! Surely not.........."

Women and people of low birth are very hard to deal with. If you are friendly with them, they get out of hand, and if you keep your distance, they resent it.

Confucius

So, my friends, now that we have put Lucky behind us conclusively, let's proceed with our learnings and enter the new world order of fairness for the working class man.

By the way, you're probably wondering what I did with the Charles blow-up doll that was given to me by Barney free of charge with the ten rolls of toilet paper that I bought from him last Sunday.

I'm saving it up for when he's made king.

The only thing I really wonder about is who is the second Royal Bugger?

Chapter 2

Hello Again Freedom Fighters

Who tells me the truth?
Who tells me the lie?
How can I choose which to go by?
Maybe the truth is from a lying man
Or the truth told from a truthful man
So which is the liar?
Who tells me the truth?
Give me this simple answer
Then I can easily decide

Kondo Popotolous (1743)

Hello again to all of my friends, including The Three Musketeers, David and Jonathan, Ruth and Naomi, Castor and Pollux, misanthropists, misogynists, Francophobes, bete-noires, Olympians and silver spoon suckers. I am, of course, including the 5,987 Royals who all think that I'm wonderful and an inspiration to the World at large.

These Royals include 5,767 divorced, 118 separated (including *Lucky*) and the three still married, but gossip has it that even this is soon to change. Please do not quote me on this. I don't normally agree with the mixed up and confused thinking from our Royalty, but on this special occasion at the very beginning of a new book, I am prepared to make an exception to this rule.

Such sincere royal patronage makes me look even more accomplished, efficacious, triumphal and foolproof to the jolly folk from Windsor where the cash flows in and never flows out. Some may consider this book nothing less than a stroke of genius, tour de force, Pyrrhic victory or just another winner from the Working Man's Guide series.

Whatever your accolades may be, you are no doubt absolutely correct in your judgement and assessment. This book of learning has been written as the second in my sixty-one book series intended to re-educate the working man, thus releasing him from impediments affixed to him as he arrived from the womb. The working class demimonde woman is barred and not included within our future plans for the take-over of this great land of ours, but more about this female exclusion charter later on, long after these bits of fluff have recovered from their anger and sulking spells.

We shall definitely have our own Sex Discrimination Act once we take over power. The troublesome female species complain about everything in life that doesn't give them satisfaction and anything that confirms their inferiority. I must ask why they bear with their descriptions in any thesaurus as women's libber, bra burner, wench, nymph, skirt, bint, crumpet, hussy, shrew or pain in the backside. Just ask your wife or girlfriend if they agree with these words as a fair description of themselves and other members of the inferior sex.

After a few hours arguing and sulking, they will eventually, come up with the usual female argument that all thesauruses are written by men and this is why descriptions are so biased and debased towards women. This female interpretation and distortion of the truth cannot be allowed to stand because if a man had written the thesauruses, the descriptions would have been far more colourful and would have included the commonly used descriptions of miserable bitch, right miserable bitch, and sulky bitch.

I am pleased to confirm that any supporters of loyal royal ilk who prefer posing semi-nude with rich bald headed advisers are invited to join The Royal Dick Head Fan Club, and are positively welcomed with open arms. However, I do request that they take urgent slimming lessons to dispose of that hideous Caucasian white flab that looks so disgusting when seen adorned across the front pages of the world's scandal magazines in full frosty colour.

Mobile phones are banned in the Royal Enclosure and in all the bars and bedrooms at the Mayfair branch of ***The Royal Dick Head Fan Club*** to avoid any additional scandal. Such scandal could be very dangerous to my prestige at the forefront of the literary world and lead to my royalty income from this book being reduced. Such scandal could be responsible for having my book pushed off the number one spot in the International Book Charts by a new book called Dick Head - His True Story.

Imagine the terrible pain of seeing your name being used without your consent, whilst at the same time somebody else is coining in all the dosh! I wonder how Lucky feels?

All oversized glamourless Royals should immediately request a copy of my book SlimDiks if they wish to adopt a rigid diet that guarantees to reduce their body weight by over ten kilos per week. The instant loss of so much horrible fat tissue will make them into royal women of great desire, on a par with Queen Baldilocks the Younger of The Fatura Islands who also has huge highly polished brass pins stuck up her nose.

I developed this revolutionary weight reduction process during my restricted spare time in 1989, that is why I am often referred to as DikDok the Dietician of Rochester. This rapid weight reduction system is presently considered as unorthodox by the orthodox medical profession. I have the greatest respect for these professionals but often doubt their sincerity. All things eventually change to a point when even the unorthodox becomes the orthodox.

Most GPs have been prescribing powerful pain killers to all Royals who have actively followed my Dikdok diet plan; a plan that unfortunately leads to some painful moments before one can achieve maximum weight loss. The pain is reported to be at its severest when one is chewing tough food morsels such as English pork chops or hard American candy.

There will be much more about this revolutionary method of flab reduction in my new publication, DikDok Weight Loss Techniques, which also contains my normal level of unbeatable humour to make the process funny, albeit very painful, during the digestive process.

Blowing one's own trumpet is better than being on the fiddle, but being on the fiddle is better than being poor and hungry. This dramatic statement has nothing to do with this book but illustrates at the start of this new blockbuster just what a literary genius I have become and that my standards never drop below perfection.

Conceit is an art form, perfected by Richard Head.

My first book, *The Working Man's Guide To The Galaxy*, has already sold fewer than three hundred million copies world-wide and has been printed in three hundred different languages and dialects, including just fifty copies printed in the Byutsi dialect for the surviving members of the Wanka Banka tribe in Africa.

Our North American edition has been edited to include a few more sex scenes and has some of the swear words substituted. Somehow I find that this American edition, with its diabolical word substitutions and added sexual flavour, somewhat vulgar, thereby lowering the quality of my prose. Did Shakespeare have his publisher pressurise him to change his words into "To screw or not to screw, that is the question"? No, he definitely did not, and yet he still became as famous as Dick Head.

This lowering of literary standards reflects the general erosion of standards in today's rotting world. Obviously I complained bitterly about these enforced changes before publication of this book in New York, but I was told clearly to "sod off!" I did.

American vulgarism apart, I am pleased to report that we have a complete and well educated regiment of B.Sc. (DikHed) graduate infantrymen now in place around the world, ready to spearhead our imminent twentieth century cultural revolution. This will eventually release mankind from the grips of an Authority that has held us all in a vice grip for as long as the squad can remember.

Hello, hello, hello! I say with genuine gratitude to our wonderful and ever increasing band of successful Dick Head graduates. Yes, I am referring to you, the clever clogs whom one can describe as intelligent, brainy, brilliant, astute, and generally being real clever dicks. This is just part of what you can achieve and you are already shining examples of what can be done after the initial first stage training that is so clearly outlined in The Working Man's Guide To The Galaxy. This first blockbusting training publication is now known to have badly upset the Authoritarians and Whatos in our midst, who are all now lumbered with very dodgy applecarts and have developed equally fragile strengths of character to boot.

Such future outcasts living within our new world order include the outdated ruling Lords, those people of privilege now running scared as nervous rabbits in Chichester. John Major has almost certainly read The Working Man's Guide To The Galaxy because he is now a DikHed convert. He recently announced his wish to abolish all automatic Honours and replace them with Honours for people who earn them. Who has earned a knighthood more than I have?

My recognition is now guaranteed, providing all of my readers write in to 10 Downing Street requesting the special form that must be filled in and returned, requesting that I be knighted in this year's Honours List. Please return this quickly, because my publishers must change the typesetting on the front cover of my next book to that of Sir Richard Head before the print deadline hits us.

Imagine buying a book with the name of the author shown as a mere commoner, when it should have been that of a privileged knight. Because of the extra three letters of "Sir" on the print line of the front cover, it may be necessary to change my name to Sir Dick Head to maintain the same impact and type size as before. I have refrained from using the common name of Dick Head in earlier publications for obvious reasons, but with the new look of Sir Dick Head I believe that this change of name is now fully acceptable to my reading public and does not offer any offence.

Our current and outdated snobbish group of inherited elitism is now rapidly erecting large walls (with broken beer bottles embedded into the tops) around their grand properties in Kensington and Knightsbridge, believing that such pathetic actions will secure for them a future as rich and rewarding as their affluent pasts. All good things must come to an end and how the mighty will fall - so will the walls.

Only imported beer bottles with "By Appointment to HMS..." labels on the side are to be used for inclusion within such wall construction. Guinness and cheapo brown ale bottles (from Pudsey Brewery) cannot be used as they are only suitable for petrol bombing in Brixton or queer bashing in Barnet. Bottles from Wankairre's Brewery in Boston are also definitely a no-no, no-go product for use on the self-defence wall construction at the Whatos ranch.

American culture has been a long time coming but its arrival is soon to be announced by Mickey Mouse on CTN in Cambodia after the corn flakes advert.

The momentum of our people's revolution shall be endless, and the taking over of society from these rich underlings is but a small part of our in-depth conversion technique that has now spread into the very core of the monarchy itself. A full regiment of battle tanks with loaded guns and armed American made cruise missiles have been recently reported within the grounds of Buckingham Palace itself.

It is claimed by the popular tabloid press that these armaments are purely to protect the Queen and all of her money, which (as a press leak from a princess has it), is more than just a few pence. This sum has recently been drastically reduced by various family settlements and the Queen paying income tax over the current tax period. Do we really believe that she will actually pay income tax based upon her true wealth? How easily the people can be fooled all the time.

I can visualise a huge sign suspended permanently across the front door at the palace quoting those now famous Royal Words, hand painted in huge orange lettering of:

This is a Royal door Dick Head
Bloody Keep Out!
By Royal Command

Very rude these royal people, but we shouldn't complain about such awful language because they are now allowed to say anything they wish within our new fairer society.

A huge amount of royal wealth has been accumulated over the centuries at the expense of the people, and this wealth is kept securely locked inside a huge pink coloured plastic piggy-bank. This piggy-bank is located within the palace cellar, next to the Chateau de Vinci 1945 vino bottles and the torture chamber.

This gigantic pink structure, made in Hong Kong by the Pink Plastic Piggy Bank Co, instantly reminds one of jolly old Prince Philip during a good day at the races. If this resemblance to the Prince on a good day at the races is to be believed, and I can confirm that this information is the truth and nothing but the truth so help me Lucky, he must have modelled for this piggy bank on the 3 September 1954 at about 3.37 p.m.. It was at this time when a Prince Philip smile was actually witnessed and recorded in The Palace Press under the headline It actually happened! This has not been repeated since, but I believe that such small criticism should not be taken as irrefutable proof that our Prince Philip is a real miserable conceited fellow of alien descent.

It was after all a horrible annus last year, or so the Queen tells me in my dreams - and I can tell you that she likes me very much and enjoys my novels. I assumed that such Latin spoken comments referred to her husband, but I cannot vouch for this, because I have not yet been invited to tea to witness for myself the prince's charm in full regal flow. However, I will be invited to the palace one day - when you, the people, demand it.

I wonder if she will call me Richard, Dick, or by some other more graphical name? Never let the unknown future worry you.

The royal press secretary insists (through a mouthful of low calorie plum juice, with added vitamin C, bought at Sainsbury's) that this mobilisation of the royal troops had taken place as a natural military precaution. This was to keep all young princesses of a troublesome nature away from those bloody journalists and publishers who are looking for even bigger royal breasts and another scandal.

I recently saw a woman in Hyde Park, running in small circles and wearing a golden crown, with *By Appointment to HMS Prince.... and anybody else* tattooed across the front of her chest. She was crying and looked at me very angrily indeed as I told her what a real nutter she looked. Please be satisfied that more royal breasts can be seen published across the world's press than ever before in the history of royal breasts, but not all of them British.

"British is Best" you may all scream, but I am not quite so sure. Personally, I think that this over exposure of royal breasts is starting to cheapen them to such an extent that very soon they will be worth nothing at all - and then where will these big breasted royals be? I could be entirely wrong because what do I know about the real value of big royal breasts anyway?

Truth is only believable when one lies for conviction.

All this unforeseen panic at Buck House has been caused by your one and only - Dick Head, the world famous author. This again proves that all our well laid plans of total take-over are starting to work perfectly according to Plan B. Plan A was just a diversionary tactic that the Labour Party fell for hook, line and sinker, and still believes to be true. Maybe they know something that I don't know about the author and what his real motives are. An even worse scenario is that maybe they don't even read my books, or possibly they're just plain thick as Scottish planks.

Please send me your opinions on this matter for inclusion into my book number 51, to be entitled Labouring Points Made Easy. To date, exactly 3,786,087 B.Sc. (DikHed) PASS certificates have been issued following the 20 Questions exam set in The Working Man's Guide To The Galaxy. Only 765 students managed to fail this most complicated of exams, which shows everybody what a great teacher I really am.

I am good at just about everything that I turn my hand to, but I must now admit my one failure in life. I find it impossible to eat cucumber, no matter how finely it is chopped up, or how hard I try.

The most abysmal exam failure received at the checking office to date, is the one sent in by a middle aged thug who was christened Fred Albert Jordan. He is a most vicious fellow who for the next thirty years will be an inmate at Wormwood Scrubs Victorian prison in London. Such a long penal sentence was handed down upon Psycho Freddy by a seventy-nine years old bald-headed deaf judge from Epping for the terrible crime of shooting down two unarmed bank tellers during a bank raid in Wapping last year.

Freddy shot them down in cold blood before they had time to tell him the safe combination numbers. These poor innocent victims were stammering out the numbers when Freddy became impatient at their babbling, lost his temper and blew their brains out with a double barrelled shotgun. When Freddy was asked why he shot them down in such a callous way, he replied to the judge, "Day wers taking de piss out off me, 'cos they must haf knows I cants count."

Freddy, of obvious chronic mental imbalance, began failing his 20 Questions exam at the very beginning of the exam paper. On question 1, which asked "Would you buy a BigDik from McDikalds?", he answered, "Are you taking the piss out of me, 'cos mine's bleedin' big enuff as it tis!"

Exam failure was finally guaranteed after he followed up this aggressive attitude to question 1 by answering question 13, "Is a bent copper worth anything?" by answering: "Yes, he's bleedin' worf a good kick in the bleedin head!"

My God, if I had my way, he would be strung up by his neck until he was very dead for the safety of mankind. A few days after issuing the FAILURE certificate to aggressive Freddy, he wrote back to me, using prison toilet paper and thick awful smelling brown ink, saying that on 3 June 2222 AD he would be 103 years old and released from prison. He went on to promise sincerely that once released, I would be his first priority and he guaranteed to slash my testicles off with a hacksaw and feed them to me for failing him in the exam.

Little does he know that there are now 267 Dick Head graduates serving time in the "Scrubs". In justifiable self defence, I recently placed a contract out on Freddy with the Wilky Gang to have his arms amputated in the bacon slicing machine and his kneecaps permanently smashed with a very large non-sterilised hammer. I sent the Wilky gang honorary M.Sc. (DikHed) degree certificates in payment for this service and that made them all feel very superior.

WARNING TO ALL PROSPECTIVE EMPLOYERS

Check back with me if you have any job applications from Buster, Wally or Jacko Wilky living at 15 Prestonian Road, Hounslow. Don't employ them!

Remember folks, when you wish to play with fire, don't muck around with Dick Head in the process because great danger is around the corner. Congratulations to Willie Heinbrekken, of Goebels-Noeballs Strasse in Munchen, who obtained a pass mark of 101% after submitting 11,569 pages of answers written in five different languages including Icelandic.

According to the rules, only the English version was marked and after all the answers were found to be perfect, he received maximum marks plus a special German perfekten bonus. To complete the exam paper in the allotted time of ten DikHours, Willie must have written at the amazing speed of 1,569 pages per hour; that is quite an achievement for an ex war veteran with no hands and a permanent twitch in both of his deformed arms.

Notwithstanding any serious doubts that could

have entered the minds of less trusting examiners, Willie also declared that he had written all of his answers using an adapted IBM electric typewriter that he operated with his teeth and nose at 150 words per minute. He also claimed that it made him very dizzy but he felt it was worth the pain - no pain, no gain, again?

Apparently, Willie also plays lead trombone in the Muchen Orkestra Filamonik, but I am afraid to ask him exactly how he achieves this amazing feat, but the mind boggles at the thought. When I flew to Germany last year to personally present him with the Degree Perfekten certificate, Willie gave me the Nazi salute and shouted out "Heil Hitler" and then burst into tears, which sadly he could not wipe away without assistance.

No matter how hard I tried, and nobody can try harder than Dick Head, Willie refused to believe my assertion that I was not a perfect reincarnation of my distant and long dead relative Adolf. Willie had admired him so much and had sacrificed his two hands for him at Stalingrad. Since my unfortunate visit, Willie has gone on a permanent hunger strike whilst staying at the KrautenZimmer tourist hotel in Grabbenarmen, a downmarket hotel paid for by the social services. He claims that he will continue to fast until his death, unless I agree to disclose to the world who I truly am, invade France and then give him back both of his hands.

The French invasion bit I agree with, but

unfortunately Willie died last night, some six hours after he had agreed to give up his hunger strike. Willie left a final message on his IBM typewriter, saying:

Dear Nurse, You stupid bitch, how go you expect me to open this tin of sardines. I'm so bloody hungry but I ....Ugh".

My God, life can be so unfair. I wonder why he learnt to speak Icelandic.

I now have £21,987,564.06 in my bank account as a direct result of royalties received from publication of *The Working Man's Guide To The Galaxy*, and further royalties are coming in at the rate of over £34,000 per week. Sales of *DikSpeks* are keeping apace with book sales and profits in this area alone adds almost £56,000 per week to the pile. Royalties from my other inventions, such as *DikFree, DikTrays, DikPegs* and *DikWissals* are increasing this sizeable income by some £167,000 per month, but currency fluctuations sometimes alter this figure, which is why I support European and world monetary union.

All in all, I am now both a clever and rich little tyke. Being rich beyond anybody's dreams, helps me to take an attitude of sheer confidence and arrogance when writing this new publication which forever more shall be known as ***Almost Anything But Lucky.*** I have so much confidence that this knowledge of my inner richness must overflow and offer extra benefits to all graduates who have decided to follow me further on this academic adventure.

Please don't cheat yourself by attempting to start your course by using this advanced book and thus bypassing the compulsory reading of *The Working Man's Guide To The Galaxy* first, because it is absolutely forbidden. Such cheating would cost me 5p in lost royalties and I can assure you that once you are found out, as you most certainly will be by the ***DikStarpo***, then vengeance will be mine in the most fiery of ways. Just remember the fate of Freddy at Wormwood Scrubs, who. after all is said and done, only threatened me physically. You will see that there is nowhere to hide if you threaten me financially.

Freddy now sings soprano in the disabled prison choir and takes antibiotics every four hours for infected kneecaps.

Anybody who has not already read *The Working Man's Guide To The Galaxy* should now cease reading this book any further at this point. You have been warned.

Insanity is a gift afforded to only a lucky few, the rest of us must suffer a lifetime of regrets.

We now accept from our readings so far, that all the old style swear words invented prior to 1992 are now made part of the new revised Queen's English. New swear words must be taught to all young children above the age of five at school and these new words will be released in book form to the academic world very soon. These new swear words have been chosen from the large number of excellent suggestions put forward by my loyal readers, following the exciting *New Swear Words Competition* as published in *The Working Man's Guide To The Galaxy.*

We actually received 11,768,564 entries and the best ten words have been chosen and will now be used in the future as official obscene swear words, all of which will be officially banned from the Oxford Dictionary. Pub Words is a 16 page booklet containing a cross section of these new swear words and is available from the Social Security Office. These ten winning words are (in order of obscenity): Frickpuss, wallygobbler, muffsneezer, wankabankapranka, prikdik, barstucker, rectosister, clapdik, crabcreep and, last but not least, ***floccinaucinihilipilificationcok***.

This last lengthy word has been voted the most obscene new swear word of all the new obscene swear words. Congratulations Glyn Evans of Llangothorellortrellon in Wales who came up with this word and I am pleased to announce Glyn wins our New Swear Word Competition. I confirm that we shall be sending him his winner's prize of violent mouth cleanser and a steel clamped *DikMask* face mask with integral *DikPeg* in the post tonight.

If only he hadn't been Welsh I would have been very pleased and sent him a decent prize.

These new swear words are considered too rude and obscene for use within my publications from now on in, therefore this is the only time that your eyes will find such filthy new language used within my books, so help me God. I am forced to print them just this once so that you can all be made aware and be fully warned that such new filth and obscenity exists. Otherwise, you would hear your kids using these words and you could be misled into believing that they actually described something delightful and innocent, such as candy bars, popcorn, edible condoms or ice cream. Believe me, such words are pure filth and garbage and are guaranteed to corrupt your kids' minds even more than their predecessors did.

Do not be conceited if you have already succeeded in your B.Sc. (DikHed) exam because this kind of restricted mentality will guarantee your final demise in the Masters exam course.

Clear your minds of any conceit and join me in a second adventure of working class education and advancement. We have only a short time on this earth of ours, equivalent to a flash of light in eternity, before we enter a new millennium of utter hopelessness. This impending disaster can only be changed by our dedication and individual efforts if we are to save our mother planet from final destruction.

Governments cannot and will not help us achieve this objective because of outside pressures from self-interest groups forbidding them to change. Only we, the common people, can take a true and positive stance and force action on a global scale to save something for our children and children's children.

You can become masters of your true destiny and make a real difference.

Time is against us because the new millennium is almost here but we can still take time by the forelock and enter a new voyage to enlightenment. Again, my friends, off we go on an adventure of masterful magnitude to seek out a better land.

Ten, nine, eight, seven, six, five, four, three, two, one.

.............We have ignition.
.............We have lift off.

You will soon be Masters of a new Universe!

Chapter 3

From Experts to Wenches

Walking with the moon is but a beautiful dream,
Given to our children as their natural scene,
Awaiting death's knell from the capitalist's machine,
Thus bearing new soldiers for society's new theme,
Morality exchanged for new house, car and cream,
Will future generations thank us for being so mean,
Destroying this land and their beautiful dream,
God please help us to become green, green, green.

"There's no crap on the moon!" Jesus Waterhouse (1989)

Are you fed up with being the same as everybody else? Are you confused about this question? Maybe you don't even understand where I'm coming from or don't really care one way or another and are not even bothering yourself to think about whether you are fed up with being the same as everybody else. You also probably don't care whether you are the same as everybody else, even if you could be bothered to think about it in the first place.

Life can get so complicated even over the simplest of issues. I suppose that I should firstly explain what the word ***same*** means in the context of this question, as otherwise some smart Dick Head graduate will lecture me on the need for greater accuracy in my writings.

In the context of this question I am asking if you are fed up with being the same as, identical to, the very same as, an imitation of, the double of, of no difference to, indistinguishable from, synonymous with, homogenous with, a duplicate of, a look-alike of, a dead-ringer of, a spitting image of, a twin like, the selfsame as, one and the same as, congruent with, looking the same as, being as like two peas in a pod like, or not distinguishable from everybody else.

Just as it can be argued by some other even more awkward people that no circle is completely round, then it can be equally argued that no single person can be exactly the same as anybody else. The answer to my question is not *yes*, but equally it would be totally misleading if it were ***no***. Therefore, for those people in our readership that like to split hairs over such basic and simple questions, I will ask an easier question so that these hair splitters are satisfied with the accuracy of my prose. They can then answer in a correct way without fear of retribution or losing marks in their *M.Sc. (DikHed)* final exam. Please read on folks.

I will now rephrase my question by asking you if you are fed up being similar as, resembling, looking like, comparable with, matching with, out of the same mould as, corresponding with, much the same as, something like, similar to, passing as, bearing a resemblance to or seeming like everybody else.

That makes it much easier to understand don't you think?

Before you try to answer this very difficult question, let me tell you an intriguing story about a wonderful man named Elton Bib who lived in the sixteenth century. The basis of this story may help you decide upon your answer to this quest for inner truth and will stop you from lying to me. Do you want to be the same as everybody else or would you like to be different like an expert?

In 1541 Elton Bib sailed to Edinburgh in Scotland aboard a small wind powered trading vessel named Almalta, as the ship's doctor and chief cook. He was in charge of the daily feeding and health of one hundred and five miserable sailors. Elton was a highly religious man, converted to the Christian faith by his father after he had returned from an extended military mission in Spain where he discovered Christ as his saviour.

During this dangerous sixteen week voyage to Scotland, six of the sailors under his care had died of various diseases and seventy-two of food poisoning. Elton decided that God was calling him to a different destiny as he had become really fed up with cooking beans and wrapping up dead bodies. Training to be a doctor sounds very romantic, but I can confirm to you that when the guts start to spill on the floor, being a holy man is a much better profession to be in. After throwing away his stethoscope and French food mixer, he jumped ship and made his way north, where, after a colourful journey taking over six months, he arrived on the Island of Curragh, a small uninhabited island located one hundred and ten miles off the coast of Inverness.

Elton commenced building a small brick house that took him seventeen years to complete. Over the following centuries, this house became *The EL-BIB Reverse Holy Church*. His reason for forming this new Church followed a vision he had received from God, requesting that he set up a Church with the sole aim of reversing the ever increasing scientific advancement and related degradation of mankind that would surely lead them to hell.

He could see that mankind was fast approaching a time when human beings would enter valleys where the cowboys would kill all the Indians and the Swiss would own everything. Whilst we maintained the survival of the free thinking Indians, the cowboys would be under control.

God had chosen Elton to form this Church so that all members of his congregation would live a solitary life where all developments of mankind ceased and true innocence would survive the ravages and rape of human advancement. The island would become self sufficient, requiring assistance from no other soul. Everybody had a full time job and had to rely upon the next man for his survival. This newly revived communal spirit would be the backbone of the EL-BIB Reverse Church and no matter what other

Churches sold their souls for, the *EL-BIB* would stand fast on what they believed in. Amen to that.

In 1560, they bought the island from Lord Pomfey Romsey for the sum of six pounds, which by today's values is a real bargain. You must remember that in those days, there was no electricity, plumbed water or gas on the island, so maybe paying six pounds was a wee bit over the top after all. However, value is what somebody is willing to pay combined with what somebody is willing to accept.

In 1563 *The EL-BIB Holy Living Book* arrived on the scene, specifying exactly how members of the Church should live their lives in love and harmony together, notwithstanding the temptations of modern society. After several name changes this book became known as *The Holy EL-BIB Book*. This book did not replace The Holy Bible, which of course was also available in the standard Latin format of the times and used by the Church.

During the following centuries the dedicated followers of *EL-BIB* merrily planted their vegetables, bred their own sheep and wove their own cloth. Because they did not conform to the current social values, inhabitants from the other nearby islands shunned them as "real strange gits". In some ways this was understandable, because they still spoke a strange Arabic/Italian hybrid language and their appearances resembled those of people so vividly illustrated in the concentration camps of the second word war. However, faith knows no bounds and at all encounters with these other islanders, they would respond with *"EL-BIB al numero uno"*, which means just what you think it means - We are the champions.

Until the introduction of portable TV cameras, isolated people could remain anonymous and be left alone. On the 1st September 1986 a nosy parker television reporter, Ranton Box, carried out a survey on the *EL-BIB* people for his satellite television station. This survey gave the following amazing results:

* *Their average life span was 179 years.*
* *They had never had one case of cancer.*
* *No cases of blood pressure or heart disease*
* *Their sexual organs were three times larger than the average.*
* *They had an average IQ of 231.78.*

Just imagines the reaction of the world's media! Within twenty-four hours, the island became overrun by thousands of helicopters carrying television crews from all around the world. In addition, drug companies sent in bribery squads to offer billions of dollars to *The EL-BIB Church*. This slush money was in return for the exclusive franchise for the special products that they obviously ate to cure all the heart and cancer diseases that allowed them to live until they reached 179 years of age.

Hundreds of thousands of people infected with these diseases chartered boats to visit the island for instant fixes to their problems. Never again would the life of the *EL-BIB* people be the same as it was. Brother Carustus, the current head of the Church gave his one and only speech to the press and the world:

"Welcome to our island my brothers and sisters. We wish you all the wealth and health that God can give you by living a frugal life free of sin but we cannot accept your modern ways of corruption and degradation which are rapidly destroying this earth of our God.

"We cannot and will not help you solve the ills of your modern society, without in return seeing a reversal of your greedy and poisonous trends. We are being forced to move our society to another place due to your uninvited intrusion into our lives. Anybody who wishes to remain here with us can join us on our voyage to another place.

"Good-bye and God help you all, but I fear it is far too late."

Within twenty-four hours, all members of *The EL-BIB Church* had disappeared forever. The day they vanished from the face of this earth, The Times newspaper printed a full page advertisement that had simply the words:

I would willingly give my life to be a butterfly for only a day.

EL-BIB

Ever since they disappeared, academics have been trying without any success to translate their *The Holy*

EL-BIB Book but even with the help of multi-lingual computers, this task has proved an impossible one. As a final sting in the tail to this extraordinary story, only last week, again in The Times, was another full page advertisement:

We are flying now with the butterflies in the sky.

EL-BIB

This weird story and phenomenon is made even more strange by the world cover-up that has occurred to block out further information on the existence of these people from the world's press. I believe that this cover-up is because our modern scientists could find no logical explanation why the *EL-BIB* people could live as they did and therefore maybe it was more than an earthly reason.

Total expertise in all things leads us to damnation

Miandini Corutia (2269 BC)

This theory did not stop our modern day experts seeking the answers to *The EL-BIB Church* secrets; they would not rest until they became experts in this subject that made the *EL-BIB* people different from the rest of us.

Despite the predictions of Miandini, I still want to be an expert. I want to be skilled and informed about everything in life, so much so that my admiring students will feel confident that I have the answers to all things.

Why am I, Dick Head the world famous author

and inventor, not already an expert? This question often baffles me because whenever I study a subject, I believe that at the end of any of my subject studies I have learnt as much as can be possibly absorbed by the human brain. With my photographic memory and gift of instant recall, I can instantly assess all previous writings by other expert people on any particular subject. Despite this, my peers do not describe me as an expert, the same as the ones I see on television or read about in the national newspapers.

What is greatly concerning is that my own opinions vary greatly with the opinions of the well known experts. So, we can say that being an expert is much more than reading and understanding all previous works on a particular subject - being an expert is a qualification in itself! Analysing any problem is 99% towards solving it. Therefore my solution is to become a qualified expert and start to understand the truths of life.

Once I am a qualified expert, I can complete my book number 22 entitled *The Working Man's Guide To Being An Expert*. This book, scheduled for publication on 31 December 1999, is being written as a celebration for the new millennium.

Miandini Corutia was born in Cairo, Egypt in 2300 BC and decided to become an expert on pyramids. He attended the *Egyptian School for Pyramid Experts* and qualified at the age of thirty in the year 2270 BC. To qualify as a pyramid expert, you had to be able to answer two million questions during a two year exam period without a single error. Some of the older students were over eighty years of age, having studied at the school for more than sixty years, failing their exams every year.

Because the exam was so difficult, you could enrol on a different two million question exam every fortnight, so that in effect you could be taking fifty-two exams over a two year period, amounting to answering one hundred and four million questions. The entire Egyptian empire considered that Miandini was a real clever expert when he was successful in his pyramid exam at the first attempt. Just imagine knowing that the ***Udah*** pyramid consisted of 46,333,333 separate stones and that the designer, Cuthbert Wilson, died from syphilis at the age of sixty-three. Being a similar expert is my aim but I carry a substantial supply of penicillin just in case it's a danger of the job.

I have telephoned all the colleges and universities enquiring about courses for being an expert. After fruitless hours of haggling on the telephone, I have since received over one ton of assorted literature describing more than seven hundred courses - but none on training to be an expert. Maybe I needed to take all the courses to be an expert. I added up all the subject study periods and they totalled fourteen hundred years, so this could not be the answer.

So how could existing experts become experts in the first place? I telephoned all the known experts from press and television with the same question - how did you become an expert? Experts are so skilled that they do not need to reply to such questions from other people who are trying to be experts. I assumed that they all already belonged to the *FYBIAQ Society* that is a well supported union for people already qualified. This *FYBIAQ Society* started centuries ago and now totally controls all aspects of our upper crust life, from aristocracy to merchant banking. How many Wally Birtwistles do you meet at Ascot in the Royal enclosure?

This total silence from our existing experts forced upon me the need to use much harsher tactics to show these people that Dick Head is unaccustomed to outright rudeness, unless flowing from my own green ink.

I commenced a telephoning campaign using an automatic telephone calling machine that I had shipped over from California because they are illegal in the UK. This fascinating unit allowed me to pre-programme all the telephone numbers of all the experts that I could track down in this country. By pressing the red start button, my plan began and systematically this machine would dial all known experts with my special message:

Hello, I am your worst nightmare because I have a secret dossier, including many graphic illustrations including colour photographs, concerning your private indiscretions which could ruin your public life

forever. My organisation knows all about your perverted behaviour.
Unless you wish to see this information and the photographs published within our national press then you must telephone Mombasa 632111 and inform me of everything you know on how to qualify as an expert.
You will get no second chance.
Have a nice day!

Don't be confused by the Mombasa telephone number because this is also a mobile telephone, owned by a friend of mine, linked to an automatic redialing machine that redirects all calls to yet another mobile telephone in Libya, owned by my niece's Libyan husband. These calls to the Libyan number are similarly transferred to an answering machine that is located in a rented office in Rochester. I saw this set-up in a recent detective story on television and it works very well indeed.

Just think about it; I'm not even a trained criminal and yet I can commit the perfect crime and get away with it. Just in case I had not committed the perfect crime and even this very smart system becomes detected, I obtained all my messages by using a mobile telephone at Heathrow Airport using a special bleeper to activate the answering machine in Rochester. I wore dark glasses and a dark blue overcoat and had a one-way ticket to South Africa in my pocket ready for instant use.

I have not yet been caught but my telephone bills from Mombasa and Libya amounted to £5,879.56 excluding value added tax. The bill for using the mobile telephone at Heathrow Airport remains unpaid because I hired it from a rental company under the assumed name of Jack Carlos. I hope he pays them one day.

As usual, I book all telephone bills to my publisher's company so that we can reclaim the value added tax from the government. Not only do I commit the perfect crime, but I also get the government to pay towards it.

Now that British Telecom is in private hands, it's no longer a federal offence and therefore my fellow taxpayers will not suffer.

After analysing all the replies, I can confirm to my readers that where mere persuasion fails to obtain results, resort to blackmail - it works a treat.

Of the 364 experts telephoned, I can give you the following analysis:

69 Told me to sod off

63 Committed suicide by varying methods

59 Shot themselves

3 Drug overdosed but survived

1 Hung himself from Big Ben

91 Left the country for good

38 Reported me to the police

40 Left messages on my answering machine!

Many of my readers may now be smirking to themselves and criticising me with comments such as "Dick Head you're a useless pervert trying to be an expert!" Smirk not ye tossers of little faith, go out asunder and purchase an American book called *How to obtain the best results from mass media telephone selling*. Once you have purchased this book for $132.50, please refer to page 1162 where you will see written:

The latest mass media automatic telephone sales machines are showing positive results of up to 7% of the total market called. Higher percentages are in theory possible but the messages require preparation by the very best promotional experts. Any results of more than 10% are considered virtually impossible.

So yet again my critics, you are quick mouthed oafs, shouting out insults before checking the facts. To repeat the words from this world renowned publication - Any returns of more than 10% are virtually impossible. Dick Head has achieved am impossibility with a return of 11%!

Now let's analyse the actual content of the 40 messages received on my answering machine:

Thirty-two people gave details of how to be an expert homosexual, by using very filthy and suggestive language including possibilities of child molesting. I have sent transcripts of these conversations to the police. Six people told me how to expose yourself in Hyde Park without getting caught. One person told me how to train a parrot without getting beak bitten (roll of Sellotape required)

And finally, one person told me HOW TO BE A REAL EXPERT! You may now shout out "Dick Head's result was only 0.274725274725% but I really don't care because I had achieved my aim. This successful message was received from Sir Robert Nancy who simply said, "Sir, if you want to be an expert, I can show you everything you need to know about everything."

I became so excited as I telephoned Sir Robert for an appointment.

After ringing for a few seconds, a reserved aristocratic voice answered in a low tone "Hello, can I help you?" I replied with my coded password of "Jack Carlos needs expert attention" to which the reply came back of "Only a real Nancy can help you". I relaxed and became less formal by continuing with "OK Bob, let's get down to business, shall we?"

"I'll give you Bob, you bastard pervert!" shouted Sir Robert Nancy in an obvious temper. I quickly disconnected the call, smashed the phone into little pieces using a big hammer, threw the pieces down a drain-hole and burnt my false beard and sunglasses.

How the hell can I become an expert? I visited Rochester library and went to the desk marked "enquiries" and asked "Excuse me but do you have a book that will teach me to be an expert." The woman sitting by the computer console looked up from her sitting position and replied with a sympathetic smile. "Yes, and on what subject would that refer to sir?" I sighed and replied "My dear lady, I just want a book that teaches me to be an expert, just like all the experts on television and in the media. I see the same people giving expert answers on any subject and I want to be an expert like them!" "Don't shout at me young man; just wait here a few moments please!" Five minutes later the police arrived, in the form of a spotty faced ex-smallpox victim, and arrested me for using abusive language in a public library.

It took over three hours at Rochester police station to convince Sergeant Plod that I was a serious famous author and inventor. To prove the point, I gave him a signed copy of *The Working Man's Guide To The Galaxy*, but got out of the nick fast before he managed to reach chapter 6. Quite a few other pages in the first five chapters needed removing to avoid more arrests later.

Becoming an expert was proving impossible, so in utter frustration I went for a few pints of Guinness (eleven to be precise) at the *Jolly Knight* pub in Rochester High Street. After the first six pints, I discussed my problem of becoming an expert with Derek the ever knowing barman. Without any hesitation, he solved my problem. "Dick my friend, you're already an expert!"

He was, of course, correct because it is not what I think of myself that makes me an expert, but it is what other people think. I had entered into a life of crime, upset the librarian and got myself arrested for no reason whatsoever, because I was already an expert!

My past self doubt evaporated away as fast as a large cognac left in the fierce Sahara sun. Just why anybody would want to drink cognac in the Sahara is a question that has always puzzled me.

Being an expert felt really good and I was very smug about it, as indeed I felt entitled. Now that I'm an expert, I can discuss and assess the various things in life that confuse other people. Crime and violence are rampant on our streets and yet our government cannot, or more to the point they will not, take any action.

As an expert, I would ban all scenes of sex, violence and crime from our cinemas and television screens. Some of our government officials are telling us that there is no proven link between the increase in crime and violence on our streets and the increase in the crime and violence on our screens. Any expert could inform these fools that their ideas are pure horse droppings.

Dick Head, the latest expert, hereby confirms that there is a direct link between television and cinema violence and the actual crimes on our streets.

Women's liberation since the 1960s has given the

old world a new extra bitchy world to live in where women constantly demand so called equal rights, providing they retain all their old feminist advantages. The sooner we return to the well established feminist values, the sooner we will eliminate the breeding of generations of psychopathic children left to roam our streets today. Liberated women are responsible for this breakdown in the family values in society today.

Home alone or with others of their ilk, the problems increase as female greed and eny increases by the year. They want equality until it begins to hurt and the blood starts to flow.

Get back in the kitchen you wenches!

Chapter 4

From KYXZANTYN to Charity

The giver of charity and kindness without reward or recognition is the true silent Saint of compassion.

Ruphus Rumbold (1919) Ypres Disabled Soldiers Fund

Alexis Alendarious arrived into this world on the 23 August 672 BC and was set to prove conclusively that you should always think before you leap, even if you are an Olympic pole vaulting champion.

I am able to report accurately Alexis's life story thanks to the very detailed information that is meticulously recorded within the ***KYXZANTYN*** almanac, that famous scripture written by the fabled ancient scribes of the Greek Emperor, Popendreous II. This fiery emperor was renowned as a bloodthirsty fighting man who ruled over the Greek empire with an iron fist from 691 BC until his death in 654 BC. Popendreous II, known as "coconut muscles" within his circle of close friends, became emperor unexpectedly at the juvenile age of thirteen following the untimely death of his dear beloved and murderous father.

His father, Emperor Popendreous the Older died without any possibility of recall due to a massive heart attack that occurred whilst he was participating in a high stakes poker game. His final game was played out with many famous people, including the King of Russia, Reg Smith (the neighbourhood pimp) and the local homosexual church warden. Death for Popendreous the Older, at such an early stage in his life, was God's way of achieving His final revenge for the tens of thousands of innocent souls that this brutal man had killed without compassion during his vicious lifetime.

He collapsed and died of burst blood vessels inside his testicles whilst holding a royal flush of hearts in his fat flabby hands, shouting out in glee "NotnowyubastardcosIvgotabloodyroyalflushaaaaaaa hhhhh!"

Life is a great leveller when you die, so they say. He won the hand but lost his life - sod playing poker! The kitty, consisting of some twenty-three pounds of gold coin, disappeared some time between when Popendreous the Older had his heart attack and when the horse drawn funeral chariot arrived to take the departed boss to his burial ground. This money has never been seen or heard of since that sad day.

I personally believe that stealing a winning kitty from a recently deceased emperor, even a murderous one, is a pretty sad state of affairs and is a crime against the betting kind, deserving the severest of retribution. The other card players in the game denied the theft, but at least one must be lying, because one of them must be the thief.

The King of Russia and the church warden, both

God-fearing men, can probably be deemed innocent and ruled out, but Reg Smith, that flashy pimp from the wrong side of the tracks, is a definite suspect. The next day after the emperor's demise, Reg stole a fishing boat and sailed away with a group of co-operative and brightly dressed ladies to a desert island near Plymouth.

Many people said good riddance to such a low class whore boss, but many of the richer aristocrats wished he would quickly return because it was found that there was a dire shortage of prostitutes in Athens after Reg Smith had left with so many of the good looking ones. The ugly ones that Reg Smith left behind did a thriving business and were able to charge twice the price for half the time. A *twenty pinter* quickly became a *diet coker*, so to speak.

Popendreous II, himself, died of a permanent heart stoppage during a hunting trip that had been carefully arranged by his devoted family as a surprise celebration for his fifty-third birthday. On this very royal birthday occasion, his six brothers (all of different mothers), went together on this unexpected happy hunting trip and brought along with them a beautiful birthday cake on the back of a horse-drawn wagon. This multicoloured iced cake was adorned with exactly fifty-two multicoloured candles, which was one candle short of the required number - or was it?

Quite frankly this shortage of one critical candle should have been a clear warning to our emperor of his family's nasty intentions - which were to put him down and out forever and ever and ever and ever.......

After the mid-morning elevenses, consisting of hot brandy muffins and three ladies of your choice, the brothers took the emperor wild boar hunting to the highest hills above Athens. Although it was considered extremely dangerous in these hills, the biggest wild boars were found to roam there.

It was later claimed that this dangerous area was chosen for the hunt to allow the emperor to demonstrate his prowess with his ancient rustic bow that had been given to him by his now long dead father. This bow can now be seen at the Greek National Heritage Museum in Athens.

Near the end of this boar hunt, Popendreous II experienced some very bad luck, which was unfortunately multiplied by six when all the arrows fired by his brothers at the targeted wild boar missed their alleged target and hit him. On a good day, even the worst nightmares will turn into golden dreams, but at this time Lady Luck was looking the other way.

All six arrows hit Popendreous II fairly and squarely in the softest parts of his body and caused his almost instant demise. If you wish to be pedantic about the true description and meaning of totally instant, then his death was not totally instant, but the excruciating pain most certainly was.

This event turned out to be of extreme good fortune for the wild boar who should have been shot stone dead. This fortunate animal celebrated such good fortune by beating the previous world record for a wild boar running the hundred metres dash by over seven seconds. Never again would this uncivilised roughshod pig laze around, bumming in the sun and scratching his backside without watching out for hunters with big prickly sticks.

As lucky a day as this was for wild boars, all was not so lucky for the Greek royal family where bad luck had arrived for the one and only Popendreous II. Not all was bad news, because he was fortunate that one of the arrows (the one dipped in deadly poison), struck him dead centre into his now rapidly ailing heart and killed him just 2.75 seconds after the other arrows struck.

If he had survived longer, three of the arrows that had made direct hits into his testicles would have given him excruciating pain beyond belief for a prolonged time, much longer than the two seconds that he did remain alive. These three arrows did not hit three separate testicles, because one arrow hit the left testicle and one arrow hit the right testicle, with the last remaining arrow striking him dead centre inside his right ear and then reappeared perfectly out of his left ear, without apparently even touching the sides.

None of the brothers showed any remorse at such a tragic family accident and indeed were seen to shove six long knives into the dead brother's heart whilst they sang the happy birthday song and ate his birthday cake whilst sitting on his stomach. The birthday cake had the correct number of candles after all.

The demised Popendreous II had been born a few minutes before sunset and the sun was still shining brightly. The candles were left unlit as a sign of respect but the cake was eaten with great gusto and tasted very nice indeed. No doubt they had their own reasons for going through with this birthday celebration when they should have been struck down in grief like any other family of the deceased. The reasoning behind such eccentric and callous behaviour is all beyond me, but there again, is it really any of my business after all?

Next time you have a birthday party, carefully check the number of candles on the cake and do not go wild boar hunting with the family.

The next day, only the youngest brother Andreous managed to return alive to Athens following this disastrous hunting trip. The other five brothers also perished by a mixture of unfortunate accidents on the short trip back to the ranch. Such an unlucky family should be careful in the future because it is unusual for so many brothers to die during one trip to kill wild boar during your brother's birthday party.

Andreous, being an impatient type of fellow, was crowned Emperor Andreous the Younger the next day, after claiming that any more delays would endanger his life from the same enemies that caused the demise of his beloved six brothers. He loved wearing crowns and eating freshly boiled fish, but he died tragically of the painful dreaded Nigerian yellow syphilis only two months after his coronation.

He contracted this terrible terminal venereal disease from his departed brother's (Popendreous II) widowed wife, Pokadu. He had forced his attentions upon her whilst teaching her to play poker with both hands tied behind her back. Revenge is sweet they say, even whilst playing cards on a poxy day.

Back to Alexis Alendarious, the subject matter of this chapter's teachings.

Alexis Alendarious was born in a stable, the son of a Greek fisherman with big feet, and a schizophrenic French mother who suffered greatly from very painful piles. They were a lovely couple together. Alexis was fated to become the most famous, saddest and generous fisherman who ever lived in Greece, if not throughout the world.

A bright star shone over the stable during this famous arrival and the very next day three wise men came bearing gifts from the East. When they saw Alexis, they said in an aggrieved tone of voice "He's not Jewish, he's bloody Greek - wrong kid again, he's going to be just a stupid bleedin' fisherman so let's go and have a pint whilst we keep looking for the next star and stable".

God, how I hate this type of person who seems to know everything. It is claimed within the text of many fabled writings that Alexis's unbelievable generosity had a profound influence upon the behaviour pattern of many later Popes, Archbishops and other highly respected people of the Church. He changed them from being normal tight-fisted self-centred holy fellows into less tight-fisted self centred holy fellows.

By pretending to adopt some of the Alexis Syndrome, these holy bosses in high places created a caring image of themselves with the poor and needy. This was required for enticing them to cough up their loot into the collection boxes to pay for the gold goodies, holy vino and nuns that they enjoyed so much.

It is necessary to convince the poor people that the Church cares for them always, because it is the poor people throughout history that have been the power base for the Church. It is no good the poor people thinking bad things of the Church, such as, "Those Church people take all our bloody money, then build churches full of gold, live in luxury, get drunk, make love to all the nuns, whilst we go off fighting holy wars and our families live in poverty and die of starvation."

No, this understanding of the truth would never do and the Church, like any good marketing organisation, knows it. This idea of conning the ignorant people was OK for as long as everybody remained ignorant of the real truth, but unfortunately for them the Magna Carta came along to upset the Status Quo, whilst at the same time the Rolling Stones upset the Church.

Soon after publication of the Magna Carta, there came the first of those great books by Magnus Cartason that really put the cat among the pigeons. This publication is still available today under the new title of You can fool some of the people some of the time.

To combat these attacks upon the Church's power base and integrity, the Holy Order marketing department pushed forward the Alexis Syndrome Theory into the public domain in a full blooded effort to make the people see and believe that everything is as perceived and claimed by the Church.

This method of conning the flock has been working perfectly well in most areas ever since, but it must be said that over the last few years some doubts have been creeping into certain sectors of the overall holy market. For example, not all is going so well for the Church in South Africa, but they have other contingency plans, including a black Pope next time around. Just watch the colour of the smoke over Cape Town Cathedral.

It only takes a small piece of generosity being handed out to the poor people whilst the media's cameras are rolling, to elevate your reputation from that of "tight-fisted holy man" into a more acceptable "that super charitable Pope with the fringe on the top". All these praises are spoken between TV commercials and whilst the church bells ring to celebrate Saint Smith's day.

Have you been to the Vatican lately to view the riches beyond description that exist there in every department, whilst the other half of the world starves? Show off your riches, let the poor die of starvation and still keep your flock - now that's what I call a real media and marketing trick. Simply control the actions of the Pope to make sure that he is doing and saying good things for just a few times per month.

Keep the subject matter always away from the real truths of life and how much money we've got. High profile stories are what the people relish and believe. For God's sake do not give them the truth

Nowhere is this "high profile" theory more blatantly apparent than with the Western hostage syndrome where a few guys were held in captivity for many hundreds of days in the Middle East. Here we have a few poor unfortunate men being held against their will for political and financial purposes, thus making great media tearful stories that are cheap to run.

The World's media went crazy in its efforts to stir up this very boring story into what it was not, because what it was not was not what they wanted it to be. What it had to be made into was good news that touched the very *souls of our hearts*. What it was not, was important news when compared with other events that were happening on the face of this globe of ours.

WAKE UP YOU MORONS!

According to the Western understanding of things, all we are doing is playing into the hands of a lunatic fringe of terrorists that fanatically and fundamentally believe that they are right in what they are doing. When looking at the world situation from their insular point of view in the overall theatre of things, such hostage taking actions are not really so evil as first appears.

History will not be quite so unkind to these people. Can the decadent West, with its drugs, violence, erosion of moral standards and inbred corruption really criticise another society's standards? I think not. The rights and wrongs of such long held beliefs cannot be discussed within this second of my educational books, as otherwise we shall become bogged down in political argument and dogma.

No, my students, the point at issue is the utter waste of time and money that was spent by the Western World over the fate of a few unfortunates. Time and money that should be better spent saving thousands of lives and caring about the world itself as we approach a new millennium.

Are ten thousand lives in Africa less valuable than a few Western hostages? What about the rest of this vicious world? What about the millions of people perishing because of our neglect? What about our own people dying because we can't be bothered to look after them? What about.............?

No, my friends, you must see this is understood as bad news and we don't want to see or hear about it, feeling our guilt every day of our lives. We want to feel tearful towards a few unfortunates that are in a jam through no fault of ours, but purely of their own. Most of you will push the infrared button on the channel changer to watch another more agreeable programme, rather than sit and watch the truth.

Mr. Media man, can you please arrange for these underfed unwashed diseased folk to die out of my eyesight, otherwise I will not support your programme in the future. This is a lousy way to live your life.

Do you know how many people die of starvation

every hour in Africa? Do you know how many people could survive if you paid the equivalent of a single pint of beer per day? Do you give a thought?

You see my futile friends and postgraduates, how easily and quickly the hostage era of the 1980s is now almost forgotten today - just a short time after the last hostage was released. Do not forget these experiences because we are living in a more volatile world now than ever before. Any trick or scheme that is successful once will be used repeatedly to meet political and financial ends.

Another hostage saga will soon cover our screens and governments will move mountains and pay millions to be remembered as the good guys in the final episode on TV. Just you watch the politicians grab a huge slice of the limelight when each hostage is released. Just watch the media mob fight for interviews and to film the next poor guy being released - a hostage fellow who has no credentials for fame and could otherwise be a sex pervert for all we know.

He will simply be an innocent victim of a hijacking who has subsequently been held in atrocious conditions for a long time, before being released into the real world again. He will have nothing to say about his capture, nothing to say about his life in captivity and nothing to say about his release. Once released, he will become a political puppet for another regime and, as usual, will be treated as a Victoria Cross hero.

The truth of the matter is that our next hostage will again be in the wrong place at the wrong time and will be just an average Mr. Nice Guy from next door. He will live out his own living hell until released and then will try to forget such memories whilst playing the part of a hero until the press forgets and looks at another Lucky scandal.

Within a few weeks of release, look out for the latest publication on the shelves of your local book store. How I survived a living hell, or a similar title will be published on the pretence that the world must know about the suffering and degradation of these evil hostage takers. Rubbish, my friends - I believe that such a publication is just to make money on the media gravy train like everybody else. Do they give all the proceeds to charity? Whatever the sufferings borne, our hero is unlikely to be buried in a mass grave in Ethiopia or Kuwait as a man with no name.

I'm lost, so lost in a sleazy life,

No hope, no love to offer you

My fellow men degrade me more

They offer up such sufferings

Who needs their help and shelter now

The cause is lost for you and me.

Joe Pikestaff (1985)

This sorrowful message was written by a poor fellow with the name of Joe Pikestaff, as he remained incarcerated in jail for ten years for the alleged rape of

Rosy Leatherbottom and her ugly sister Mandy. Last year he was found innocent and given a Royal Pardon, "I the Queen do pardon you". Thank you very much your Royal Highness, have a nice day.

This pardon came after twenty-seven men came forward to inform the police how they had all been sexually attacked and raped by the same Rosy Leatherbottom and her ugly sister Mandy. These rapes took place during a very lively birthday party held at Rosy's house after the rugby club dance. Each of these poor unfortunate men had been warned by the ugly sisters that "we shall shout 'rape' if you talk about this affair to anybody, let alone the police."

Only after these raped men eventually read the details of Joe Pikestaff's sad case in one of the cheapo left-wing tabloid Sunday newspapers, did they realise that justice must be done. This feeling of guilt combined with the fact that the sisters were both lousy lovers, decided the issue.

When the police first listened to this fantastic story of the raped rugby gang, they joined in the rugby club humour and initially ignored this outrageous possibility. Eventually, after much protestation, they decided to question Rosy and her ugly sister about these accusations. The truth was revealed.

In outrage at such accusations of gang rape, Rosy claimed that all twenty-seven of these terrible men had each raped her and Mandy during her birthday party. She was asked by the police inspector how she could laughingly sing the happy birthday song, blow out the candles with a cheer and then go away for a flexible weekend with her boyfriend and his four brothers following the alleged gang rape. She retorted with a laugh, "I always like being gang raped whilst I drink gin and blow out the candles or indeed blow anything else that needs blowing, if you know what I mean."

After the appeal, Joe Pikestaff was released from jail, complete with the gracious Royal Pardon. To date, he has not yet actually received any phone call from the Queen asking how he's getting on and "will you pardon me?", but we hear that this is because she is very busy spending our money at Balmoral and paying off a few royal relatives. God blesses the Queen and all who smile with her.

Joe's health has deteriorated to such a dangerously low level that he needs the help of a walking frame to help him move even the few yards to his outside toilet. His mind's gone completely as he permanently spits everywhere and mumbles, "Rosy's a lying bitch! Rosy's a lying bitch! Rosy's a lying bitch!..................... "And so on and so on. Eating fish and chips has become difficult and he can no longer add brown sauce.

He has just been committed to the Dunkfield Institute for the Insane by a young social services officer who otherwise abuses young children in care when not flashing himself in the park. Joe lives alone in his sad far away world of idiocy, where he can mumble on until his heart gives out one of fine sunny law abiding Queen's pardoning days.

The point at issue in this sad story is that poor old Joe Pikestaff was just as maltreated as those hostages who hogged all the headline news during the 1980s, but who gives a damn about Joe? Nobody cares and certainly no television crews have asked for his story, because he is ***bad news***; not exciting enough for the caring public. Joe Pikestaff will not be writing a book for anybody, unless it's to be called *"Rosy's A Lying Bitch"* or *"The Queen Pardons Me After I'm Knackered"*.

I must stop wandering off the subject. Alexis grew up quickly under the pressures of Greek poverty to become an expert fisherman. In just one four-hour fishing trip in the bay of Athens, he could catch over one ton of fish in his boat The Greek Kipper Clipper. Upon returning to shore, he would gut and clean all the fish and prepare them expertly for sale. He mixed up all the leftover guts, heads, skins, etc. together with pure Greek grass seed and ducks' eggs, using a special mixing machine, and from this mixture he produced a large quantity of his special Crapolis Fish Pies.

These pies became famous throughout the region for their awful smell but wonderful taste. You could hear many a comment such as "bloody awful smell but great pies!" throughout the width and breadth of Athens. At 4.00 p.m. every day he would open up The Alexis Fish & Pie Shop (written in ancient Greek of course), where he would sell his fresh produce at very high prices to the aristocrats of Athens who lived in the Croppo high above the city.

The people from the Croppo were also simply referred to as "those rich lazy sods on the hill" (again spoken in ancient Greek) by the folk who lived as virtual slaves in abject poverty. Nothing really changes in this world, does it? By about 6.00 p.m. every day, the Croppos had usually purchased all the good lobster, snapper, cod, prawns, etc., leaving all the remaining cheapo fish and all the Crapolis Fish Pies, which they considered as too crappo for the Croppos. Alexis would then proceed to hand out these leftovers to the poor people free of charge to help them survive on the living side of starvation.

This charitable act kept many poor families alive during the months after Alexis started this free food hand-out every afternoon. The poor thankful recipients of the free fish treated him as a saviour and indeed he was referred to as Saint Alexis the Fisherman from God by the men, women and children alike.

After these initial months of hope being offered by these free handouts, huge crowds started to build up every day, awaiting the free food handout. Before this time arrived, if a rich Croppo purchased any fish, the crowd would boo and hiss, pushing and hitting the purchaser in a hysterical way and shouting out vulgar comments like, "Leave me bleedin fish alone". This treatment of the Croppo purchasing public led to only one result within the capitalist environment of Ancient

Athens: the Croppos cleared off to buy their fish at another fish shop.

This new shop was run by a Jewish man and there was no danger whatsoever of him giving any fish away. Now I am, of course, aware of another Jewish fellow giving away fish, but this story takes place long after Alexis started the trend, even including the bright star bit............ Now on with the story.

Eventually, Alexis was forced to work twenty hours every day catching and preparing the fish for giving away to the hordes of some twelve thousand people that now came to his shop to obtain their free ration. No Croppos came to purchase fish anymore because it had become far too dangerous. They had a real fear of attack by the mob who shouted out, "This is our fish!"

Alexis earned no money but he felt morally obliged to continue feeding the poor. Eventually he could not catch enough fish to feed all of the ever increasing crowd that came with pleading eyes to his shop. On the first day when he could not feed everybody, the crowd realised that being first in the queue meant first being served with their guaranteed meal.

Massive fights broke out amongst the people in their efforts to be fed. Those at the back of the queue started shouting at Alexis, "El Bastardo!" This obscene shouting is reasonably self explanatory in most languages, and started a massive riot.

The rioting continued for several hours and spread to the rich areas of Athens, killing some 634 people, 321 of them young children. Alexis was arrested and charged with inciting a riot and being responsible for the death of 321 innocents and 313 other lower class people. He was taken to the Upper Court within the Acropolis (Croppo-land) where the full list of charges was read:

Causing Riot.

Causing the death of 321 innocents.

Causing the death of 313 low classed people.

Not supplying fish to the Croppos.

Contravening the fixed pricing laws.

Being a general nuisance.

In summing up the case, the Prefect stated:

"Alexis Alendarious, you have been charged with these many serious crimes upon which we find you guilty on all counts. Your absurd generosity led to a shortage of lobster for our leaders of society which meant no Surf and Turf on the menu at the emperor's table. You've completely knackered the structure and stability of the fish prices in the Athens fish market and you've shown yourself to be an unmitigated idiot! You are sentenced to 50 years hard labour where you will work as a boat loader in Athens docks. Send him down and bring me some more wine!"

During the next 50 years, Alexis loaded 11,231 boats, gave no more fish away. He decided that if he survived these 50 years of hell, he would take up a profession where there would be no temptation to give anything away free of charge, such as being a lawyer or bank manager. During his four quarter hour rest periods each day he wrote books and poetry, his most famous book being Only Imbeciles Give Charity.

This is available today in thirty-seven languages, although the translation of the word bum on page 1234 has been difficult to achieve in some languages, because the meaning can get out of context. The translators did their best but in the German translation this has proved totally impossible. The word bum has been substituted by the words "Herr Rectum".

Poetry was by far and away his favourite way of expression and on his 25th year of boat loading he wrote the now famous *Fish Bloody Fish* poem:

I was only a simple minded fisherman,
Each day I brought in the fish again,
Sold fish to the rich,
Gave fish to the poor,
Those greedy freeloaders always demanded more,
I pleaded to the hordes please go on a diet,
Their instant reaction was to go on a riot,
Now I'm loading boats with wood and black coal,
Alexis the fisherman you're such a sad soul.

Students, oh students, have you reached your conclusions on the lessons of this truer than life story? Did Alexis do it all wrong? What should he have done instead? Do you know???

The basis of this story is one of pure greed caused by people awaiting something for nothing and how it should be controlled. Such greed cannot be controlled by the *greedy something for nothing people*, but only by the generous people ready to feed the greedy people. Once you give something for nothing to a person a second time, he then believes it is his right to receive it freely every day, no matter if you can afford it no longer.

This is the situation in our society today, but the country can no longer finance such a lifestyle. It is a warning for all of you to beware of the something for nothing brigade who will be queuing outside your door the moment they see a chance of taking an advantage without having to work for it. This is a sad reflection upon our world society but this attitude has existed ever since Francis Drake had his bowls pinched whilst he was away defeating the Armada.

Francis Drake finished his game of bowls before taking out the English Fleet to destroy the famous Spanish Armada, thus saving England from the dago threat. "Rise Sir Francis" spoke out our monarch, Queen Elizabeth I, as she knighted the great national hero with her Sheffield steel Sword of the Realm. The wink of her eye betold much ado about everything me doth think.

In conversation at the Knighthood party held that knighting evening, Sir Francis discussed the strength of the British spirit with the local aristocrats. He spoke of the victory, including the bounty ships captured during the battle. "Me thinketh that this famous victory doth for the common good for all, doth send thine Dagos back to their Paella pans for a vereth long time. The bounty ship, *El Dagoby* hath beeneth given to me byeth our Majesty and containeth some two hundredth tons of huge onions that tasteth liketh silk witheth a tear in myeth eye. Frometh now, all peoples of Plymouth willeth groweth and eateth these onions. So be-eth!"

Not everybody was completely happy about this forced eating of dago onions. It was in an act of revenge and in retaliation for such an imposition upon the common man that the greenkeeper stole Sir Francis's bowls. He left a note in the box from whenceth they had been stoleneth. It readeth:

Sir Francis defeated the great Armada,
With Englishmen full of fight and ardour,
Rise Sir Francis the Queen spoke out so bold,
He was given the ship Dagoby, which he sold,
He kept those bloody onions, full of disease,
Forced all in Plymouth to eat them with cheese.

Despite losing his bowls, Sir Francis Drake enforced his will upon the population of Plymouth; they would grow and eat the Spanish onions every day, no matter the medical circumstances. The situation became so serious that whenever anyone in Plymouth referred to the strange Sir Francis Drake or his onions, one spoke in a whisper. Anyone heard criticising Sir Francis, did so with the fear of vicious reprisals. Similar punishment was handed down if they were caught not eating their daily intake of Spanish onions.

Even when toilet tissue was impossible to buy in Plymouth, due to the fierce demand and hoarding that took place, he would not relax his rules on onion eating. Eventually, this severe attitude led to whispers of the *Drake-Onion problem* that had besieged the city, and this word has now become part of our English dictionary to describe such tough conditions of life.

This story about the Armada has just reminded me of something that my old grandpa told me about whilst I sat on his wooden leg in front of the old coal fire in Northfleet as a young boy. I'd better tell you about this piece of history told by a very brave man who fought for his King and country during the First World War and lost a leg in the trenches.

One of the first radio show quizzes broadcast after this war of useless slaughter was, *Long forgotten sayings by long forgotten people* and my grandpa was invited to take part in this show. He had answered all the questions correctly in six preliminary shows and eventually reached the grand final. If he won the grand final he would become the champion of champions and be rewarded with a grand prize consisting of a trip to Paris for two and a new fully mechanised wooden leg, complete with spare batteries for walking up to twenty miles without recharge.

The two other contestants on the show were questioned before grandpa and they both answered only two of the three questions correctly. Now it was my grandpa's turn! He only needed to answer all three questions to be the champion of champions and win all the prizes.

"Mr. White", spoke Walter Winterbottom to my grandpa, "Your first question is: who was asked by his brother, what is the common habit of a Mexican queer, and what was his answer?" This presented no problem for grandpa who smiled and said in reply, "This long forgotten saying was by Captain Horatio Brownbottom whilst he was visiting Mexico in 1793 and his answer to his brother was, Never let a day go by."

"Correct Mr. White, now for your second question. Who was it who was asked, 'have you ever been to Mount Olive', and what was his reply?" Good old grandpa smiled and spoke with the confidence of a winner. "It was spoken to Popeye in the film, Popeye's Birds & Bees, and his answer was, Yes, I went to mount Olive but by the time that I got there she had gone."

"Excellent Mr. White, now for the last question, which if you answer correctly will give you the champion of champions award. Your last and final question is, who said 'what the bloody hell was that,' and then died shortly afterwards?"

My grandpa racked his brains and after the buzzer went to indicate his time was up, he said "Mr. Winterbottom, I have studied this subject of long forgotten sayings by long forgotten people for over fifty years and cannot recall anybody quoted as saying such a thing. I must pass on this question." Wally

Smiling Chops sounded like a vicar at a funeral as he spoke out sadly, "Mr. White, you have correctly answered two of the three questions and passed on one. On the one you passed on, who said 'what the bloody hell was that?' The answer to this question was The Captain of the Titanic."

My grandpa received a less valuable prize of a battery operated foot (without leg or batteries) plus a cheap day trip to Southend on the bus.

Referring to homosexuals for a few minutes, I would like the government of this country to allocate special queer areas throughout the country where these members of our society could exercise their ways of life in private. This would be great for them because in these special sanitised rooms they could feel like normal people, without subjecting the majority of us other people to watching their antics.

In my opinion, a homosexual can behave in any way he wishes, providing this behaviour does not offend my wife, my children or me. Joking about them is similar to joking about Jews, rabbits, Churches, the Pope, transvestites, God, Jesus or any other subject that can give a laugh to a large number of people. There is no particular animosity towards this group of people providing they do not offend others.

If they object to jokes about themselves then maybe we should lobby our MPs to pass an Anti-Homosexual Sarcasm Act, which is a great subject for another joke in itself. The nearer the nub we reach with jokes or criticism of a minority group, the more they become dangerous and violent, like rabid injured dogs. The more violent they become then the more truth is likely to be present in the subject matter under discussion.

Homosexuals are a minority group, looking for recognition and promotion of their faith. We, as the *silent majority,* would like to have homosexuals fully identified so that they can be avoided, joined with or congratulated, whatever be our choice. This shows that we are really all in agreement and not at odds with each other.

Will all my readers please help me to examine this subject in greater depth by sending in your answers to the following questions:

(1) Are you a homosexual and are you proud of it?
(2) Do you blame homosexuals for the spreading of Aids?
(3) Do you want your children to be in contact with homosexuals?

Once all of your replies are received, we can publish the result of these completely unbiased questions that will be printed out from my Korean made IBM compatible computer. This electronic wizard operates with my own bespoke software programme, developed after eighteen years of study into this subject.

It's strange how in previous polls the answers given by homosexuals are completely opposite to the answers given by non homosexuals, and I expect this trend to continue in this new poll. So, do we carry out the wish of the minority or of the majority? This, is a very interesting question my friends. At the moment we are led by the noisy rabble of the minority, rather like trade unions really.

Whatever your feelings, I wish to make my position very clear. I don't want my children in contact with them, I don't want to be influenced by them and I wish that homosexuality was illegal. Nothing personal, but maybe you would be happier dressed in fluorescent pink suits with a large H on your forehead so there would be no need for contact magazines. Now that I've allowed another minority group to speak its mind and have a balanced debate, let's continue.

As a believer in equal opportunity, I welcome any published homosexual comments relating to the perversity of Dick Head and his writings.

My homosexual students should have no fear for their chances in their *M.Sc. (DikHed)* graduation, because it is your ability we are testing, not your sexual preferences. You will still receive your Dick *M.Sc. (DikHed) certificate*, but it will be overprinted in four inch high letters saying *HOMO* in pink ink. This is to identify you as part of this minority group which you are so proud of, to your friends and employers alike.

As an added benefit for the HOMO graduates, the Dick Head's Old Boys Club in Fulham has recently opened the Pinko Room that is exclusively for you. It is fitted with dressing tables complete with ten shades of lipstick and mascara, plus double settees with aircraft type seats. Special rose emblazoned note paper is placed at your disposal and a senior surgeon is on call to discuss any type of sex change operation that you may desire. Unfortunately the President of the Club, Prince Rudolf, is somewhat strict on the club rules and refuses to allow kissing or any other acts to take place inside the club. However, the club next door, *The Bent Boys Bar*, is more understanding towards such indiscretion.

The rich man's morality is very often regarded as totally immoral by the average working class man; so what value can we place on your individual morality my smirking liberal minded readers? "What the hell is he talking about in this chapter?" you are most probably mumbling, but soon you will regroup your thinking on the morality of mankind - on that you can be sure.

Where does morality for giving charity start? Does it start here at home within the Land of Hope and Glory, or should we just take a peek over the page of the world's book of suffering; forcing ourselves to face the truth of how fellow man treats fellow man.

"Charity starts at home," says the well bred and well fed pub drinker. "We've got to look after our own lot first, mate. Look at all them old ladies dying of cold, we gotta help them first!" Yes, yes, my charitable readers of the tabloid newspapers, but what about true morality and helping one's fellow man, what do we do to help?

"It's no good giving to charity, mate, because those bleeders in the fancy cars; those geezers that runs the show, they spends all the money. Nothing reaches those poor buggers in Eathy - bloody Opia," spouts the man drinking his third beer, having spent enough on booze to have saved several lives in Eathy - bloody Opia. This is a standard excuse heard many moons ago; a standard excuse spouted for the umpteenth time.

How about those poor old ladies (let alone the poor bloody whales) dying of cold? How on this charitable Earth of ours can it happen? Just look at the total lack of care that exists for these dreadful things to happen.

Firstly, all the family members of these poor frozen dying old dears must have the morality of a sewer rat to allow gran or auntie to live in the cold and squalor that we all know exists today in this wonderful consumer society. A society where electric windows and aluminium wheels on the new family chariot take up all of our concentration and attention. "By the way, poor old Aunt Bessie is starving and dying of hypothermia, can you hurry up and choose your car so that you can take her a slice of bread and twenty pence for the gas meter? I know it's none of my business mate, but if only ...."

All this is to no avail, because Aunt Bessie was buried last week, the family wore black, everybody cried, all felt guilty and drove home in the new limousine with electric windows and aluminium wheels. Poor old Aunt Bessie, she was a grand old lady - they don't make 'em like that any more.

After the family lets Bessie down, we look towards the caring neighbours, those lovely folks believing that their night noise and drunken singing will help keep Bessie warm and drive away the hunger. Such wonderful neighbours last spoke to Bessie in 1967 and asked her "Why don't you cut your grass every week as we do you silly cow, otherwise you will lower the value of our property."

Obviously, old Bessie at 79 years old was considered fit enough for this task, as indeed she was considered capable of doing her own shopping. Much better she walks those one and a half miles to the local supermarket every week pulling her shopping trolley behind her; even better when it's pouring down with rain. The walk there is much easier than the walk back, so let's leave it to somebody else; why should we get involved because she would become a burden and you wouldn't want that, would you?

The Social Service ginks, direct from the University of Moscow, also attended poor old Bessie's inquest to put in their presentation. They gave their pre-printed speech, "We consider that we have followed all the necessary guidelines as specified in How to let old people pass away cold and hungry, when dealing with Mrs. Bessie Brinks. Everything possible had been done by the Social Services Department to help her in her hour of need. It is indeed tragic, however, that more could not have been done and had sufficient Government funding been available from this Tory dictatorship, I have no doubt that the life of Mrs. Bessie Brinks could have been saved." Amen, my little left wing idiot. You have defended your beliefs and stupidity with the normal aplomb as expected of all Government officials - "It's not my fault, and if only.........."

Just imagine one day, a civil servant actually saying in straightforward English: "My friends, we in the civil service are to blame. Mrs. Bessie Brinks was literally murdered by us because we are employed to ensure that she did not die of squalor, hunger and of a broken heart. Yes, I submit to you that we should be fired from the civil service and tried in open court for our shortcomings. After all, we are human beings just like everybody else."

Stop! Stop! Dick Head, you always wander off into dreams of fantasy. Next you will be suggesting that we give free electricity and free food to Aunt Bessie and those like her- No! No! How can we do that, we must save enough money for more important matters and don't forget the cost of saving the whales must be paid for as well.

If all else fails, the Church will take over. Bessie had attended church until the age of 68, until her closest friend Elsie Plonkervist (Dutch extraction) died. After Elsie's death, Bessie had grave doubts regarding the practicality of believing in a God and Church that allowed Elsie to suffer so much at the end. Because of this, Bessie did not attend her local church any more, and she quickly found out that if you don't believe, you don't get help - you've got to believe me on this. For several months, the father from her old church called to give comfort and counselling that consisted of saying prayers which Bessie objected to based upon her feelings over Elsie's painful demise. After the fifth month of trying, Father Donald Duckworth decided to utilise his valuable time elsewhere with people who had a greater need and had greater belief than Bessie.

You see, if you don't believe, you may not go to heaven, but if you are in a similar position as Bessie, you will most certainly suffer in life.

OK, so Bessie was failed by family, Social Services and the Church, but what are you really getting at Dick Head? What I'm really getting at my greedy freaks is who really cares about anything? Who is prepared to make personal sacrifices to improve this world of ours? Stop putting a few coins into the collection boxes and start really caring - let's fight the people who don't care and then give us the impression they do care. Let's become a caring nation!

Christ, Dick, you do go on about Charity.

Yes, I do!

Chapter 5

From Roads to DIK 1

Common logic is considered a danger to the bureaucratic raw power base and is treated as an unacceptable challenge to their promotion aims

Joseph "White" Hall (1898)
Shadow Minister for Transport

During a recent visit to the famous Sproutzenbrau second-hand book shop in Brussels, I was fortunate enough to find and purchase an original leather bound edition of that wonderful book of guidance, *Straight Roads and Bent Priests*.

Written by Father Marcus Eindelhus in 1645, this fabled writing gives full praise to the simple logical minds of the Roman road builders, during the Nero era, for building all of their highways in dead straight lines. This was a far cry from the later post-Nero period when the road building programme was severely disrupted by the local politicians. It was decided that most of the local taxes should be spent on improving the Rome Fire Brigade system (which had come into some serious criticism then due to the arsonic nature of Nero himself).

A proportion of these local taxes was spent by Nero on constructing thousands of wooden crosses to which faithful Christian activists were attached with large nails for long periods of time, or until they were dead. Singing or any other form of enjoyment was forbidden once you were crucified, but rarely did this occur.

Our belated gratitude goes out to the Tarmaccidi family of Villa Strada, Rome's premier road building family for over six hundred years. These beer swilling builders were the catalyst and driving force behind the Roman road building programme. This construction allowed the multitudes of fearful Roman troops to be kept on the straight and narrow, heading far afield to pillage and rape in distant lands, lands yet to be conquered and to experience the taste of crappy Italian food. I am definitely *anti-pasta.*

Father Marcus Eindelhus eventually died of infected haemorrhoids following a traumatic encounter with a strange looking Icelandic penguin whilst he was swimming off the coast of Greenland. This unsuspecting penguin was stranded upon an iceberg and suffered from severe concussion following this event. The penguin was given the name of Jacob and she quickly became our holy man's cuddly toy at night.

The happy couple went to live in a vicarage in Wrexham where Jacob was immediately infatuated and finally became addicted with eating over fifty chocolate covered biscuits per week, bought from Tesco's every Friday night

Not everybody was happy when Jacob turned up at Brussels Cathedral on a bright summer's day to attend the funeral of our scribe and father, Father Marcus

Eindelhus. Jacob was dressed in multicoloured matching Indian saris which she had purchased from a Hindu temple in Dover just before boarding the ferry for the short trip across the English Channel to attend this sad event. One of the badly dressed jealous deacons was heard to whisper to his assistant, "What's that bloody penguin doin' 'ere then?"

Jacob now runs a fish and chip shop in Bishopsgate where most of the British born penguins live in peace and harmony.

After carefully studying any one of the many thousands of modern brightly printed and over priced road maps, you will see a mass of multicoloured spaghetti lines splashed across the page, depicting the incredibly idiotic British road system. Standing regally apart and superior from this Technicolor mess, you will witness many bold red lines clearly indicating the survival of the original Roman roads. These roads are as straight today as the day they were first born.

This survival of pure straightness is more than can be said for the six hundred toothless holy fathers from Ghent, so described on page 67 of *Straight Roads And Bent Priests*. An updated version of this Father Marcus Eindelhus's ancient publication is being published by the Belgium Bint Press and is due for release early next year. The title of this modern rehash, describing the active priests and their road preferences, is *Bent Roads, Even More Bent Priests And Two Postmen Deliver Everything*.

This latest edition will not be leather bound like its predecessor, but will be available in a paperback edition at the bargain basement price of £6.00. Progress in these modern times really is becoming cheap and cost efficient because £6.00 for this publication equates to only one penny for every toothless holy father and even less for every offence described therein.

For those amongst my readership not having yet learnt to read, do not despair at the thought of missing out on this indulgence just because you are an ignorant git. You will not miss out on all the lovely dirt, because you can also interpret the stories by following the one hundred and fifty pornographically illustrated coloured pictures that are located at the back of the book.

This costs you illiterate race only four pence per dirty picture, which, compared with the lesser quality of porno video films available in the local sex shop, is still excellent value for money.

The present British network of cochlear, convoluted, whorled and coiled roads require the IQ of a genius to allow you to interpret them correctly, let alone being able to plan a trip from Walton to Wigan. This self-degenerating hideous mess of progressive bureaucratic diarrhoea is now completely out of control, but by pure poetic justice and coincidence, these modern convoluted road shapes resemble closely the rear ends of the bureaucratic fools who designed these lunatic highways in the first place.

The building of roads in today's advanced society can be, and should be, a very simple and uncomplicated occupation. It involves such basic procedures as drawing a straight line, digging a big trench, filling it in with hard core and then laying a top surface to suit the conditions for which the road is being built. Hence you have a straight Roman type road.

Some additional mechanical help to the road construction gang is normally given by the employment of several types of huge yellow earth diggers and a few thousand happy Irishmen half smashed on Guinness. If Guinness had been available to the Romans, then Rome could certainly have been built in a day.

It was our friends from Nazi Germany (now our European friends and partners) that made the greatest job of building a complete network of fantastic dead straight roads. Herman the German named them autobahns whilst at the same time he placed his towel on the sun lounger by the pool as the sun rose each morning in Spain. These autobahns were specifically designed to accommodate the Germans' huge fleet of tank transporters, which were a very common mode of transport during the pre-1939 nationalistic days in Germany.

Those were wonderful heady days for living in the heart of the Third Reich, that great teutonic empire for the master race as perceived by Adolf Hitler, my distant relative on the kraut side of the family. In 1943 it is estimated that there were over fifty-five million men (and some six million women) living in Europe and sporting small Hitler type moustaches and wearing black shirts. A later study carried out on Christmas Day in 1946 concluded that not a single Hitler styled moustache was to be viewed anywhere in Europe, but some sixty-seven million turkeys had just gobbled their last gobble.

I'm just a simple cock robin,
With red plumage upon my breast,
I'd rather be an archbishop,
Or a footballer like George Best,
It's so cold outside at Christmas,
My turkey friends are in a mess,
Plucked and stuffed for roasting,
Which they regard as fully dressed?
I'm so happy to be a cock robin,
With red plumage upon my breast.

Jack Bird (1986)

Road building and killing forty million people has nothing to do with cuckoo clock making and is far less skilful as a trade. This concludes that Adolf was a more powerful mortal than my father, but far less skilled with his hands. Since ending the European slaughter of the second world war in 1944, the German autobahns of mass military transportation are now converted over to a more domestic use. This conversion is now part of the German Miracle that allows hordes of blonde haired conceited German tourists to invade the rest of Europe with a high degree of success that was denied to them during the second world war. Iss goodz, ya? The Fourth Reich is already created and distorting our minds, my friends. We are all so busy scratching our backsides, pulling our plonkers and complaining about not getting enough of the something for nothing being handed out by our governments, that we fail to see this real danger.

Working hard for Herman the German is, however, a much better proposition than slaving for a non-European culture that is quietly but surely taking over our entire industries and destroying our cultural heritage.

Just use the divide and rule tactics to incite the greed that is our main factor of life. Very soon we may all be crouching like crabs on the dining room floor whilst eating raw bloody fish from Osaka with Joe Tow and his sword. Pearl Harbour is a lesson on Japanese culture that should never be forgotten, if we are to survive economically and culturally in the future. Long live black pudding!

As I was saying before the bus conductor came upon the scene, when at first you don't succeed, then try, try again. This famous piece of advice was first given to Adolf during his final inventive days on earth in 1944. He gave little attention to this advice, which he considered as relatively unimportant because he was otherwise involved with more important matters. He was fast heading towards becoming more than just fractionally annoyed because things were not going quite as planned on all fronts. Adolf was not renowned as being a great listener to other people's theories and certainly this long held trait continued during this terminal ending of life crisis in 1944. Adolf became so annoyed, that despite his relationship with God, he could see that the world was turning against him and his future was very insecure.

He was heard to shout out in a drunken anger "Ziss itz bullshitz!" just before pulling the trigger of his Italian pistol, which he used on this final occasion as a thank you to that tosser Mussolini. Adolf thus departed this world at a rapid rate of knots heading for the land reserved for losing dictators situated in the blue beyond.

Have you noticed how the marketing department within the Vatican Church has never proposed or authorised a *Saint Adolf's day*, despite the co-operation during the war? Never trust an ally when the chips are down or when the vino runs dry, particularly if they speak posh Italian with a Vatican accent whilst working for a holy bank. Who did cut his hair anyway?

A recent edition of "Palace Observer" magazine quoted a comment made by the Queen during her recent visit to meet the Pontiff. It stated, "I don't recognise the fellow in the white cloak reading the Bible, but the guy just behind him reading a comic book and scratching his bum is Dick Head the famous author." I refute these royal allegations and intend to tell her so personally the next time I am honoured with an invitation to the palace!

Who knows what state the world would now be in today if only Adolf had taken notice of the other piece of good advice given to him in 1931 when he was told "clear off back to Austria you Austrian midget". It was a dark skinned bus conductor who gave this advice with considerable venom, whilst Adolf complained about the weather in Berlin. This man of non-German blood was eventually shot in revenge by a citizens' firing squad on Easter Monday in 1938.

The firing squad was made up of twelve unhappy bus commuters, all of them with a grudge to bear against bus conductors. They were personally selected by Adolf over a period of six days during which time he carried a placard to the bus stop. The placard had a message in bright yellow lettering saying, "My name is Adolf Hitler, I am not a daft short Austrian midget and I require twelve miserable commuters to shoot the rude dick who sells us overpriced bus tickets."

The German military, and others of sympathetic mind, readily and speedily responded to this request and over seven thousand people volunteered for the job, all bringing along their own weapons of various types to make the job quick and cheap for Adolf. Over seven thousand unhappy and unsuccessful volunteers left the selection hall in a real teutonic huff, including an ex-artillery major, Johan Verbitzenberg III, who had brought his 150 millimetre howitzer with him, pulled by two huge white horses that he had named

Hyne and Rick. The twelve successful volunteers were all very short, sported small black moustaches and were as daft and short as Adolf.

As I was saying before Adolf led me astray, when at first you don't succeed, then try, try again. I can inform the world, including my faithful dedicated students, that this famous and classical turn of phrase was written into the history books by Deondeneno the famous astrologer on the 25 December 1478. These words were at first hard to decipher from the scrawled lines that were written just before his passing away in agony and frustration. He died of worn out feet whilst looking for the edge of the world. His worn out feet refused to support him any longer, causing him to fall onto his face and break his very thick neck.

Deondeneno was the 132nd honourable elected president of the *Portuguese Flat Earth Society* that had its headquarters located above a famous boxing gymnasium situated in the centre of Lisbon. Deondeneno was the perfect physical specimen of a man, becoming a very famous athlete within his country, culminating in his winning the fifty mile walking race at the 1472 Olympics held in Venice. These Venetian Olympics are recorded as the most tragic of all the Olympic games, such tragedy caused by the huge torrential rain storms that hit the Venetian coast during the second day of these games.

This torrential downpour caused the sad demise of some 356 French athletes who were drowned after lightning struck the gondolier taxis being used for their transportation from the mainland to the Venetian shores. This terrible tragedy happened during the earlier days of civilisation, long before the industrial revolution or even before the French had managed to irreparably infect and destroy the culture of Canada and North Africa. However, no matter what the historical clock reads, at the time of this disaster, the rest of the world already really hated these arrogant French people with rubber covered legs and stinking breath.

Such an attitude was reflected by the assembled audience that decided that watching these French athletes drowning in agony was a far better choice than watching the preliminary heats of the Olympic races. A great cheer went up from the watching crowd, which consisted of some 170,000 spectators happily very merry on grappa, as the last sinking gondolier taxi finally submerged below the surface of the canal.

The few survivors were milling about in the water and started screaming for assistance that was never to arrive. Some members of the French swimming team were amongst the few initial survivors and due to their supreme aquatic abilities, they eventually reached the canal bank, adjacent to St. Marks Square, where they attempted to clamber to safety. With great enthusiasm, the spectators along the canal bank pushed these poor souls back into the deep end of the canal using gondolier punts, to the absolute delight and rapturous applause of the watching happy and ecstatic throng.

Eventually, the crowd became bored at this French side-show, and so the last three surviving swimmers were held under the water with gondolier poles to finish them off quickly so that everybody could continue watching the real games.

What a fantastic day was had by all. It took so long for the drowning to be completed that almost everybody missed seeing the men's 4 x 400 yards relay race, which was actually won by four milkmen from Hong Kong. The French team won no medals in the swimming competitions that year and sent letters of complaint to a Mr. Condomani, President of the Italian Olympic Committee in Rome. These French letters were put on file for future reference.

Deondeneno, as president of *The Portuguese Flat Earth Society*, was increasingly coming under great pressure from a long bearded weirdo professor by the name of Rhondo Globulus, who was president of *The World Is Round Society*. Just imagine this long bearded Greek prat from Athens standing up during Deondeneno's annual address at his conference and stating in front of all these dignitaries that the world was definitely round and not bloody flat!. So mad was our Olympian champion, Deondeneno, that he shouted out in unrestrained anger across the hall, "Right you daft nincompoop, I challenge you to walk all around the world and end up where you started, if the world is so round!"

Globulus jumped out of his seat and retorted with great glee, "This challenge is accepted on the basis that you must also walk to the edge of the world and fall over the edge you stupid idiot!" So, the great *Round or Flat competition* started out on its way on the 25 May 1476 from the church gates of Biggleswade at exactly midday.

Biggleswade was chosen as the starting point for this race because it was reckoned to be the epicentre of a flat earth by *The Portuguese Flat Earth Society* and the most detested township in the world as specified by *The World Is Round Society*.

To cut a very long and sad story short, and to avoid giving details of his terrible sufferings, I can tell you briefly that Globulus returned home from the opposite direction from whence he departed, some twenty-three days after he set out, thereby proving that the earth was round. Deondeneno, however, was never seen alive again. A bottle containing inside a note written by him was found some 206 years later.

The surviving Globulus was a huge hit and hero with all friends and foes alike, because he had proven that the world was indeed very round and not very flat. Nobody thought of calculating that by walking a maximum of thirty miles per day, then if Globulus had truly walked around the world as he claimed, then the world had a circumference of only 690 miles, less than the length of Great Britain. It's a small world, isn't it my friends, even though it's not flat.

On the 30 September 1684, a young lad who answered to the name of Snotty Dick or Signor Tossa (whatever you preferred to call him), espied a green glass bottle floating up the river Thames on the evening tide. Thinking only of the two farthings reward that the local brewery would pay him for delivering to them such a handsome beer bottle, Snotty Dick quickly stripped himself down to his Marks & Spencers shorts and swam out to the centre of the river to retrieve his treasure.

Once safely back onto the river's bank with the bottle secure within his filthy grasp, Snotty noticed that there was something foreign inside this strange looking bottle. This foreign item quickly turned out to be the last testament from Deondeneno. It had been found! The rest of this story is now written down into the annals of history, including the *Deondeneno Death Ode* that is now more famous than those two postmen.

The Deondeneno Death Ode consists of some 245 pages of beautiful poetry (it was a very big bottle) that ends with that famous line of endless logic, "If at first you don't succeed then try, try again". It is reckoned that more people around the world can quote this Death Ode word for word, than can quote the Bible in the same way. Amen.

Roads are designed by highway engineers and are then constructed to allow us, the common tax paying motorist to travel in the shortest possible time from A to B in a safe condition. To achieve this objective, a huge sum of money is extracted from the good old car driver in the form of fuel and road taxes. In return for paying these huge taxes, we have the privilege of driving a car, upon which another huge car tax plus vat is added and collected by the government. Not satisfied with these rip-offs, we are then forced to pay tolls to cross bridges or to go under tunnels that have been built with our money in the first place.

You want to park somewhere? Be prepared to pay even more money for the privilege of using a space of the road that has also been built with our money. All these taxes are paid by the motorist from his income, which has already again been taxed by the government at source under the guise of income tax. Furthermore, we pay a local tax to the local authority, part of which is supposedly used for local road building.

We must also ask what happens to all the other billions of pounds of other taxes collected by the ever grabbing exchequer in London. Indeed, the Government can, and does, charge whatever it likes and when it likes, only controlled by the voting bribery that becomes common place with all parties just before election time.

We mere mortals of the highways just continue paying and paying and paying because of our love for an independent life and the glory of driving our twentieth century chariot in full view of our peers. It takes minimal brain power to understand that once we buy our dream car, the last thing that we then want to do is to walk to our destination

This simple fact has been noted by our civil service in Whitehall and is taken as a sanction to allow their official stealing of money from the car driving taxpayer under false pretences to continue.

That is why we are stuck daily in a bloody great traffic jam on the M25 motorway around London! Can any man of even the lowest sanity level really imagine a bigger farce than that of the building of the M25 motorway around our capital city of London? It reads like a tragic comedy, with everybody in authority blaming somebody else in authority concerning the cause of this permanent hundred miles long car park.

With experiences gained in Paris, Tokyo, San Francisco, Madrid, and hundreds of other cities before the M25 was built, the good old reliable civil servants at the transport department made an utter balls-up by ignoring these past lessons.

Imagine that if any of my first year Dick Head undergraduates were requested in their final exam to plan the M25 with absolutely no prior experiences whatsoever of road transport problems, could you really make a bigger mess of it? The answer to this really simple question is that even my parrot Betsy could have done a better job by simply placing droppings on top of a London road map to indicate just how it should have been built

If we could have listened in on the original planning meeting before the M25 had been finalised, the conversation might have gone like this: "Right Fred mate, now let's build a new big ring road around London to ease congestion and to keep the traffic of our great capital moving. The road users pay so much money every year in the form of various taxes that they deserve a decent road."

Fred replied, "Great idea Jack, but what about all the traffic from the M1, M2, M3, M4, M11, M40 motorways and all the other trunk roads that are already permanently chock-a-block in the morning. How can a motorway around London cope with all of this traffic? Taking all this traffic from these existing motorways and cramming it onto a circular motorway during the rush hour will be a tremendous task for us to achieve."

Without blinking an eyelid, happy Jack responded with a great deal of glee in his eyes: "You're right mate, if all these existing motorways are already chock-a-block every day using only three lanes on each one of them, then when all this traffic joins this new M25 motorway, then at least ten traffic lanes will be essential to avoid a complete snarl-up every day."

With a great deal of irritation Fred snapped back with his sharp reply: "That's bloody obvious mate, do you think I'm a bleedin' idiot or somefing". To defuse this fiery situation, Jack spoke in a low-voiced conciliatory tone: "No, you're right Fred mate, but after we finish these plans, we must get it approved by the Ministry for such an expensive road."

The Ministry employs trained monkeys and a few people complete with computers and lots and lots of statistics to prove that Fred and Jack are fools in dreamland, both wishing to overspend the meagre funds available from the road building budget.

Peter Owen Nicholas Clive Edwards OBE, the chief planning officer, chaired the meeting that made the final decision on the planning of this massive road building project. He spoke up like a queer weasel.

"Gentlemen, after close study of all the statistics, it is clear that the planned M25 motorway need only be constructed incorporating three lanes which is considered sufficient to handle all the traffic that is projected to use it over the next 25 years.

"I know that all other cities in the world have found it necessary to have at least eight lanes on their orbital motorways. However, with the added benefit of incorporating the new British designed computerised system of Controlled Handling Of Cars Keeping Easy Roads (CHOCKER), from a new centralised computer station, we can now move twenty times more traffic over the same length of motorway in less time.

"In the unlikely event of a road accident causing delays, we have special road blocks to be lowered from helicopters, known as CHOCKER BLOCKS, to bypass such delays. In the future, the M25 will be synonymous, and known around the world as the motorway with the CHOCKER BLOCK principle."

This decision can only be compared with the C.S.E. Examination in mathematics, where a pass is given for simply turning up for the exam, remembering your name and trying. These planners had decided that 3 + 3 + 3 + 3 + 3 + 3 + 3 + 3 = 3 which in the C.S.E. Exam would give you a good pass at grade 3.

Unfortunately, in road building it represented a disaster for millions of motorists. The government says it is not to blame. Did anyone get fired for building this because our waffling fools at the Ministry of Transport blamed the miscalculation on the government figures for future road usage.

An official statement from a Ministry official said, "We did as we were led to believe was correct from the official figures - don't blame us".

I seem to remember another time during the war crimes' trials after the second world war when this excuse resulted in multiple hangings. Perhaps we should ask if the same type of trials should happen over the M25 debacle. I shall be requesting that the government hold a referendum on this important matter, with the clear penalty that a yes vote will result in all the Whitehall wonders responsible for the M25 being hung, not by their necks but by their testicles.

Is it not a fact that over two hundred Members of Parliament have already volunteered to be the hangman and prepared to place the rope in its allocated position? I have informed these politicians that there would be £150 in it for every hanging, to which most of them pleaded poverty and requested that we allow them a period of two years in which they could pay this amount in instalments.

We all know that the M25 is such a stupid idiotic mistake made by idiots at the idiotic Ministry of Transport, and yet it is amazing that we listen to P.O.N.C.Edwards from the ministry spouting the same old garbage to the media. I quote, "Based upon our traffic projections, the M25 should have been sufficient to handle traffic until the year 2100, but unfortunately, these projections are now revised by six thousand percent and thus we can now visualise that some problems may exist. But, you must remember that .... " ugh!

Obviously, the permanent delays experienced every day over all of the M25 are now described within the Ministry's dictionary as "some problems". By appearing on the TV programme Question Time, my question to the minister responsible for this grandiose cock-up would be a winner. "OK sleaze box, now tell me why, within twenty one minutes of the M25 motorway opening for traffic we had a three hour delay on the section between the M40 and the M4 motorways and this particular delay has been a permanent feature ever since? Perhaps the traffic increased by one thousand percent overnight?"

After putting this question, panic would set in and greasy hands would not answer the question but would waffle for the remainder of the programme about how the Tories had spent 267% more than the Labour Party on new roads over the same period of time. All very interesting stuff for the few boring Professors of Statistics that may be listening in the audience. It is of very little relevance to 230,000 punters of the road that sit hour after hour in the pollution of the M25 traffic jams, being forced to pass the time away by scratching the lower parts of their body. Just try to calculate the horrendous cost to the country because of this motorway stupidity that locks away hundreds of thousands of top business people inside their steel cages for several hours per day.

Stuck in cars, rather than acting as our captains of industry earning the export business so badly needed to pay off our National Debt. Certainly, these lost billions would pay for a twenty lane motorway, let alone a four lane motorway. Do you think anybody is clever enough to work this out? Maybe, just maybe, the solution is known but it is hidden away so that nobody needs to make a decision that could influence their civil service careers.

Yes, my drivers of despair, it is all a planned plot to keep us locked away each day to be sure that we cannot become agitators against the government. Fuel tax is earned on every drop of petrol and diesel, whether we are stuck in the M25 traffic jam or speeding towards Glasgow on the A74. In Russia they have food queues and in England we have M25 queues - very similar indeed except we don't go hungry, do we?

Just look at the total effort and waste of human material that the local authorities put into screwing the motorist, because he has no defence and is guilty as charged on every occasion. Imagine if all the people employed collecting road tax, VAT on petrol, traffic wardens, painters of yellow lines, traffic police, etc. were disbanded and transferred to a town police organisation, then we really could protect the citizens against the criminals and nutters that have turned most citizens' lives into a nightmare of fear.

"But Dick Head, we must have these people doing these important social jobs, they save so many lives!" scream the town hall idiots who do not have the benefit of knowing what exists outside of local government and do not possess my inner knowledge of street life.

Undue pressure is only exerted upon the motorist because the authorities can never lose - they achieve their own internal targets at the monetary expense of the tax paying motorist, spouting out statistics to prove their points. The Minister of Transport stands up in the House to reply.

"To answer the question just put by the Right Honourable Gentleman from Prickly Central, I am pleased to confirm that although the M25 is not running entirely as originally planned by the previous Government, our new rear seat belt law is. It has resulted in a reduction of 3.874% in the number of accidents occurring with young children on this same stretch of motorway this year as compared with last year."

Very good my statistical Minister, but how about improving the lot of the poor old motorist? I've yet to meet any motorist who would complain about the price of petrol, motor tax or other motorists' charges, providing they could be sure that the income was spent in a sensible way. It is very clear to me that simple things are difficult for the government to understand. The next time you are sitting in your car stuck in the M25 jam, or any other motorway jam, just calculate the cost of all this wasted time to this nation.

I reckon that I am personally held up at least 500 hours per year on our motorway system, by jams and go-slows caused by overcrowding. If the average is only 250 lost hours per year for the twenty million drivers on our roads at a cost of say £20 per hour for this lost production time, then we are talking about a loss to the nation of a staggering **ONE HUNDRED MILLION MILLION POUNDS PER YEAR**.. Add to this the wasted petrol, wear and tear on our cars and lost export orders and you can more than **DOUBLE THIS TO TWO HUNDRED MILLION MILLION POUNDS.**

Discussing the additional fuel being burnt with its effect on the environment is yet a more serious affair and one that will be studied in book 7 entitled It's A Gas! I expect a writ to be issued upon me by The Ministry of Transport disputing these figures of mine, followed by the publication of a 2,768 page report by a special select committee set up to confuse the Government and the general public, and to discredit my calculations. My figures may not be perfect, but they are near enough to simply emphasise the unbelievable stupidity of governments over the past five decades.

Please add up this loss together with the car tax and fuel duty and value added tax to see just what is being screwed out of us with nothing in return. How about a new motorway network covering every city in the UK with ten lane motorways?

The alternative is further chaos, but there again this problem will be faced by a different government. "How about the costs, Dick Head?" "Yes, minister, and how about the three million unemployed people doing nothing who could be building our road infrastructure." "But.................."

On the question of cars themselves, I have noticed the wonderful "extras" that our car manufacturers con us with by working upon our snob personalities. Just notice the SRi, SL, L, GTi, etc. badges shining on the back of most cars as you drive along. You must then ask yourself how much you look to see if other cars on the road are a higher specification than yours.

The government have brought in new laws enforcing the wearing of seat belts, no kids in the front, no holding phone handsets whilst driving and a vast extra range of restrictions to hamper the motorist. If they brought in a new law tomorrow specifying that all cars must have ABS anti-locking brakes fitted on all cars, this would save more lives than all other related laws put together.

ABS brakes cost less than the average array of glitter and aluminium fitted to most new cars, so what is the value of your family's life, buster? Aluminium wheels and a sun roof, are they more important? Another ridiculous situation is that a car with ABS brakes driving in front of a car without ABS brakes becomes a serious road hazard likely to lead to death in the event of emergency braking. Does anybody care about this?

Whilst the motorways have been falling apart, the road traffic police have become even smarter; they have developed a new gang approach of hunting in packs to get the motorist at all times. How can you judge the efficiency of a motorway policeman if you are his superior officer? Perhaps you say "Well done Officer Plonker, I see that you controlled your motorway section so well this week that no bookings were necessary."

I don't think that this would be the approach taken by any senior officer. I believe that Constable Plonker would be told, "Officer Plonker, why do you think we install special radar equipment and cameras in your car? Why are you issued with mobile radar guns? Why is it that

Officer Vicious booked over three hundred speeding motorists last week and you booked only one?" No bookings mean no promotion, my son. Now let's talk for a few minutes about our road traffic police. These are a very special breed, born and bred to become hated public enemies to the general motoring public.

Not all people in one profession can be branded the same way. I must admit that in 1954, a road traffic policeman on the A1 in Yorkshire is reported as having smiled and said please to an old lady in dire distress after she had been attacked by a police dog owned by his brother. This old lady died of shock as a result of such kindness from the traffic policeman. Despite this sad ending, we must give the fellow the benefit of the doubt that his action was meant as a kind gesture, instead of being his usual arrogant self. No other cases of traffic police kindness have been reported to me since 1954 to match this level of pleasantry but updates will be given in each of my new publications should any future reports be received.

Some couple of years ago, I was merrily driving my four year old Ford Granada southwards on the M1 at 78 miles per hour in the outside fast lane. I was then listening to Rod Stewart singing "Gasoline Alley" on my Japanese stereo radio, thinking about God, pretty birds and making love. I was driving in the traffic flow at the same speed as all the other traffic in this outside lane. I was wishing ill will to nobody and thinking what a great day it was for all. Suddenly a police car pulled out from junction 16 and chased up behind me with a blue light flashing and a sign saying "stop police".

Now the sign read OK to me and I would support any such new proposed law, but obviously there must be two different meanings to this instruction. I stopped on the hard shoulder and lit up a cigarette to cover my nervousness - I was afraid that I had knocked somebody over without knowing. A giant thug-like character walked up to my open window and I trembled. "Right sir, I'd like to talk to you about the speed you have been driving at" said officer Puddingbottom with a definite hint of bad B.O. floating across the universe. With a stammer, I replied, "Yes officer, if you'd like to talk to me about my speed, then I have plenty of time and would like to talk about it as well. Now officer, tell me just what you'd like to know about my speed?"

"Please step out of the car sir!" spat out red-faced Puddingbottom with a teutonic guttural voice. "Now have you been drinking?" he requested of me. "Well my kind hearted and polite police officer, it is natural for me to drink eight times per day, at the very minimum. Now is this a quiz and was that my starter question for twenty points? Can you please tell me what the full range of prizes are if I get all the questions right?" Old happy Puddingbottom is obviously from an epileptic family because at that moment I thought he was going to bust a blood vessel as he shouted angrily in response, "OK clever Dick, now I'm nicking you for driving at 104 miles per hour! How about that?"

I wondered how he knew my name. "Serves you right Dick Head," I can hear you police supporters shouting at me in glee at home. That taught old Dick Head a lesson! Indeed it did my boys in blue, it taught me what I had suspected for many years, that many policemen are arrogant lying sods, only happy when they are practising their Gestapo tactics out on the poor motorists. Why motorists? Simply because as a motorist, you are guilty as hell from the moment you are stopped - you have no chance to defend yourself - you are an easy target for the Gestapo mind.

Once you are booked you are guilty, guilty and guilty. Try pleading not guilty and you will quickly find out that you are still found guilty but fined four times as much than if you had pleaded guilty first, plus you pay all witness costs - great British justice. You don't believe me?

Well, my readers in safe havens, I sincerely hope that you never have to experience similar treatment, which if you are a young, middle aged or old lady with big breasts, then you have nothing to worry about.

My booking was based upon a lie and took up the time of two policemen for almost half a day, resulting in me being fined £78 and banned from driving for three months. Imagine that at the same time as I was being booked an old lady living alone in the same town where I was taken to the police station could have been battered to death because no one was available to respond to her distress call in time. Still folks, the traffic police got their man!

Ironical isn't it how police get their priorities so wrong and act as a different race of people to the average working class man. How many policemen do you socialise with and how many of them drink in your pub? Interesting Ha? If they don't know how to, or don't want to socialise with the average guy, then how can they really understand him or expect co-operation from him? This is police policy after all.

A policeman's lot is a hard one, but they all know this when they join the force and understand the difficulties involved plus the advantage of the big pension at the end of the day. We have some great coppers to be proud of (fourteen at the last count), but the proportion of cheats and arrogant ones is increasing alarmingly. OK, OK, OK Dick Head, that's enough, where's your proof to back up this libel, shout all the daydreamers. Proof is proof if you can prove it.

If it's my word against a policeman, then what? The problem is, I can't think of a better way of policing our country under the existing democracy.

God, I'm in trouble when the police next stop me in my car, registration number

DIK 1.

Chapter 6

From Harpoons to Chat Lines

The goodness of mankind is inversely proportional to the cost of giving.

Bert Dole (1905)

At certain strategic God inspired moments throughout the history of our human race, a man is born (never a woman) with the planned objective of severely altering the direction in which this world continues flowing along its chosen road to obscurity and eventual destruction.

One such preordained bodily subject was an inventor who went about his life being referred to as Mr. Foyne of Norway by his friends, and by other less flattering names from his enemies. Mr. Foyne of Norway did not consider himself a real cruel Norwegian, but simply as a male of the human species destined to grow up to be a very clever, albeit cruel, inventor destined to change the direction of mankind and to control the extermination of the ***Whelsh*** population.

His clever inventive thoughts came forward into his active and progressive mind shortly after he began understanding the value of gold. He quickly decided that it was better to be very rich than very poor. This decision set his direction in life - he must live in the fast lane, which in itself drove him to his inventive ends. Such inventive ends were destined to be the beginning of the beginning of the end for one of our fellow mammals, those beautiful and defenceless whales of the deep blue seas.

Mr. Foyne of Norway was, of course, the jolly fellow who invented the shot-harpoon in 1870, which guaranteed that from that day forward, man could greatly increase the number of whales that could be killed during any single bloody whale hunting massacre on the high seas.

Up until this Foyne shot-harpoon, our fellow *Whelsh* mammal community had been content for millenniums, troubling nobody in particular and could be seen quietly burbling along in the waves of the oceans of the world singing that 'ammers song of "I'm forever blowing bubbles".

How quickly things can change for the innocent creatures of this world when gold is involved.

So horrendous and tragic was this new killing tool that Mr. Foyne became known by all the well educated whales as "*That Norwegian dick with the big prick that sticks*". I cannot condone abusive language being used for pure unadulterated blasphemy from any whale, but who can blame them for using such debased language under these circumstances?

This new shot-harpoon method was perfected even more in 1949 by the introduction of the electric harpoon that guaranteed even easier killing of even larger numbers of defenceless whales. This advanced harpoon was a much more efficient killing machine, passing an electric current into the whale's body after the harpoon had embedded itself into the body, thus paralysing or killing the poor animal without any other effort required.

A full range of soaps, candles, margarine, corsets, cattle foods, fertilisers, perfumes, pet foods and other commodities are by-products still derived today from the whale after it has been mercilessly slaughtered and processed.

Once this new equipment was made available for mass killing of the innocent whale, so began another example of man's commercial greed that would eventually guarantee the beginning of the annihilation process of another species of our fellow creatures from planet Earth.

To a common or garden sperm whale, having a whale of a time involves having a bloody great harpoon stuck in your ear and 10,000 volts injected into your body free of charge with kindest regards from the ship's captain, but without any overload protector being fitted. There is no electricity bill problem for you my *Whelsh* friends.

Have a nice day my fellow mammals, the world at large will always say that it really did worry about your survival, but we're still going to finish you off because it means we can make more profits whilst we exterminate you. The rarer you become, the more money per kilogram we earn from your flesh.

Do you know what the *mysticeti, odontoceti, Vladimir Remek* and *Tahl-Tan* are? If you don't know what the hell I'm babbling on about, then I consider that you must be an ignorant fool. It will be necessary for you to fully understand all of this by the time you reach book number 11 when my specialised Mother of Nature Knowledge will be essential for the completion of your studies on the *Whelsh*.

Those poor old whales, we must help save them from extinction! They will soon be a *Whelsh rarebit*.

Do you remember that prolonged saga concerning the dramatic life and death struggle of just a few unfortunate aquatic kings of the ocean - the ones stuck in the Arctic ice in 1985? They were stuck in hard and fast, flapping and thrashing around in sub-zero temperatures, appearing as frantic bees trapped inside a jar of Lebanese honey on the White House table at breakfast time. Twitching and fighting for freedom, yet being instinctively aware that Mother Nature's blessing will not be forthcoming to them without a helping hand from the caring human race.

Never trust people bearing gifts.

Those same charmers that had invented the

electric harpoon and fried fish with chips were going to help them in their hour of distress? The dying whales could not understand why these humans were so worried about their welfare when they fully expected to receive a big harpoon stuck in their necks together with a generous dose of electricity for good measure. Little did they know that during their hour of need, this was not a convenient time for killing them, but was a time for saving their lives because the people of the world were watching this exciting life or death saga in full colour on television.

People watching television meant money in the bank!

You don't kill the money-maker, do you?

First on the scene to maximise the commercial possibilities were, of course, the Americans and their marketing managers, called observers by the world's press. These observers were supposedly sent to gather data and report the latest situation urgently back to the President who would in turn discuss this in greater depth with his advisers. These advisers would in turn advise the President.

After studying this situation for a few days on the ice, the American observers were unable to make any true assessment because they could not converse with the whales about their plight. Those poor creatures were not able to understand or speak the English language. Personally, I can't understand a single word any American says, and I'm not even a whale.

When in deep trouble - think big!

Guy Fawkes (1756)

I'm not sure if any of these American observers knew anything about Guy Fawkes, but as they were supposed to be the good guys in this media opera, they had to start thinking big. They could not get the poor whales to follow any of their instructions given in their well intentioned effort to get these fellows released from the ice. If only these good American guys had learnt the aquatic *Whelsh* language, as understood and spoken by the frozen and panicking whales, then they would have understood the true meaning of their heart rendering screams.

Such screaming was of course being made to the *Whelsh God Blubbermouth*, located way up in blue seas up above. They shouted at each other in utter frenzy and distress, the heart rendering cries of, "What the hell's that American fool saying?" and "Moby Dick please help us!"

When in trouble, call in the United Nations.

American Good Guys (1993)

To improve international relations and to save the image of old Uncle Sam, the United Nations (USA and a few lackeys) were called into the frozen *Whelsh* act. The United Nations sales image ("We're the real good guys") was now at stake. It was decided during an emergency session in New York that something drastic must be done to rectify this very serious language problem. Action must be taken to help both the whales that needed saving and the people that wanted to carry out the saving. Life can get so complicated.

A German multi-lingual scientist, Herr Doktor Viktor Mercedes Krautenlink, was chosen by UN decree, "Get your backside over there!" He was sent as the liaison officer between the dying whales and the various multinational rescue teams that had by this time accumulated at the central spot of activity.

Our friendly Herr Doktor was personally instructed by George Pattern on behalf of the Secretary General of the UN to oversee the situation as he saw fit. He must make sure that fair play was maintained between both the Russian and American rescue teams so that the Americans obtained all the credit from the media and the Russians were made to look like inefficient and vicious communists.

Why change a habit first started in 1945?

Such was the competition to be the first country to be seen saving the whales, that George Pattern considered a serious conflict could erupt unless extreme care was taken at this early stage of the great whale rescue proceedings. The Americans must be seen to be the victors and take all the credit. The Russians must get no credit and be shown to be second class.

One must consider world armament sales at all times.

Herr Doktor went to a great deal of trouble during the first three days in the dangerous sub-zero temperatures of Arctic winter to teach the mother whale (who was the most intelligent of the freezing family of whales) to speak his mother tongue of German. No matter how hard he tried, his efforts were not a complete success, because Viktor quickly realised that you cannot teach a frozen dying whale how to speak German fluently in only three days, even if you do threaten her and her family with a gun.

Despite these severe limitations, some limited success could be positively verified after the Swedish rescue team reported hearing the mummy whale crying out repeatedly the words, "Ya vowl, itz verr damz coltz heerts."

Unfortunately, nobody from either the American or Russian rescue teams could understand a single word of this broken German language being spoken by the whales. Therefore, these wonderful creatures continued to freeze to death, albeit a little bit at a time. Ziss itz snotz gootz enufts!

The American and Russian rescue teams were not only wary of each other, but were also extremely jealous of Victor's close relationship with the whales. This jealousy stemmed from the vast TV coverage that gave even more fame to this kraut egghead from the UN than to them.

Who won the war anyway?

Why appoint a language teacher with a stupid name from the losing side? Sticks and stones are one thing, but a kraut egghead should not be allowed. After a few days of the rescue teams getting increasingly excited and agitated with this unfair media exposure projecting Viktor as some kind of people's hero, it was decided at a joint rescue team meeting that something must be done to put this kraut vonderkind in his place.

They arranged to have Viktor sent home in total disgrace, by working out a scheme where he would be arrested on a trumped up charge of multiple whale rape. He was accused of doing it with the mummy whale in front of her dying children. Viktor, far from pleading his innocence, admitted to the offence on the pathetic pretence that it was fully and legally justified because whilst teaching her to speak German, he found her much more responsive when he made these advances.

He also claimed in court that the physical exercise helped to melt some of the ice and this assisted the rescue efforts. He said in his defence that mummy whale paid more attention to her German lessons with this method of tuition than she did otherwise. He claimed that such molestation was justified when one took into account the magnitude of the event and the tight time schedule allowed by the good guys. "If you don't believe me, then try it out yourself!" he shouted.

All his pleadings were to no avail and Viktor was found guilty of this serious offence, lost his lucrative job and was sent home in total disgrace. This is where the saying "having a whale of a time" originated from. As a footnote to this sad affair, after three months of brooding over the loss of his lover Spermlove, Viktor realised that life was not worth living without her.

He purchased a large second-hand ocean yacht from a boat yard in Hamburg, whence he set sail for the waters of the Arctic Circle to search for his lost loved one.

You can still find him today searching and crying for Spermlove his only love as he sails the length and breadth of the Arctic. Our love sick pervert transmits a pleading message to Spermlove on a continuous basis, using an underwater sonar transmitter, "Diss itze Viktor thee humantz lovertz hoostz lovetz yootz".

His hopes were raised in March last year when he heard a BBC World News programme reporting the sighting of a family of twenty-four whales that had been spotted near Iceland. The reporter stated that all the whales had swastikas tattooed on top of their heads and carried huge beach towels in their mouths, with the inscription of, "This is my swimming pool because I got here first - so clearenzeeoffen."

Is it true that all sperm whales are of the male species?

We still had our dying whales awaiting nature's call to the shiny pond in the sky where only soft warm waters flow and whales are still kings of the deep blue seas. Little did these very unhappy whales (with frozen cobblers) know that things were about to change for the better - da de da! The TV media goons in the United States of America had found a way of making huge capital out of this painful emergency where the Blubber family were trying to save their futile fatty skins.

The secrets in this international media "save the whales" game was to use all the marketing skills known to mankind to create an international rescue operation of Hollywood proportions to be shown live on prime time TV. Such dramatic filming was sure to set the ordinary stupid citizen's brain alight with intrigue and wonderment.

"Jesus Haitch Christ, did you see those poor bloody whales stuck in that ice!" will be the catchwords on everybody's lips for quite a few days - just think of the advertising revenue.

To obtain maximum exposure and success, we must not rescue them too quickly or too easily, this would give the folks in Commonland the impression that the crisis was rigged and not the real thing. Only a long drawn out crisis can create a real heart rending syndrome that is convincing enough to be believed by the population of Dallas. A large number of people around the world will love this live feature showing the eternal goodness of mankind attempting such a difficult rescue operation of our fellow creatures.

Due to the lack of food and water, television and radio sets, the people of starving Africa don't care much about these stupid whales. They also don't buy hamburgers. Everybody else around the world; those with food, water and television sets, will be on the edge of their seats, wondering if these poor whales will survive until tomorrow or freeze to death today.

The sale of popcorn and cola will increase by several hundred percent for the duration of Operation Whalebuster. Have you understood it all yet my goggle eyed TV freaks?

Yes, I fully remember this pathetic Save the Whales exercise, as though it happened only yesterday during the eleven o'clock performance at Sea World in Florida. My memory is failing me fast during these later years of life and therefore it could have been as though it only happened yesterday during the four o'clock performance, when the tickets at Sea World should in my opinion be at their cheapest. If it didn't happen as though it only happened yesterday, then it was probably that it happened as though it only happened the day before yesterday. It may also be that it possibly happened as though it only happened two days before yesterday.

Whenever it was when it seemed like it only happened, this entire dingbat world of fools and me, gave central attention to this event using the full power of all the media hype.

On the front page of the multitude of semi-pornographic type cheapo tabloid newspapers could be seen tear-jerking pictures illustrating in full colour the titanic struggle of those magnificent whales, stranded and locked inside the ice floes, trying to survive whilst we continue to eat our breakfast on the patio in peace and quiet.

Famous headlines covered the front pages of all the world media, headlines so famous that they have now been carved in marble to remind us forever of this huge news story that changed the direction of newscasting for a few days. Headlines carved into the marble structure of the *British Newspaper Museum* entrance hall where tourists can daily witness and feel the mood that existed on the day that the world saved the whales.

This museum has long since become a great memorial to our brave and trustworthy defenders of the truth and free speech. Located at 4578a Fleet Street, you can see those famous headlines etched in marble for forever and a day, screaming out to the conservationists of the world such unforgettable and blood curdling headlines of:

Blubbermouths in Trouble
Spouting Dangerous
Crisis in Tokyo Chip Shops
Fat Chance
Whale of a chance!
Sperms in danger
Poor Bloody Whales

Such blubberlust hysteria was created to excite all of us buffoons, jackasses, cretins, morons, wallies, jerks, suckers, tossheads, politicians and two postmen from Wapping. The enormous 94% majority of the common people was at this point in the proceedings shouting loudly in total support throughout the land, "Give us a bit more of the old whales stuff!"

The media naturally obliged to such a request and gave these dikiots a lot more of the old whales stuff, with scant regard for the minority of people within our multi-racial democratic society who did not want any truck with the old whales' stuff. This ignored minority prefers watching the Black and White Minstrels Show on TV, or big breasts on page 3 of their newspaper, but were forced to absorb even more *Whelsh* garbage in which they had not one inkling of interest.

Whales for the majority were ***in*** and painted singers or wobbly knockers for the minority were definitely ***out***, Oh You Tee (effing OUT). Got it?

Just imagine folks; for the first time throughout all of television history, we were able to receive live television pictures depicting magnificent dying whales directly onto our television screens. Pictures of absolute clarity in full colour were being transmitted by state of the art satellites, beaming micro waves of suffering across millions of miles of dark space for the world to view. The ultimate in technology being employed for this one single story, marketed for human consumption and playing up to the average stupidity of tax paying and TeeVeeHolic public.

A street-wise gang of fools that must be shown absolute junk on a regular basis to allow them to maintain their permanent illusion that they are normal caring human beings living in a great caring country. Here we go, here we go, here we go, here we go, here we go.......

It has been calculated by ***MESS*** (Media Expenditure Survey Station), the leading world media research organisation based in an old blue caravan in Lima, Peru, that some $156,763,985.76 dollars was expended by the world media during this ice carnival floor-show of tragic proportions. That's the bad news, but the good news is that the advertising revenue received by the media during the corresponding period, reached an astronomic $569,342,952.76.

That, my capitalist student, is really good and positive economics - dying whales or not.

Those dying whales got into their own tidy mess Stanley, and the world's media simply made sure that it was exploited to maximise their advertising revenue.

Compared with the mind-boggling events happening across the world at that same time in Africa, Israel, Iraq, Russia and Skelmersdale, involving millions of lives and billions of ice cream choc bars, who really gives a care about some stupid whales who managed to get their balls stuck in the ice?

Do we know what happened to these temporary stars of the silver screen and newsprint today, after the public became rather pissed off with seeing stupid whales on their TV in the morning noon and night?

After the heart-pulling period of the first few days, the media ran out of steam with this international con game and moved on to some equally insignificant story elsewhere. I will repeat the question to all of you my aspiring genii of the future; do we know the outcome of this story and the final fate of these whales? More importantly, do we care one little bit? Ah ha! Now you're starting to feel guilty because of course you don't know what the hell happened to them and you don't really care one little bit - do you?

Yes, my whale caring folks, during this typical American craze of trying to present this new package of Saving the Whales and seeing the World in ten days, all hands were placed on the pump of the money machine. You must move quickly now you guys, because we move on to Rome tomorrow and Amsterdam the day after that.

"We've got a great story Jack, just imagine how much advertising space we can sell during the six o'clock news. Providing we show real live pictures of those big bloody whales thrashing around like pigs stuck up a gum tree - I hope the silly sods don't die on us before we transmit these great pictures, because The DuoCrank Detergent Company are paying us 60% above premium rates for this prime advertising time. However, this is providing the whales are seen alive and without too much blood around to upset the kids. They don't give a doodly bit about our advertising space and will cancel out if those bloody whales freeze to death or if the kids start crying because one of the whales gets a nose bleed. Maybe we should send a few barrels of brandy and a box of plasters to the iceberg just in case." Very touching don't you think?

Even the Presidents of both the United States and Russia helped out during this crisis because such sympathy touches people's hearts everywhere and this really influences world opinion. The power and goodness of mankind are unyielding, but if you're a whale reading this book, then it is understandable if you disagree. In any case, I must say that I admire you as an advanced aquatic clever blubbermouth able to read who is completely out of your depth so to speak.

My advice to all of you whales out there is not to take too much encouragement from this single episode from my book highlighting man's magnificent behaviour. It is completely out of character and in any case we must not forget that mankind still intends to kill you all off - but only when the cameras are switched off and the squeamish people are in bed. All whales should immediately cease reading my book at this point and make haste to the greatest depth possible in the Atlantic ocean, hold on to your balls and swim as fast as possible in a westwardly direction, making sure that Tokyo is always directly behind you. Do not listen to the false words of any smiling Japanese sailors offering cheap radios and jewellery whilst encouraging you to come to the surface and drink Saki cocktails with them. They are wolves in sheep's clothing, whilst at the same time looking like slant eyed gits with big swords.

Finally, never sell your story to a British Sunday newspaper because if you do, nothing remains sacred and you will become just another one of those idiots from Whales, left high and dry to die.

If we had had no media coverage of this event then we would have had no world opinion trying to save the whales and therefore the whales would have frozen to death with the virtually extinct and unknown *Arctic Wobbler* penguins looking on in amusement. I'm not sure if these rare penguins eat whale meat, but apart from this possible stealing of the penguins' potential food supply, we must admit that the media coverage of this episode of world stupidity was not all bad.

Just as well that this tragedy occurred where it did though because imagine how much help they would have received if they had become stranded on the sandy beaches of Tripoli or Cambodia. Some help the goodies from the West would offer them then. Same old whales, different media situation - no bucks in return for this location.

We don't like Tripoli or that land with bad memories of our hidden guilt, so hard luck to the whales.

"Don't criticise us" the media guys will scream when they read these comments written in green ink by my golden pen. "We must show the people the truth, thus ensuring that they understand and appreciate the sufferings of these fellow creatures living on this planet of ours."

Such artificial attitudes from these perverts of true morality are of course total rubbish. The sad fact that drives these pariahs of the civilised world towards this type of scoop is that their moral corruption is so deeply inbred into their souls, that these guardians of truth actually believe in their fantasies that have convinced them that only they depict and present the truth.

The quiet minority of people who really care about the plight of the human race must helplessly watch on, to witness the raping of Mother Earth carried out continuously on such a massive scale. We must start fighting back for the sake of future generations yet to be conceived and born, unable to protect for themselves this almost lost heritage. Otherwise left they will condemn us for our desertion of responsibility.

We should start this regeneration process now by asking these slick well dressed media marketing executives some simple questions. "Excuse me, top executive of the media, but now that the whales are saved from the ice so that they can be freely harpooned by the Japanese whaling fleet next week, what will you report to your viewers next? Will you please spend the equivalent amount of $156,763,985.76 showing the true details covering the present horrors of deformed children in Cambodia? And, by the way, can you also arrange a live interview with the senior government officials responsible for those atrocities? Will you also arrange a programme on why we didn't have a war crimes trial after the Vietnam war similar to the Nuremberg war crimes trials?

"You see, my friend of the media, a lot of the ordinary thinking and caring people of this country are very confused and see a great similarity between the Nuremberg war trials and the crimes we committed against the Cambodian and Vietnamese people.

"Be sure to run these stories and interviews live on the six o'clock prime time television otherwise the people who want the truth will not witness this truth.

"You will still have about $95,000,000 in change to spend elsewhere after this series is completed, compared with the cost of the idiotic whales story.

"We feel sure that you will want to show the truth about war crimes because, surely, the lives of all these people in Asia and the hundreds of thousands of deformed children being born every year are more important than the two whales which are now being fried with chips in Tokyo."

Do you think that Rupert and the other equally daft media executives will respond to this question with a sensible response? Maybe they will answer like, "What a fantastic idea Dick Head, we'll run a twenty week series showing these deformed kids with pus running down their faces with some good close up shots. This awful exposure of our foreign policy and criminal murdering politicians will most certainly shame the people and the country as a whole.

"We'll lobby the President at the White House to such an extent that he will have no alternative but to arrange The Chicago War Crimes Trials of American war criminals to clean the slate of the American conscience. Dick, my friend, we thank you for bringing this to our attention and guarantee that all this will be shown live on prime time television!"

All this is but a useless dream, my students of a new educational age. Rupert will not reply to my question with such a moralistic answer, because such an action is not profit making and in any case would put him out in the bright lights ready to have his ears shot off. Rupert, like most of us, finds that having ears is very useful and will at this point apply some of his college waffling technique. He will probably say something like "sod off you commie agitator".

This very crude response to my simple, yet very searching, question leaves little room for doubt concerning the level of interest in such suggestions. He definitely does not agree in any way whatsoever because we, the common street people of all democratic countries, only want to be told the truth that we would like to hear; the truth that satisfies our egos.

Please keep all the awful truth off our television screens, thank you very much indeed!

Let's discuss for a few moments why we completely devastated this area of the globe and assess the noble reasons for this. Certainly it was not in the name of freedom because if that was the real reason, then why in hell did we pull out when the going got tough? No, my cringing readers trying to convince yourselves that we in the West are the shining knights riding to the rescue of underprivileged masses, we must face the truth even if it really hurts us.

Remember how the people back home in America, who generally supported this "fight for freedom" in earlier years suddenly didn't want to defend freedom in later years when the going got tough? Losing lives, whether of our loved ones or of the hated enemy, is horrific at any time in history but is a necessary part of any war that must be fought to defend good over evil.

It is unforgivable for a government to expend our young blood for a useless cause that can have no useful outcome.

In a future world democracy, all soldiers will fight only in the wars when they believe in the cause as nobody will turn up to fight wars with such stupid causes then the problem will be automatically solved. The only stumbling block is that the politicians will still control the manifesto and therefore the truth.

Serg "Bollox" Bilko (1959)

You are able to live in your cosseted and spoilt lives because of the sacrifices made by millions of brave defenders of freedom from previous conflicts.

In Vietnam (yes, we can say the word!), why did we wreck a country whilst defending nothing, yet creating a wilderness of hatred against the American people. If this war can ever be justified, then we should hang our heads in shame at the outcome and the resultant show of cowardice. If the war was not justified in the beginning then we should still hang our heads in shame at the outcome.

It is convenient and very simple for the consumer society of today to forget, but history will never forget, the moment of ultimate truth depicting the moral fibre of the American nation at war. This judgement will remain as a permanent reminder to all nations of the strength of will of the American people, even if national guilt forces us to hide the truth away for today and possibly tomorrow.

Just spend a few months studying this subject of American disgrace to see the depth of depravity that America fell into during this stain upon its history. This war of killing the innocents will not be forgotten, even in a thousand years time, and has most certainly changed the future direction of mankind forever. God blesses America.

I'm not a pacifist, I just want to see my twenty first birthday, get married, have children, play golf, buy a house, and believe in God. The alternative offer is to get my balls blown off defending a pile of sand inhabited by people that hate our guts. To save oil, I'll walk to work.

John Emlyn Wayne II (1973)

America should content itself with shooting at small countries where, because of their advanced technology, a quick victory will be a certainty. Defend freedom providing that in doing so the other guys can't really fight back.

Unless attacked, America has shown its lack of ability to finish off the job when the going gets tough.

The latest Gulf war and its unfinished business highlight this fragility of nature within the American government and hence within its people. The world now knows this as a proven fact and future disasters will surely be caused because of this knowledge. This will all come back to haunt us one day in the future as sure as eggs are eggs.

God helps us all and Mother Earth.

Oh to be a happy worm,
Of that I dream with some concern,
In dark black holes I eat the earth,
To progress down for all I'm worth,
Work all day and work all night,
This simple life of an hermaphrodite,
A squirming creature yes it's true,
But when I'm cold I don't get the flue,
It's such a great life, I do confirm,
Oh to be a happy worm.

Harold Buttons (1917)

Was the fighting of communism in poor countries worthwhile? Maybe in one hundred

years the socialist (communist included) countries of today will be more democratic than the democracies of today and the democratic countries today become more socialist.
Time will tell my friends.

Back to my whales.

Regarding the President of the United States, who fully supported the action to save the whales, this in itself led to a most unbelievable situation. As a *Limey* author, albeit a world famous Limy author of blockbusting novels of excellence, I visited the White House press department to obtain valuable extra information that I had planned to pass on to you in this book

During this visit, I found it extremely difficult to obtain any of the data essential for me to complete this chapter with absolute accuracy. A chapter having such delicate political impact should be compiled using absolute facts that would pass all media and political tests and stand up to the denials that were guaranteed to explode upon us once the truth displayed within this book became public knowledge. It would be bad enough with an unknown author, but with Dick Head involved............?

During a press conference at the White House, held to enlighten the world's press about the President's attitude during the Whales crisis, I was eventually able to put a question to Burgundy Weinburger the President's press officer. "Sir, is it not true that the President is very fond of whales and that's why he's spending more money on saving these trapped whales than required to ease the poverty in the slums of Harlem this year?"

Burgundy formed a toothpaste trained smile upon his granite featured face and looked me squarely in the eye before replying with sugared venom. "Welcome to the White House Dick Head, I am pleased and greatly honoured to have such a famous award winning author here from England to record this historic event. The President has decided that mankind must at last halt its economic progress, based upon greed only, and must start assisting its fellow creatures in distress.

"I can confirm to you all here today that our great and wonderful President is now taking personal charge of this rescue of the whales operation. The world will be able to witness all of his action live on all main TV channels tonight during prime viewing time".

A very good reply from Burgundy, straight to the point, whatever the point was, but not to the point requested in my question. This evasion of the political question is the greatest skill essential to any political animal who is expecting to succeed within this industry of corruption and conceit. Despite many requests for clarification on the issue posed by my question to old Burgundy, the whale saga has now been long forgotten and become redundant for media exposure.

I had my chance and fluffed it and another war in the offing diverted all attention away from the whales and other matters. Too late, Dick Head, you must obtain your information from other sources. Burgundy had succeeded in evading the truth without telling any lies for over fifteen years and today he is now being put forward as the next Senator for Kentucky. There is some suspicion that he drove his car into a river whilst under the influence of alcohol, killing a young girl, plus being unfairly accused of a rape or two, but this is not enough bad news to lose him the nomination at this stage in the proceedings. Murder and rape with no extra witnesses are OK because it can all be covered up by political clout and money, but never, never, never, tell a lie where it can be recorded on a tape recorder and come back to haunt you.

With all this in mind, Burgundy may yet become President providing he learns to play golf and avoids screwing female assistants in public.

You must research into the internal functioning of a multitude of separate departments within the White House to understand the reasoning behind the President's involvement with these Arctic whales. All departments are staffed by very tall, individually selected and highly educated, special agents. Daily hormone injections are required to make sure that these giants retain their rapid growth pattern that is so essential in these positions. An American secret service agent must always be taller than his Russian counterpart.

How things have changed over the past few years with the Gorbachev revolution (and his downfall), the Gulf War, civil war in Yugoslavia and a new fragile democratic begging Bear. Hormone injections are no longer compulsory in today's new world order, just the ownership of a few thousand cruise missiles. End of newsflash - now back to the whales period in our political life.

After ten years at the White House, you either become a successful politician or you can join almost any top basketball team as a star player. If you are born as a short midget with a stammer speech defect, it is of very little use applying for a position within the White House for any of these agency positions. Your chances of being selected for any of these positions can be compared with the chance of any Zulu warrior or Asian prince being the King of England.

Maybe I shouldn't be quite so sure about these comparisons. Democracy has no influence upon the maintenance of the royal family in England, such a fair and green land. For sure, a white shonkee with strange habits will remain in power at Buckingham Palace until well into the 21st century. All things must come to an end and this includes the racial background of our royal family.

At the present birth rate applicable for each racial group in Great Britain, it is estimated that over half of the population of the United Kingdom will be a greyer shade of Anglo-Saxon white by 21 June 2067 AD. If this situation comes about as predicted by the Black Velvet Society then I for one would find it most offensive still to have the same white skinned dynasty in power at Buck House.

These outdated royals that consider a poppadom a style of fuzzy hat worn by the coloured minority when attending the Epsom races must then be replaced. No, my student of regal taste and racial growth and integration, when this time arrives it is far better to have the royal speech on Christmas day starting off with the words, "Diss iss your king speakin'....."

Our first black king will be in power, and not before time I must say. Buckingham Palace would naturally be repainted in bright purple and yellow stripes, with the horse guards regiment riding camels down The Mall, complete with ostrich feather headgear.

This, my friends, will indeed happen to our royalty, without a shadow of doubt (so to speak), because it is right and just to all the people of this land and will avoid any racial bloodletting in the streets if we don't have an acceptable royalty.

We look forward to our new king ruling over British people holding British passports, and all other nationalities that evade our immigration officials to join their families here. These people, the lovers of a new free land, are all simply wishing to live out their lives in peace and harmony without fear of daily persecution.

Here they receive the immediate benefit of free dole money, all paid for by the long suffering general public who can ill afford such generosity. If the general public object to contributing towards this massive generosity and withdraws such financial support, they are eventually sent to prison. This is quite an incentive to support these new British residents.

The capitalist Chinese from Hong Kong will also become aware of the possibility of becoming the ruling class within British society and thereby having a Chinese King of England, providing they make the right moves. Just watch them (so to speak) take the necessary actions with the expectation and surety of gaining their first Emperor and King of Great Britain by 29 August 2189 AD, providing they don't develop a condom that can be put on with chopsticks.

The future Great Britain will, with my total consent, abolish the futility of having any queens because we only want happy monarchs.

Back to the White House story.

The prime job of these secret agents is to keep the President in power and to keep him out of trouble by using whatever means is necessary, legal or otherwise. During the whales saga on ice, it was agent Joseph Josiah Jinzenovich who alerted the President to the possibility of gaining an advantage by becoming involved with the safety of the Arctic dying whales.

Joseph, an egghead with tiny balls, was lovingly referred to as 3J by his work colleagues in the *Voting Tactics Department*. He daily fed data connected with the "general attitude of the American public as related to the President's popularity" into the giant purpose built IBM computer nicknamed *The Word of God*.

This strange and rather sarcastic nickname for the computer was in 1971 shortened to that of *The W.O.G.*

This name caused some complaints from the few floor cleaners working for the contract cleaners then but they have since all left to open takeaway shops. Ignoring these few complaints, the White House changed over to a Korean run cleaning company, and the whizz kids then shortened this computer nickname even more in 1979 to just *WOG*.

So endeth the story of how *WOG* was born onto this earth of ours.

My information is unlimited.

WOG was linked by platinum wire to two hundred and thirty-six gold plated keyboards and had the massive power of some presidential six million megabytes; now that is a lot of thinking power - yes indeed! After inputting the full set of data concerning the dying whales, only a mere

1.765 milliseconds (*WOG's* thinking time) had elapsed before *WOG's* assessment of this complex situation arrived in the form of a 3,765 page report.

The comprehensive presidential report came complete with pie charts and other graphics, all printed by a colour laser printer that made a very attractive presentation. It is claimed that this laser printer has the possibility of printing over one million different colours. That seems quite a feat of ingenuity, although just why the human race needs over one million different colours rather passes me by.

This presidential report included every piece of data and computed assessments that electronic brains could produce. The main and final assessment from WOG read:

If the president supports the effort of saving the whales there will be an increase in his popularity by 7.4532% within 4.76984 days of making his first whales related TV sympathy speech on national TV. This speech should preferably be on the six o'clock news, or on prime television time. Warning: Do not overdo the support of these whales - withdraw support after five days if we reach any scenario where the whales die or bleeding whales are seen on TV. If this Whelsh support must be withdrawn, we must look for other sympathy subjects, or invade a country of high profile but of low competition to our armed forces.

Do not inform the British or French beforehand - end of pure factual assessment.

Did you know that it has been said that John F. Kennedy tried to get the name of the White House changed to *Black & White Minstrels House* during his first year in power? Presidents will do anything to get what they want, just ask some of Marilyn Monroe's friends.

In aid of improving your American Governmental knowledge, *The Voting Tactics And Spying On Opponents Department* was first established in 1946, just after the end of World War II. This department was originally for making sure that no person of German or Japanese origin ever had the opportunity of becoming President of the United States of America. It has never been explained to my satisfaction why no reference was made in the department's guidelines to exclude a Russian from becoming President.

This department very quickly became the largest of all departments inside the White House, employing some 2,675 agents. Each successive President decided that this department gave him such an advantage over possible pretenders to his throne, that the terms of reference were continuously changed to increase their power base. Indeed, was it not said that assassination of political opponents was approved in 1959, providing that nobody found out that the White

House was involved in such illegal skulduggery. If the public were to become aware of such assassinations, then the particular agent involved was aware that he was on his own and ran for cover.

If, despite all precautions to the contrary, the guilty agent was caught by any law enforcement agency that had not agreed to this assassination charter, then good-bye agent Smith, off to the gas chamber you go. Your family will be well looked after - trust us because we love you and have a nice day.

In 1960 it was rumoured that it was now possible to allow persons of any nationality to run for President, providing that the C.I.A. agreed to the choice of the candidate on a time by time basis. A few Arab names were definitely excluded, but this was considered to be a personal vendetta carried on by the President himself then.

This extension of its responsibility and power base guaranteed that the department grew and grew until some 27,543 agents were employed by 1968. The department had grown so large and cumbersome that it was found necessary to separate it into three separate sections, namely, *Administration, Locksmiths & Forced Entry* and *Telephone Bugging & Surveillance.*

These departments offered brilliant careers to the brightest and most forward thinking people of the time and this quickly caused a critical shortage of locksmiths and telephone engineers within the Greater Washington area. It became so critical, that if you unwittingly locked yourself out of your house, it was quicker and less expensive to smash down and replace the front door than wait six weeks for a locksmith to fly in from New York.

In commercial business, the old slogan of where there is a will there is a way is no more perfectly applied than by *Ra-Ajar Door Replacement Inc*. This company became a huge success by offering a four hour service for door replacement - no matter what type or shape of door you required. They could replace your smashed down door with a replica of your old door within four hours - no matter how fancy your door design happened to be!

All it took was less than two kilograms of magic glue every year and a few thousand hypodermic needles to keep these guys in business. Doors from the most expensive houses were measured up whilst the occupants were away at the office and were unaware of the con being planned.

A perfect replica door was produced at the company's modern factory, all ready for when this future client had door trouble, which was preordained. Trouble came the very next day in the form of magic glue being injected into all the locks fitted to the front door by using sub-contract labour temporarily employed on a commission basis from the criminal fraternity.

A company van would then be parked just across the street to await the homecoming of the target client. This new client was about to be in dire need of an emergency replacement front door, all paid for of course by the insurance company. Whatever your feelings may be about this illegal and shady type of trading, you must recognise that it is non-violent and helps more people than it hurts (which is none). It also helps to recirculate money within the local economy and keeps over one hundred people in full time employment, all of them paying taxes.

The insurance company paying for the new door is not unhappy because the premium levels are set to reflect these problems and to give an acceptable profit to the shareholders.

Prompt payment of the claim goes to show the value of having your doors covered by insurance in the first place and encourages more people in the area to insure their own door just in case the same misfortune strikes them.

The insurance company gradually increases the premiums to all door owners as more doors are replaced under the insurance scheme. These increased premiums are paid for by the customers with money that has been taxed at source by the government, thereby giving the government a higher revenue that can be spent on better care for the old people and nuclear submarines.

Some of my close friends, who are senior officers at the Exchequer Department, consider that this door scheme is a really efficient way of redistributing wealth without the government even being involved. They calculate that if 25,657,567 doors were replaced every year then income tax could be reduced to only 1% of earnings.

With self motivation and wealth acquisition being involved, the system operates very efficiently indeed, and all this because of a dire shortage of locksmiths. That's capitalism for you.

The lack of telephone engineers has had no effect upon the average person in Washington, but is playing havoc with my friend's wife's underwear parties, also with the escort agencies serving the top politicians in town.

These shortages apart, the department ran very smoothly and expensively until that dramatic time when the New York Times presented the first episode of the *Watergate Soap Opera* (final episodes yet to be written), published and shown across all stages of the world.

As soon as the mess hit the fan, agent 3J immediately fed all relevant data related to this slightly embarrassing balls-up into *WOG* and before a bat could fart, *WOG* spewed out his report on the six colour laser printer. The electronic advice was simple:

It would be prudent to disband yesterday the Locksmiths and Forced Entry and Telephone Bugging and Surveillance sections and rename the two as a single new Voting Tactics department.

The President's aide immediately agreed with *WOG* (but refused to sign anything) and the department had its name changed accordingly. All records of the previous names were removed from *WOG*, and 3J fell under a train in the subway the same evening. 3J did not recover from this trauma and he was buried in cement packed inside a partially filled plastic carrier bag.

A severe staff shortage came about within a few days of this rapid change around because most of the locksmiths and telephone engineers purchased cheap group travel tickets and emigrated to Colombia. I feel sure they are now using their expertise in a productive way in their new homeland without the democratic interference experienced in the USA.

So much for loyalty to the President, but he never knew anyway, or when he said he didn't know, he didn't actually mean he didn't know because what he meant was...........

The *WOG* computer also strongly recommended that the President switch off his tape recorder unless he one day decided to tell the truth as interpreted by everybody else. During a recent internal audit by the fraud squad at the White House, no evidence could be found of any later purchases of recording tape after Watergate became Hollywood news. You see folks, even the President learns very quickly indeed; once bitten, twice shy as they say.

The internal auditors did find that there had been a huge increase in the bulk buying of toilet paper during this same period and this is now being investigated to see if there is any connection with this same crime.

Forced by the Watergate development, the President yet again placed extra overtime strain on *WOG*, which was now installed within the recently renamed *Voting Tactics Department* where 3J's successor fed in all the latest bad news and asked *WOG* for a rapid escape route for the President.

After a few milliseconds, out spurted the answer to his many prayers. This is such an important part of yet unrecorded history that I feel obliged to tell you about, and to quote WOG exactly and precisely:

The President is in deep, deep, trouble. Dramatic action is required by the President, including the President to keep repeating "I didn't know about the buggings."

Future actions can be suggested as follows:

Bomb Libya.

Invade Switzerland and share out the gold with all our people. Confirm that this would save the day and give the President an overwhelming 67% of the vote in the next election.

President to make a cowboy film but no shooting of indians to be included. Conclusive data proves that the people are attracted to film stars in cowboy films but indians hate seeing other indians killed by cowboys.

President to train as a fighter pilot. Conclusive data shows that the people love fighter pilots. Warning: Do not substitute this with joining the State Troopers, even if father has influence, this will positively lose votes.

Don't join the National Guard at any cost - claim invalidity.

Offer to cut the National Deficit by half in three years.

Offer to cut taxes.

Make Russia a state of the USA.

Marry a lesbian and let her do all the talking.

If all else fails, destroy all tapes, start singing opera and claim you're a nutter.

Move to Libya.

These *WOG* suggestions prove conclusively that computers can have independent visions of the future, because how could *WOG* have known that a cowboy actor and fighter pilot were soon to become presidents of the United States of America?

I cannot imagine why *WOG* did not suggest that the President didn't start cultivating peanuts.

If only he had taken *WOG's* advice, the world would have become his oyster and history would remember him as *Richard the Great* and not Richard the ——er. Afterwards, in the euphoria created by such resounding successes, who would have cared about a little break-in and some petty lying anyway? Everybody tells a few white lies some time in their life, so why not the President of the United States.

Just read about the history relating to the rise and fall of the Roman Empire to appreciate that the President was a saint compared with those guys in charge of Rome with their world-wide assets. In comparison, he just stole a sugar lump or a piece of candy from the larder so to speak. In those days he could have been referred to as The Saint of Buggers.

Come to think of it, Lucky could become Lucky the Saint of the Bugged.

Without doubt, my graduates of history are now smirking with glee and thinking, "OK Dick Head, what about the history related to the rise and fall of the Roman Empire? Answer that you know all big headed author!"

Firstly, in answer to your stupid question, I don't have to answer you doubters at any time or place because I'm writing this book, not you. Secondly, and most importantly for you lovers of lies to remember, is that America is growing stronger day by day, unlike that of Rome! Don't now start carping about "how about Vietnam?" "What about the drugs crisis?" "Why do we have so much poverty?" "Why do the Japanese own 99% of America?"

You are too late with these extra questions. You had your chance of making a valid criticism and you have failed dismally.

Look out for my book number 33, *Questions From Troublemakers Answered.* That book should suit your mentality perfectly.

With the benefit of hindsight we now realise that some of these *WOG* suggestions have been utilised by later Presidents with a great success rate. No other President since Watergate has been fired (impeached if you prefer a nicer word that the working class can't understand) which proves the value of a *WOG*.

In a certain way, we must also be extremely prudent and careful not to give any *WOG* too much power because

I remember vividly a film where a *WOG* style computer almost took over and destroyed the world, just because some young fellow phoned in to play games!

Let's be careful lads, concerning the dirty games played out on those chat lines, the ones that the government says they are trying to ban. If they failed to ban these lines of filth over the past five years, what hope is there for us in the future? In my ignorance, I thought you just disconnected a few wires and the phone stopped working, but there you are, my friends, nothing is ever as easy as it appears.

There again, what do I know about chat lines?

Chapter 7

From Getting Stuffed to A False Dawn

A partner lost,
A reason found,
Now we're apart
No longer abound.

"Bad Joss" James Floyd (1972)

"But Mr. Parrot, if you're a taxidermist, then why can't you stuff my husband Fred and then dress him in his Royal Marines military uniform? I want to stand him up smiling in all of his glory in a glass cabinet located in the front entrance hall of my house so that we can all remember him as he was. That was Fred's everlasting wish, sob! sob! sob!"

"But Mrs Friendly, I'm not at all too sure if stuffing Fred and putting him on display in a cA partabinet in your entrance hall is within the law, let alone having him smile at visitors for hundreds of years to come. Just imagine, if everybody did it then we would have three billion stuffed people by the year 2001, and that takes a great deal of stuffing," spoke out our friendly taxidermist, Ivor Parrot, in a most concerned manner.

"Mr, Parrot, my husband Fred Friendly was such a happy fellow that he was known as 3F by his thousands of friends and his very few enemies. It's in his will that he wants to be well and truly stuffed, ensuring that you fix forever a big smile on his face by securing his cheeks and lips in position with staples and using taxidermists' face spray lacquer. Fred had a bet with Zacharia's betting shop for a stake of £1,000 at odds of 1500 to 1 that he would end up stuffed and placed in a glass case in his hallway.

"Fred hated the owner, Zacharia Jeremiah, and reckoned he had lost over £10,000 in his betting shop over his lifetime. Imagine Fred's smug satisfaction in heaven to know that Zacharia was having to pay out £1,500,000 after his death. Mr. Parrot, I am prepared to pay you £500,000 to carry out this work of stuffing Fred, even if you are breaking the law" said Mrs Friendly.

"Mrs Friendly, I am sworn by the oath of the *B.S.A. (British Stuffing Association)* to uphold the laws of the land and to only stuff those creatures as allowed by law. *The 1902 Stuffing Act* doesn't actually forbid the stuffing of humans, but I must check with my stuffing association first before I can give you a positive decision."

"Thank you, Mr. Parrot, please call me as a matter of urgency, because the sooner Fred gets stuffed then the happier he will be and the sooner Zacharia is hacked off and becomes a Christian."

At that she strolls out of the stuffing shop and heads across the road to the *SUNCOAST* travel agents. It's not often that you win £1,500,000 just by arranging to get your husband stuffed. In this modern age of a fifty percent divorce rate in our society, Fred is a very lucky man indeed.

Ivor Parrot rang the *B.S.A* that very afternoon and asked in a nervous tentative tone, "Hello Mr. Willy, I have a woman who wants me to stuff her husband and I thought it better to telephone you first to check upon the regulations." Mr. Willy was somewhat bemused and asked Ivor if he intended to commit a sexual offence against the deceased, which really upset Ivor who was nervous enough as it was.

Eventually, Ivor made himself clearly understood inasmuch that the amazed Mr. Willy ultimately checked the reference books and found that indeed there were no laws to prevent Fred Friendly being a well and truly stuffed Fred Friendly. Ivor went away and commenced an in-depth study of the stuffing of the human body to find out why it was not a common occurrence. He found out that the human skin is so weak and thin that it would be virtually impossible to stuff Fred without him bursting out all over.

"Mrs Friendly, there are indeed no regulations to prevent Mr. Friendly being stuffed, but unfortunately it is not technically possible due to the weakness of the human skin. Just like a conker, the skin would need soaking in vinegar for six months to toughen it up, and that of course is not practically possible."

"Mr. Parrot, for £1,500,000 anything is possible! I must inform you that my sister Ethel owns and operates the SEASPREY fish and chip shop down the road and I know that she really loved Fred and would do anything to help me out."

It came to pass, so to speak, that Fred Friendly, wearing only a very colourful pair of Hawaiian swimming trunks, was gently lifted up by four temporary labourers from the dole office and placed upside down inside a huge eight feet tall green tinted glass jar. This oriental looking jar had been purchased from the British Rail Lost Property Office and was of the type that had previously been used for smuggling in drugs from India during the 1960s.

One end of a thick coil of rope was attached to Fred's feet, whilst the other end was tied to the top of the Coke cooler. This allowed Fred Friendly to be rotated each morning, thus resulting in perfect marinating and hardening of all his body parts. For decency's sake, his very attractive swimming trunks were removed only during night-time hours to make sure that the hardening process was completed perfectly on all parts of his body.

When the malt vinegar bulk tanker called the next day, the marinating and toughening up process of friendly Fred Friendly was continued by pumping in two hundred gallons of premium malt vinegar inside the glass jar with Fred. Fred, a non-swimmer in life, loved gherkins and pickled onions, so they poured in twenty pounds of each of these items on top of the malt vinegar to make him feel more at home.

Pickled Fred became the talk of the village, county and country and very soon the national press took up the story. *"Pickled Before Stuffing!" "Fred and Onion Stuffing!" "Man pickled in a jar!"* The headlines were endless and the people came from all over the land to see Fred Friendly suspended upside down in a green jar of malt vinegar wearing brightly coloured swimming trunks and having pickled onions and gherkins as company. Photographers from all the world's press, periodicals and television engulfed the *SEASPREY* fish and chip shop to witness and record this most unusual of events.

Sister Ethel did not miss a trick and charged £25 for cod and chips wrapped up in newspaper with a story of Fred Friendly printed as the headlines. These newspapers are today worth over £150 at auction each but smell very badly indeed.

As the weeks went by, Fred's skin went from a pure white to fawn, to brown and eventually to a pitch black; all this unbeknown to Mrs Friendly who sat at home collecting her royalty of five pounds on every portion of cod and chips sold by sister Ethel. Mrs Friendly awaited the £1,500,000 from Zacharia once Fred was stuffed. She had never before realised how life can be so good for you, even though it was far too late for Fred.

When Ivor Parrot telephoned to say that Fred was pickled enough for stuffing, she was ecstatic, jumped with joy, and immediately phoned the *SPENDALOT* travel agency to book her first class six months around the world tour at a cost of £18,560.88 including travel insurance. This may seem a huge outlay to mere mortals, but appeared to Mrs Friendly as a drop in the ocean under the current circumstances. Thank you Fred.

It was a Sunday, the sun was shining, the dole office was closed and Ivor could not find four willing volunteers to help him lift blackened, hardened and marinated Fred Friendly out of the green malt vinegar filled jar. He was forced to pay a backhander of forty pounds, plus as many pickled onions and gherkins as they could carry, to four on-duty policemen as they were about to walk into the Four Cocks pub, a low class drinking establishment situated opposite the *SEASPREY* fish and chip shop.

These four burly men of law enforcement ilk hoisted Fred out of the green jar feet first and carried him to the canal at the back of the premises to wash off the awful smell of marinated human skin, pickled onions and gherkins. The washing process worked very well because after drying him by using powdered fish batter, Fred smelt only like ordinary shite, which was a slight improvement. Ivor blamed this awful smell on the polluted canal but the policemen simply said "What a fucking awful smell!" and left Ivor to do the rest on his lonesome.

Notwithstanding that Fred smelt very bad indeed, he was now a very tough skinned individual, even though his skin colour had changed to that of shiny coal. It took six days for Ivor to stuff Fred good and proper, including the painting of his exposed skin using Dulux eggshell white emulsion paint to bring him back looking something like his true racial background. A generous quantity of "Old Spice" aftershave was liberally sprayed all over his body in a useless attempt to hide the very bad crappy smell. This tactic was not a complete success but after some short consideration, Ivor concluded that Old Spice and crap were a great improvement over crap alone.

"Hello Mrs Friendly, Fred is stuffed, dressed in his corporal's uniform complete with medals, smiling and ready to come back home! Get the £500,000 cheque ready and be prepared for your round the world holiday. This is a great day for Fred and the two of us." "Great news Mr. Parrot, can you bring Fred over now because the glass showcase has just been delivered and it looks really great!"

So Ivor paid the foreman at the local builder's

yard ten pounds to borrow a pickup truck for the morning and, with the help of the milkman and the postman, loaded up well stuffed Fred. He covered Fred in two old blankets and proceeded to deliver Fred to Mrs Friendly's house. He had, however, forgotten to bring any mode of transport or lifting tackle for shifting Fred from the pickup truck to Mrs Friendly's front door, a distance of some four hundred metres.

To overcome this oversight, Ivor put Fred upon his back and carried him into Mrs Friendly's entrance hall - even though old smiling very dead and stuffed Fred does smell rather crappy, vinegary, oniony, gherkinny and Old Spicy. Once in the hall, Mrs Friendly greeted him with a big kiss and presented Ivor with the showcase. "Voila! Here is Fred's new home." On the outside of the showcase was a huge engraved brass plaque saying:

Corporal Fred Frank Friendly
Stuffed and not heard,
but to Zacharia it's all so absurd
(1932-1993).

Oh Boy, what a wonderful showcase, manufactured from solid Korean mountain mahogany with real Polish glass crystal doors on all four sides and sixteen disco lights mounted inside. On the top of this wonderful example of cabinet making was mounted eight huge stereo loudspeakers, linked to the disco lights and to a multi-play CD player located in the base.

"Fred loved disco music, so I thought it only correct to make him feel at home whilst I'm away on my round the world holiday. Would you like to join me on this trip Ivor, we can both afford it now!" Ivor, being lost for words, was panic struck thinking that he wouldn't get his half a million quid unless he went on holiday with Mrs Friendly; and friendly she was certainly turning out to be.

"Mrs Friendly, let's get old Fred inside his disco first, get the cash from Zacharia and then we can sit down having a drink to discuss this wonderful holiday offer, eh?"

So that's exactly what they tried to achieve but like so many previously well planned projects, it went disastrously wrong at the critical moment.

Needless to say, stuffed Fred was too tall for the cabinet, but all was not lost. "Don't worry Mrs Friendly, anybody can forget that the cabinet height is not the same as the height of the body to be fitted inside. All you need do is to order another cabinet that is four hundred millimetres higher, you can certainly afford it, ha, ha, ha!" Mrs Friendly glared at Ivor in an unfriendly (unFriendly) way and spat out a venomous response. "Ivor, you stupid prick, I'm going on holiday around the world tomorrow and I must get the cash from Zacharia first. I refuse to leave Fred in your workshop all alone for a full six months. You'll have to find an answer - NOW!"

They discussed many ideas for solving this time delaying problem, including removing the top of the cabinet so that Fred's head, complete with army beret, protruded out the top as though he was in the trenches. Ivor suggested that they set him up with a pair of binoculars as though he was on guard duty and searching the horizon for the enemy, but Mrs Friendly thought this was in bad taste and chastised him for such a horrible idea. Eventually, following much bickering, Mrs Friendly exploded in wrath and rage. "Ivor, there's only one answer, CUT HIS BLOODY FEET OFF!"

Cut his feet off Ivor most certainly did, using an electric carving knife from Mrs Friendly's kitchen. This knife is totally knackered after cutting through Fred's leg bones and Mrs Friendly has given this cutting instrument to Ivor for future limb removals. Mrs Friendly can now buy a replacement electric knife from Comet and still have £1,499,987.83 (less Ivor's fee) in change.

The greatly shortened version of Fred was then placed in the cabinet with his amputated feet placed inside a sealed garbage bag that was tucked inside the rear of his army tunic where it could not be seen from outside of the cabinet.

"Mrs Friendly, don't think that I'm trying to cause unnecessary trouble where trouble can be avoided, but there is definitely something wrong with Fred's appearance." Mrs Friendly raised her eyebrows, inviting Ivor to continue with his speech. "You see, Mrs Friendly, we've reduced Fred's height by four hundred millimetres and as he was already a short little runt, his new reduced height is such that his eyes don't even reach the height of my belly button." Mrs Friendly's reply was very positive indeed. "Ivor, just shut the fuck up and take me to Zacharia's betting shop so that I may collect my winnings; I'm dying to see his face. Let me first put on the CD player and disco lights."

Mrs Friendly switched on Rod Stewart's recording of "I'm Sailing" on the CD player and set it to the automatic repeat play mode. Fred was going to get awfully pissed off with Rod Stewart by the time Mrs Friendly returned from her six months round the world holiday.

Mrs Friendly and Ivor drove down to Zacharia's betting shop and found a big sign outside that simply said: Permanently Closed Down Moved Away. Mrs Friendly went crayzeeeeeeeeeee, and Ivor said "oh my Godddddd!" After about three hours, Mrs Friendly calmed down and then took notice of a further sign that said: Enquiries: Please phone 00654 23487

After driving around the area for over two hours, Ivor found a working telephone kiosk and telephoned this number where a recorded message told him: "Hello all my creditors, my real name is Maxwell and I have been stealing your money for years. I've now decided to leave before being caught and go to a better place. Have a nice day and sod all of you!" Mrs Friendly was driven to despair and shouted at Ivor. "Ivor, you must now help me to bury old Fred, because I'm so poor that if I was to see Fred in the cabinet with that goddamn grin on his face every morning it would remind me of all the money I have lost and how rich and happy I should be. He annoyed me when he was alive, but he is driving me nuts now that he is dead. I want to bury him in my back garden underneath the bloody compost heap that he loved so much!"

Ivor was flabbergasted and replied, "You can't bury Fred in your back garden!" Over the next four weeks, Ivor and Mrs Friendly met with all the relevant government departments and at the local village church and they found out that Fred could indeed be buried in Mrs Friendly's back garden and there was nothing anybody could do about it. It was not even necessary to have the church consecrate the plot - just dig a hole and drop old Fred in and all was OK.

So it came to pass that Fred had his legs sewn back on and was buried in the back garden under the compost heap. Some six months later, around the time that Mrs Friendly should have been returning from her round the world holiday that she could not go on due to lack of funds, Ivor woke up with the most wonderful money making scheme on his brain. Why stop at burying old Fred in the back garden, why not bury hundreds of people and charge for it?

This could be a gold mine. Mrs Friendly was very enthusiastic towards this business proposition because she was totally broke and living on social security. How the mighty do fall. So was born the *Friendly Back Garden Funeral Service Limited.* This new company placed advertisements in the personal columns of all the local newspapers:

FRIENDLY BURIALS

Place your loved ones in the hands of a loving family where only nice people will be accepted for burial with existing nice people. Save 90% on funeral costs or have us invoice your insurance company the current rate and receive a cash pay back of the difference! Special burial package including plastic reusable flowers for £999.99 including a Noddy plaster of paris headstone.

Call Mrs Friendly at Friendly's Back Garden Funeral Service.

This marketing method worked a treat and *Friendly Back Garden Funeral Services Limited* were burying an average of twenty-two people per week which meant invoiced sales of over one million pounds per year with almost no overheads

Ivor dug the holes with a second-hand JCB

digger that he had bought for £2,000 and the plastic coffins from Taiwan were obtained at £45.78 per dozen in assorted colours. The plastic flowers cost £15.78 per dozen but lasted at least six years before being replaced. A nice little earner you might say.

Ivor calculated that by removing the garden shed, demolishing the conservatory and filling in the fish pond, they could accommodate about three thousand six hundred burials. This equated to about six million pounds in sales and made the money that was lost to Zacharia for having Fred stuffed a mere pittance. All looked good for the future.

Back garden burial did not prove popular with the neighbours, who formed the *NABOURS* (Neighbours Against Burials On Utilised Road Systems) protest group. They claimed that the value of their properties was being adversely affected and it was becoming impossible to sell any house in the same street as the Friendly Back Garden Funeral Services Limited, where up to three thousand six hundred bodies were due to be buried. The sight of the hearses drawing up and the coffins being moved into the back garden did not help the property prices. Mrs Friendly and Ivor claimed it was the most popular street in the area, but unfortunately most of the occupants were dead. There is no more powerful group of protesters than that of private house owners when their equity is threatened. Despite these vehement protests, there was absolutely nothing they could do to halt the profitable Friendly Back Garden Funeral Services Limited where business thrived.

The bigger the protests, the greater the media coverage and the more people became aware of the company and wanted cut price funerals for departed relatives whom they hated.

It was after the first fifty burials that Ivor had complained of a bad back and had purchased the secondhand JCB digger from WIMPEYS that was "sold as seen". It turned out that Ivor had not the first inkling of how to drive this huge earth digging monstrosity, let alone on how to operate it safely - here lay the Achilles heel of the venture. On his first attempt to operate the monster, Ivor knocked down the chimney-pot from the Jones' bungalow next door, which crashed down through the roof and killed both Mr and Mrs Jones whilst they were watching Columbo on television.

Fortunately, Columbo's assistance was not required to solve the demise of the Joneses because this was done by P.C. Stanton from the local police station. He wrote in his report:

The Joneses were definitely dead when I arrived on the scene; died by brains being smashed caused by falling chimney. Chimney broken off of house by a Mr. Ivor Parrot whilst he was driving a knackered JCB digger in a drunken state without an operator's licence to dig holes in the Friendly graveyard situated on the next door's property at the back of the house.

Ivor was fined £400 for drunken driving of a JCB in a graveyard, but all other charges were dismissed because the offence took place on private property where the other civil laws did not apply. Mrs Friendly offered to bury both of the Joneses for a special price of only £200, including plastic flowers, but the Joneses children did not take up the offer.

By the 1 January 2001, the whole Friendly graveyard was full up with 6627 happy occupants. Ivor had squeezed in the extra 127 people above the original estimate by doubling up the occupants on a few plots after he had thoroughly checked that the first inhabitants had no living relatives. Being a cautious man, Ivor used instantly removable screw-in plaques on these double-up graves, just in case some long lost relative turned up.

What to do now? Both Ivor and Mrs Friendly had become accustomed to a high style of living and without much effort because operating the *Friendly Back Garden Funeral Services Limited* was too easy for words. The answer was of course obvious - buy a huge mansion house, one big enough to bury hundreds of thousands of people in the grounds. They looked around for a suitable property and eventually settled upon Bryant House, located on the outskirts of Canterbury, which had grounds of over six hundred acres, mostly real crappy marsh land. Marsh land is no good for tennis courts, but really fantastically easy for digging holes in. Then the real problem reared its ugly head! Mrs Friendly insisted that they take Fred with them, but this time they could afford to buy a tall disco display cabinet for him that would be placed in the trophy/snooker room at Bryant House.

"OK my dear, he's preserved well enough; all we've got to do is dig him up and place him in the cabinet." As soon as Ivor started digging old Fred up out of the ground, a slant-eyed man from the Home Office arrived with a warrant for his arrest. In court it was disclosed that the Home Office agreed that you don't need a licence to bury anybody (or any bodies) in your back garden but YOU DO if you wish to dig them up! Ivor was fined £5,000 for disturbing the dead and warned that any future similar offence would be treated gravely and lead to a statutory prison sentence. He tried to explain to the judge by saying:

"My Lord, before we buried Fred, we marinated him, stuffed him, covered him in Old Spice to stop him smelling so bad before we cut off his legs and put him in a beautiful display cabinet. Mrs Friendly has purchased a beautiful new display cabinet complete with disco lights to keep Fred happy, and we only want to dig him up to put him

in this new cabinet. This time we won't even cut off his legs! It's only right that a wife should be able to take her husband back with her once he's been stuffed. I'm sorry about the original sawing off of his feet but this was an arithmetical problem that required solving."

All of Ivor's wonderful speech was to no avail because Mrs Friendly was distraught to the point of suicide. "Are you bloody well telling me, you bloody body stuffer, that we can't dig up old Fred and take him with us!? How about the other customers in the back garden?" Ivor was very careful regarding the tone of his reply. "Sorry to say Mrs Friendly, but that's the law."

"Bolox to the law you silly man, we're going to dig up Fred and take him with us tonight!" Fred was indeed dug up, decrappitised and taken to Bryant House where he still stands on display to this day.

Mrs Friendly invited an estate agent to come along to value the old house that was now redundant to their requirements. Ivor explained that they were prepared to take a slightly lower price than normal due to the nature of the previous business operated from the premises and the "few hundred" people who had taken up permanent abode in the back garden. "But they don't cause any trouble" confirmed Ivor to the somewhat confused young fellow.

When they entered the back garden and the

estate agent actually saw the 6,500 gravestones, including one empty grave that he thought had been vandalised by grave robbers, he was horrified and had to sit down to recover his breath and composure. This was not a normal day. After spending a few minutes composing himself, he prepared himself to speak in as serious a manner as he could adopt under the current circumstances.

"Mr. Parrot, having no previous experience of selling a detached house in a good middle class area complete with several thousand graves in the back garden, including one emptied out by grave robbers, I find it difficult to give you an instant valuation of your property. The fact that every house in this street is already empty of occupants and all have For Sale notices up also has an affect upon the valuation. You also tell me that the purchaser must allow relatives of the back garden occupants to visit the graves at any time and that they have become accustomed to having tea and biscuits served on Sundays. You further request that the plastic flowers be changed every six years.

"There will obviously have to be a large discount applied to this property as compared with a similar property in a similar street where no graves are located. I would estimate that under normal circumstances this property would be worth around £265,000 but you should advertise an asking price of £20,000 for this property and also consider any offers."

It came to pass (so to speak) that the house was eventually sold to a homosexual Welsh social sciences teacher from Cardiff, a gentleman who had a morbid fascination for graveyards and occasionally killing old people with big axes every time Wales lost a rugby match. Contracts were signed on the 1 April 2001.

Ivor and Mrs Friendly got married with Fred standing in as best man. Fred smiled continuously and looked great in his uniform, although his smell is getting much worse as the years go on. Mrs Friendly felt so guilty about marrying whilst Fred was still around watching, that as a compromise she convinced Ivor to change their name by deed poll to Mr & Mrs Friendly-Parrot.

I, for one, wish the Friendly-Parrots a very happy and prosperous future.

They read in the paper that Her Royal Highness Lucky was still smiling on the front page and that Maxwell (alias Zacharia) was found drowned last week and had left all his companies' shares to them - what great luck they thought.

Little did they know that the worst was yet to come and that today's news was just a false dawn.

Chapter 8

From Wally Bean to Very 'umble

Humility is the greatest sacrifice.

Siegfred Wallington (1834)

Wally Bean is probably the happiest man I have ever had the pleasure of knowing during my own life of serenity and literary satisfaction. When I say that he is the happiest man I have ever encountered, I don't mean to imply that he made me personally happy or even made me laugh. I would go as far as to say that Wally Bean made me very unhappy, purely because he is the happiest man that I have ever encountered.

I would have been much happier if I had been the happiest man and Wally Bean was the second happiest man I had ever encountered. However, one must accept one's lot in this life of trials and tribulations. If, as a stranger, you were to assess Wally Bean's lifestyle, he should have been positively the unhappiest man in the world, but instead of this he was probably in the top ten list of "people who are very happy but should be bloody miserable!" Got it?

Wally Bean was in charge of the toilets at *Patel's Cheapo Pie Factory* where the multiracial blend of workers spent a great deal of their time. Have you ever worked within a pie factory that employs one hundred and eighty-seven people, each one having individual eating, crapping and ablution habits?

Have you ever considered or analysed the vast range of food items consumed by these people? Have you ever studied the long list of medical, stomach and bowel complaints that so many workers suffer from as a constant part of their lives? Have you also ever considered the hygiene level of these same workers in this Asian owned pie factory? Of course you haven't; you self- centred moron.

You are not the least bit interested in such a range of unsociable and somewhat obnoxious questions, are you? Speak up or forever hold your tongues! For those people who wish to hold their tongues and need to use both hands, please see my book *The Working Man's Guide To The Galaxy* for details of how to purchase a DikPeg.

As an aside, I would like to discuss a different bean for a few moments. Did you know that 91.6% of the world's population does not know how to open a tin of Heinz baked beans? Admittedly, 87.9% of the world's population have not yet tasted Heinz baked beans, but even so, the statistics are amazing. Before we go on any deeper in the beanz direction, I want to know if it should be Heinz's or Heinz baked beans - what do you think? If it should be Heinz baked beans, then it should also be Kellogg cornflakes - but it is not! It is Kellogg's cornflakes and therefore it should be Heinz's baked beans. If Mr. and Mrs Heinz and their six windy offspring were going out to dinner with the 57

Varieties, you would say *"the Heinz's are coming to dinner tonight"* and you would not say *"the Heinz are coming to dinner tonight."* We also say *"the Queen's subjects"* and not *"the Queen subjects"* because it would sound stupid.

We all now agree that as from this day forward, we shall order only Heinz's baked beans on toast and nothing else will suffice. I have heard it said that until the 18 June 1993, just over 63,000,000 billion, billion zillion beans have been baked by Heinz's and that requires an awful lot of ovens. We must only say "Beanz meanz Heinz's." Now concerning the problem of 91.6% of the population not being able to open a tin of Heinz's baked beans, I can see that this is a big problem.

Now back to our subject bean, Wally Bean our toilet attendant.

"Dick Head, my old cobber, everything is in the mind and nothing is really as bad as you first think because there are always more important things in life to consider and worry about," said Wally Bean to me one day at the pie factory. He took a similar approach whenever I tried to discuss the reasons why an apparently intelligent man would do such a lousy job and worked with it every day. Throughout the world, the job of bog-house cleaner (Crappenhausenmann, Il Turdopersono, etc) draws ridicule and guarantees that the recipient is left as an outcast in the society in which he lives. Just imagine you take your wife to Wally Bean's house and he personally cooks and serves you up a big plate of steaming minced beef curry, whilst informing you glowingly, "Yes, my friends, this was cooked with my own fair hands." Being sick on the dinner table is the norm under such situations.

Furthermore, just what can you talk about during such dinner meetings when you are drinking your brandy? You could, of course, discuss the effect of the climate upon the bowel movement of Chinese immigrants, or the variation in crapping techniques between the various ethnic races, or even the toilet paper consumption statistics. No, I consider that it would be better for all toilet attendants to permanently hold their tongues and refrain from holding any dinner or barbecue parties.

So, as expected, Wally Bean became the joke of Patel's Cheapo Pie Factory and an outcast of society. That was of great concern to me because it was a complete injustice. However, no matter the level of ridicule heaped upon him, Wally Bean remained a happy and contented man at all times and to me became an enigma.

There came a moment on the 1 July 1981 that was the beginning of a discovery that would eventually change my whole attitude towards life, Wally Bean and all toilet attendants.

On that special day, I awoke early at 6.32 am for the first time in many years, and decided to take my reliable Ford Granada on a spin into the countryside and experience the real feeling of nature. Fresh air and country smells were only a gallon of petrol away.

An accident only becomes a disaster when the insurance company won't pay!

"Going Broke" Chris Tenterten (1967)

I headed into the countryside and dreamed of joyous moments in my life and other less enjoyable moments in the past when cars have been the root cause of trouble. Humphrey Bogart immediately came to mind and made me smile to myself. I came across this gentleman some six years ago.........

"Mr. Head, my name is Humphrey Bogart and I am the chief claims manager for the *Screwyou Insurance Company* who are your car insurers," spoke this squeaky voice on the telephone in my kitchen. "I have phoned you personally to discuss the claim you have submitted concerning the accident and damage relating to a Mercedes car, registration number DIK 1. This accident as reported appears very strange to me and it is not definite that we shall be paying out on this said claim."

At this point our highly trained company con artist from the *Screwyou Insurance Company* stopped talking and awaited my nervous response - all as taught to him at the *Screwyou Training School.* Silence is golden, so I refused to answer him. I remained silent.

"Hello Mr. Head, did you hear what I just said?" Silence remained golden and I did not respond - a technique taught to me by my father as a sure fire way of unsettling the opposition during moments of conflict, and guaranteeing to get them really annoyed. "Hello Mr. Head......Hello Mr. Head, are you there?" More silence from Dick Head the expert negotiator. "Hello Mr. Head, oh fuck me I've lost the silly bastard!" spouts out our upset Bogeyman and he slams down the telephone.

Everything comes to him who waits, and waiting for Humpty Dumpty took only nine seconds, thus proving that he is a very dedicated chief claims manager and that he almost certainly has last number redialling on his telephone. I can't be absolutely sure of this, but it's a pretty fair guess. I pick up the receiver and the fun continues.

"Hello, *Richard Head Investments*, can I help you?" I said, speaking in my best Irish accent. "Ah, I wonder if I may speak to Mr. Head please?" says Humphrey in a very annoyed tone. "Which Mr. Head would that be?" I asked in a friendly way. "Mr. Richard Head!" barks out the chief claims officer. "One moment please" and I push the mute button and await his next move. After exactly one minute and seven seconds (I've got a call duration clock on my phone), Humphrey Bogart starts asking, "Hello, hello....Jesus Christ what the bloody he.." and at that moment I release the mute button and answer "Richard Head, the silly bastard here, how can I help you Mr. Boggy?"

"Ah, Mr. Head, sorry about the bad language on the phone, but I thought that the line was dead; by the way my name is Humphrey Bogart not Boggy." It is at this point, my graduates, that perseverance along a planned route must be maintained at all costs if you are to succeed in your well laid plans. It is far too easy to think that the nut is already cracked and decide to reach out for the fruit. This would not be the correct route to take - no siree, not at all. Please read my booklet entitled *How to annoy an insurance investigator and take the spoils*.

I remained silent as Humphrey continued with his monotone voice, "Mr. Head, I wonder if you would mind answering some simple questions relating to this insurance claim on your Mercedes Dik 1?" Silence. "Mr. Head are you there?" Silence "Mr. Head, Mr. Head....oh the shitty bastard is avoiding answering my questions and has cut me off!" He throws down the receiver and the line goes dead.

Everything is going according to plan and I await his next call. He obviously required time to cool down and this call arrives some six minutes twelve seconds later. "Hello, Richard Head Investments, can I help you?" I said, speaking in my best Irish accent. "Ah, I wonder if I may speak to Mr. Head please?" says Humphrey in sickly nice tone. "Which Mr. Head would that be?" I asked in a friendly way. "Mr. Richard Head!" squeaks out the chief claims officer, trying not to lose his temper. "One moment please" and like before I push the mute button and await his next move.

After exactly one minute and sixteen seconds, Humphrey Bogart starts asking, "Hello, hello....Jesus Christ not again"....at that moment I release the mute button and answer "Richard Head, the shitty bastard here trying to avoid your questions, how can I help you Mr. Boggy?"

"Ah, Mr. Head, I'm so sorry about the bad language on the phone, but I thought that the line was dead at the time; by the way my name is Humphrey Bogart not Boggy." I remained silent as Humphrey continued with his monotone voice, "Mr. Head, I wonder if you would mind answering some simple questions relating to this insurance claim on your Mercedes Dik 1?" I responded at last. "Mr. Boggy, I'm sure that you must realise that being called a shitty bastard and accused of trying to avoid your questions is rather offensive. You do realise that you are talking to a world famous author and inventor I hope?"

"Mr. Head, let's make a fresh start, shall we?" "Mr. Boggy, my friend, I find that your understanding is very touching. Now how can I help you?" "Mr. Head, do you have a copy of the insurance claims form that we are referring to?" "No I do not." "Mr. Head, can I therefore fax you a copy so that we can then discuss it on the telephone in a few minutes time?" "No we cannot because my fax machine is broken."

Humphrey is becoming very nervous and finally takes the plunge and asks me, "Mr. Head could I read out your statement concerning the accident so that I can then ask you some questions?" "Certainly Mr. Boggy, go ahead at your leisure." "Mr. Head, I will now read out your statement as received by us from you:

"I was driving along in my Mercedes car at the slow pace of 29 miles per hour in a 30 miles per hour area on the A10 heading for Cambridge. Suddenly, a huge bright yellow greyhound dog ran in front of me and I instinctively swerved to avoid hitting this beautiful K9.

"I hit and demolished the front of a Rolls Royce showroom, thus doing great damage to my own car and at least twenty brand new cars in the showroom. I immediately jumped out of my car, said 'gosh!' and shouted out 'Rover, Rover.' No large bright yellow greyhound appeared and therefore we can assume that the dog's name was not Rover or it had pissed off home double quick for lunch.

"There is mucho damage to zee krauten car and at least twenty Rolls Royces! All because of a bright yellow greyhound"

Humphrey clears his throat and says, "Does that sound correct Mr. Head?" "Yes Humphrey, I'm sure that you have read it out word for word. If I wrote it then you've said it!" "That's good Mr. Head, can you tell me anything more about Rover?" "Nothing about the dog, but I think their cars are crap."

"OK Mr. Head, can you therefore explain your comments of 'there is mucho damage to zee krauten car and at least twenty Rolls Royces!" "Well Humphrey, I'm no coachbuilder - just a world famous author, but I would say that on top of the £32,670 you've got to pay for my written off Mercedes, there must be a further £200,000 to pay the Rolls Royce garage. It was a shame about that beautiful convertible. That's what I mean by mucho damage. Is that all you want to know Humphrey?"

"Well not exactly Mr. Head, I also phoned to ask you to explain your sarcastic undertones on your insurance claim, which we also considered very insulting!" Now for the finale - da, de, da!

"Really Humphrey, would you consider that my helpful attitude, albeit considered by you as sarcastic and insulting, is as bad as you calling me a silly bastard and a shitty bastard? I think we should hold a meeting and let your superiors decide." Humphrey is lost for words but manages to bluster out "Mr. Head, I ah, well maybe, ah........"

"Humphrey, my friend, why don't you go and screw yourself!" "Mr. Head, if I had my way you wouldn't get one single bean!" So here again we come back to beans, but I am pleased to report that the Screwyou Insurance Company paid for DIK 1 and Humphrey is now learning how to stick labels onto soup tins at the local canning works.

From one bean to another, the stories go on and on and on and on. Back to our Wally Bean.

My mind reverts to the present as I joined the main A345 road where my attention was drawn to a field of cows and Wally Bean thumbing a lift alongside his broken down Fiat rust tub. As with any other good Christian or Samaritan, I stopped and asked him what the problem was. "Wally, my old bean, what the hell's wrong with your rust bucket today then?"

Wally Bean smiled gently before answering in his quiet reserved way, "Dick Head, my true friend Dick, my car has unfortunately given up the ghost and I am desperately trying to reach Dartford." At that very moment a cuckoo flew directly over the top of my head.

"Wally Bean, my friend, here is your Dartford carriage and I am your Dartford carriage driver. Jump in alongside me and we will have you there in just a jiffy, before you even close the door! To what address shall this personal taxi take you?" I considered this to be a witty comment under the circumstances - what do you think?

"Thank you Dick, just take me the nearest bus stop as I can get a bus to where I'm going to in Dartford as I don't want to put you out too much." I felt somewhat insignificant as I replied, "No, no, Wally Bean, please tell me where you want to go to because I've got all day and nothing to do." To this remark, he smiled, showing his shining white teeth and said, "That is very considerate of you Dick, please take me to Auburn House in Watling Street. I'll show you the way but let me load up a few boxes in the back of your car first."

It took just over twenty minutes to load up several heavy boxes and following Wally's instructions to reach a large house that had a huge driveway from the main road. As we drove into the driveway, we passed under an overhead sign saying *Auburn House VETERANS HOSTEL*. At the end of this curved driveway we approached a huge white painted country house, looking as though it belonged more on the edge of Blackheath Common than stuck away on the outskirts of Dartford - it was a beautiful building.

As Wally exited from the car, he spoke very quietly to me, "Dick, why don't you join me today whilst I take my friends to the seaside?" Boring can be described in many ways, including being totally pissed off, Making love to the girlfriend or drilling a hole in the ground. I was definitely off sex since last night with a nymphomaniac postwoman, I have no interest in oil prospecting and therefore you are all correct in assuming I was definitely pee eye ess ess ee dee of eff eff, with a capital Pee and Oh. This being the case, I answered Wally with my best beaming smile, "Wally, you Bean, I'd be honoured to join you and your friends on a trip to the seaside, my old mate!"

I could have replied "that's a bloody good idea", but this would have been too shocking for Wally who looked as though he had just been ordained as a priest that very morning, or at the very least as though he had just found God.

Now I would find out what a toilet cleaner did in his spare time. At least none of the other lads at the pie factory would ever find out that Dick Head was socialising with the outcast from the toilets, so I was safe from such ridicule. Bogs, crappers, shithouses, piss holes, johns, etc are all ample descriptions for what we in Europe politely refer to as the toilet, or in lower class areas as the lavatory. Our higher class American cousins have developed the camouflaged names of wash room or rest room to avoid describing what actually goes on there.

With all of today's hygiene regulations forcing everybody to conform to any one or more of over 245,768 regulations in force in Europe alone, you would think that the washing of bums after using the toilet would be compulsory. We are all aware of this unhygienic part of life, and yet we accept sitting upon chairs that have been sat on by other people, whether these people are washed or not. Out of sight, out of mind.

This is not good enough for Dick Head and I have written to my local MP, Walter Bothhammer (ex barrister and practising homosexual), as follows:

Dear Mr. Bothhammer,

RE: WASHING OF THE BUMS

Following our recent telephone conversation, when I tried to explain the need for you to propose a new Bill in Parliament regarding enforced washing of the bum after use in the toilet, I am sorry to see that you appeared to find this subject somewhat offensive and called me a "pervert". However, as all MPs also have bowel movements, some say more than ordinary folk, then you daily experience such hygienic risk.

It is positively today's most dangerous health risk to allow people to walk around without such enforced washing being applied. I would go as far as to say that it is perfectly disgusting that this rotting excreta is left to be a breeding ground for all types of germs and apart from this, it stinks to high heavens. It is therefore a matter of urgency for you to promote this Private Members Bill for "Compulsory Washing Of The Bum After The Toilet" to eliminate this health risk.

To be sure that all people of this great land are prepared for this new procedure, it will be important for a full television advertising campaign to graphically promote the procedures to be adopted and to highlight the benefits to the health of the nation. All public conveniences must be installed with new automatic anus washing machines to carry out the new procedure in a soft and painless way.

Just like parking meters, they can be coin operated; say 20p per wash and 10p a dry with an optional payment of 5p for talcum powder application. All such machines must be government controlled to avoid the possibility of a sexual connotation being brought into this area of public health.

On the basis that everybody uses these machines at least three times every day, they will generate a massive extra governmental income of over £15 billion per year. For this huge sum, it is worth the government ignoring and accepting the almost certain new nickname of "crapper tax" that would quickly describe this item.

This would allow the government to make even more foolish mistakes as they would have another £15 billion to throw away. To enforce such a law, we shall require a new group of "Sniffer Wardens" who would be dressed in dark brown uniforms including the regulatory peaked cap of authority.

I believe that personal sniffing is impractical and would lead to physical assaults upon the sniffer wardens by the populace at large. I make this statement following my recent discussions with my former workmates at Patel's Cheapo Pie Factory on the desirability or otherwise of personal sniffing. Pastry Pete was furious and became extremely agitated before he stood up and shouted, "No poofter in a brown uniform is going to sniff my arse!"

You have nothing to worry about Mr. Bothhammer, because even this problem can be overcome following the results of a meeting recently held with the UK Rottweiler Breeders Association that is located in the dungeons of Rochester Castle. It is a proven fact that these rather vicious beasts (often described as dogs), can detect the faintest smells from a distance of over two hundred metres.

To check on this extraordinary claim, I carried out my own tests to be totally sure that these animals were the answer to our sniffing problem. I can happily report that the results of these tests were positive. The test involved employing twelve of my old work mates from Patel's Cheapo Pie Factory, six with freshly washed bums and six with unwashed bums.

As they left work at knocking off time, I released six of these Rottweilers to sniff out the vulgar and unwashed ones. Yes, you've guessed correctly; the six unwashed workers were attacked by these beasts and the six washed ones left unharmed. I am pleased to report that the six workers attacked by the beasts were saved from serious harm when the trainer recalled the dogs by blowing a DikWissal.

All six are in hospital and are expected to make a full recovery before Christmas; which is very good news indeed. We therefore propose that each sniffer warden has his or her own Rottweiler to enforce the regulations, knowing that no offender is likely to offend a second time after being caught by these beasts the first time.

Obviously, we must allow some extra cash for the hospitals to pay for the new CUA wards that will be required. So, Mr. Bothhammer, I think you can now see just how important it is for the new Bill to become law as a matter of urgency. The sooner this is done, then the sooner we eliminate the filth walking about our streets every day of our lives. Please contact me at any time should you require any data to support this new Bill.

Yours Very Truly,

Richard Head

World Famous Author & Inventor

PS: Unless we enforce the whole Bill, it won't be worth a bean.

I'm now awaiting progress of this new Bill and will keep you informed in future *Working Man's Guide* books. Now, from one bean, back to Wally Bean at the Veterans Hostel and our trip to the seaside.

As I walked across the gravel drive with Wally Bean towards the main entrance to Auburn House, the door opened just before we reached it and an elderly man in an army uniform, complete with red beret, came out in an electrically driven wheelchair and greeted Wally. "Nice to see you major, I thought you must have had some kind of accident because you've never let us down yet!"

Now my mind was in a real spin; what the hell is all this major stuff and who is this guy in the wheelchair wearing action man gear? "Hello RSM, nice to see you again, I'd like you to meet a close friend of mine, Richard Head who is quite a famous author and inventor of things. My car broke down and Richard was kind enough to pick me up and bring me here. He's joining us on our trip to Brighton today. Has the colonel phoned regarding the Aldershot bunch?" Our friendly RSM replied, "Hello Richard, I'm very pleased to meet any friend of the major's" as he shook hands with me using a very firm grip. "Yes major, the Aldershot bunch will meet us at the hall around 2 o'clock for drinkies and sandwiches."

Some forty minutes later, twenty-six of us, including twenty-four disabled ex-soldiers had been loaded up into an air conditioned coach and we were on the M25 heading for Brighton. The wheelchairs and crutches were stored below for safety.

All these old soldiers were wearing the very smart uniform of the Parachute Regiment and full rows of ribbons depicting I know not what. Wally Bean opened up the huge cardboard boxes that he had brought on the back seat of my car and inside were twenty-four bottles of all different types and brands of alcoholic drinks; one for each one of his soldier friends, especially selected to suit their favourite individual tastes. Then came the smoked salmon sandwiches and cold beef rolls, followed by an array of Danish Pastries.

I was very confused, but by sharing in with twenty-four types of drink, I very soon became very confused and very merry. Being nosy is a trait associated with famous authors and I am no exception. I approached our friendly RSM, who was sitting at the back of the coach with some of his friends, well out of earshot of Wally Bean. "Excuse me, RSM, but could you tell me exactly how you met our mutual friend Wally Bean, because I'm somewhat confused?" Have you ever been looked in the eye by a person with such intensity that you feel his telepathic power burning into you, trying to pass on secret information that should remain unspoken? No, nor had I until that moment in my life - it was a neck tingling experience.

"Young man, Major Bean is a fellow soldier of the Airborne Veterans Association, even though he is from a different generation than us few survivors of the Second World War. All of us are the survivors of a drop into France on the night before D-Day when we dropped directly on top of a German fortified position. I know how a pheasant feels during an organised game shoot young man, as all of us here do.

"Brigadier Bean, Major Bean's father, was awarded The Victoria Cross for incredible bravery during this turkey shoot for the Germans, where only seventy-two out of an initial four hundred and sixty survived to see the daybreak of D-Day. Of these seventy-two survivors, only twenty-four were able to walk home and the rest are as you see us here today.

"Brigadier Bean was unbelievable that day, in ways that can never be described in words. It was as though he had been temporarily invested with a special Power from God that helped him help us to survive, but it eventually cost him his life. Whilst gasping through his final living moments, he asked me to look after his boy Walter, the man you call Wally Bean.

"This regiment never forgot Brigadier Henry Arthur David Bean and we looked after his son and eventually sent him to Sandhurst where, in 1962, he passed out as top cadet and carried the silver sword. Without hesitation he requested a posting to his father's old regiment and the regiment felt honoured to have him as one of their officers. He quickly obtained his crown and due to his bravery and ability was expected to reach the very pinnacle of the army establishment. But for the Official Secrets Act, I could tell you stories about the major that would make your hair stand on end.

"Major Bean was sent to Vietnam during the height of the war with America as an official army observer and it is here that his life was changed forever. We will never know exactly what happened to him over in that hell on earth, but when he returned, he resigned his commission.

"Auburn House had been the family house of the Bean clan since 1798 and when the major's mother died in 1981, he gifted the whole estate to the Veterans Association. We all wrote thanking him for such a wonderful gift that improved the quality of our lives beyond belief from our previous squalid living conditions in institutional care. Major Bean emigrated to a small farm on the Falkland Islands in 1979 where he kept himself isolated in an attempt to come to terms with the cruelty of mankind towards mankind. With the Argentine invasion, even this privacy was to be destroyed forever.

"He returned to this country about three years ago and once we heard of it, we invited him to become President of our Veterans Association immediately. This he accepted and ever since has worked his every possible hour assisting us in any way he can. God only knows how he copes with the work load and how he finds the cash to do all the things that he does. If we need something badly, then Major Bean will get it.

"Now young man, how do you happen to know Major Bean?" I replied in a very quiet voice: "The major is an executive in my company; I work for him."

That night after I arrived home, I felt disturbed and so very, very, very 'umble.

Chapter 9

From Respect & Dignity to Up Me Bum!

"Modern science endangers the very Soul of Mankind by replacing personal dignity with a greed for progression without individual assertion."

Ernest Einstein (1890)

Mankind has an incredible ability to advance its learning at such an unbelievable pace that it would surprise and possibly amaze a visitor from another solar system. Each successive generation understands the utter absurdity of watching Earth's warlike people ignoring all the past mistakes and continues heading towards future catastrophes. We know the dangers, but we refuse to take heed and therefore we must sit idly by as the bombs start to fall upon Bosnia.

This learning from previous mistakes is the real value ensuring that the teaching of history is a compulsory part of our children's schooling and for us adults to take the same notice in our daily lives. I am hoping that one day we shall all decide to learn from our mistakes and live in peace and harmony but have no great confidence that this will ever happen.

Should I be elected by God to create a better world, then my New World would have both respect and dignity located within every breathing human being as my first measure towards reform. Dignity would replace existing priorities where we prostitute our lives and personal morality purely for material gain.

We sacrifice all other things that dare to cross our path. My new path would put a permanent stop to this rape of our planet Earth and the corruption of its peoples; which is laughingly described as progress. This chapter will sow an eternal seed of hope and pride inside you that will grow and grow during your study of Dick Head's *Working Man's Guide* series of educational books.

This seed of hope will spring into full bloom once you comprehend the real meaning of respect and dignity of the human race. This new inner feeling will allow you to experience a new flow of respect and dignity that has been missing from your thoughts since the first day you were born. From birth you have been cast into a world of greedy unscrupulous people, prepared to take away the basic rights of man, even away from themselves in their evil pursuit of everything except respect and dignity.

The Roman chariots may have changed into executive black limousines in New York, but the results are still the same.

"I hate that bloody Prime Minister," shouts out one of your friends when John Major appears on television whilst you down a few jars at the *Cock's Whistle* in Walthamstow. Everybody feels obliged to add their own expletives to this innate comment, just to be in song with the consensus in this bitter school of learning. Look, thick heads, how can you hate the Prime Minister, until you decide what you hate him for?

Like all moments of working class hate, it is this total lack of brain power to truly assess the subject matter that keeps you as a daft ignorant sod. No doubt you are half drunk and nodding your head at every half-witted comment made by any idiot in your messy pub, lost in your world of alcohol induced stupidity that makes you stay exactly where you are for the rest of your sodden life.

If you are happy where you are in life, then please don't read any more pages of this book because you are a bird-brain of the lowest order. Even worse, you are just wasting my valuable time and I have much better things to do than worry about you. Just be brave and ask friends out loud (come on now!). "Is there anybody here in this pub who can read and would like to change from being a drunken idiot and become a highly respected leader of our society with a highly paid job and a *M.Sc. DikHed* degree?"

You will be mobbed by people looking for this opportunity, and indeed by next Friday your pub may be empty. When you say in the pub, "I hate that Dick Head!", there will be nobody else there to agree or disagree with you because they will all be at home or at the local community centre reading this book. Who wants to mix with an ignorant sod like you anyway.

So when the people that took over your book reach

this point in this study course, you will then look doubly stupid. By then you will be an outcast in your own public bar, left playing darts and pool on your own because you are so ignorant. Your old friends will be heading for the top jobs of the future. Their high flying employers are never going to hire a stupid fool like you, are they? You should start planning to live on the dole and cheap beer for the rest of your life.

No matter the warnings I give at each important juncture of our historic trip to change society, it must always be understood that some people really do think that they already know it all. These people should cease study of the Master degree course at this critical point because the going is now starting to get tough and they are never going to make it.

For those of you with a stronger character and a positive will to continue, despite this temptation to jack out and go back to the *Cocks Whistle*, then God be with you.

Just make a note of the names of those working class cowards who have dropped out, in a special book for future reference. This book should be named, *Fools not to employ in the future* and you should treat these people with the respect and dignity they deserve, no more and no less - after all, this is the subject in question. For my persevering millions - onward we travel!

Hate is a wasted emotion and a wasted word, because if hate exists in your body then your whole soul can be eroded and eaten away, piece by piece, without any true logic or meaning to it. Hate from deep within is something that you must consider fully in an effort for you to come to terms with the reasons that created this negative force. Hate only helps to destroy the dignity of your life and to a similar extent damages the dignity of your family and friends.

Accepting other people's rights to individual free thinking and allowing them to live a different life style than yours is the first concept for my students to understand. All is not as you are led to believe by our blood-sucking media; this guiding hand of society that finds a giant pair of restyled silicon breasts more important than the lives of millions of our fellow human beings.

You must learn to believe that the other person has a viewpoint that he believes in just as strongly as you do - so why should we always be right? In more cases than not, the viewpoint of the victor, after a conflict is settled, is shown to be in error by later generations. When the conflict occurred it was essential for the working class people to be misled into believing in the official story released by Authority to guarantee support for its unilateral actions during such a conflict.

Sheep follow the leaders; just watch any football or political riot on television to prove this case in point. Unless you eradicate hate from your heart, you can never pass this subject of *Respect & Dignity*. Your exam paper will have an endorsement written,

Still a hateful Sod! and you will be failed, even if you pass with distinction all other subjects; such is the importance of this section of your study course.

Analysing the reason for any particular hate is a deeply complicated process for the layman starting out for the first time on this subject for softening up your character. Analysing the reason for anything that disturbs us in life often leads us into realising that there is no real point in being disturbed for such idiotic and insignificant reasons in the first place.

Let's take the prime example of "I hate my mother-in-law", where after a full analysis we have the following answers and conclusions upon which to correct our position.

She's a miserable old cow .

She's an interfering old bitch.

She hates my guts.

You hate her guts.

She's the most ugly person you have ever met.

She's always rude to you.

You argue with her at all times.

She speaks badly about you to other people.

She's the most rotten person in the world.

This list does of course perfectly describe most mothers-in-law, but many people have found ways of living with these feelings, or the cleverer people amongst us have analysed the situation as follows:

I'm never ever going to make her smile unless I kill myself.

She's going to be an interfering old bitch unless I cut her hands off, cut out her tongue and send her to Japan for twenty years.

Sticks and stones may break my bones but this bitch will never hurt me.

Hating her guts is a loss of my personal dignity.

Yes she is very ugly.

Yes she is rude to me.

If I don't talk to her, how can we argue?

Other people must recognise her for what she is.

Yes she is the most rotten person in the world.

Now that you have analysed this problem, don't you feel less hate? Not yet? Well, we must now dilute the problem to change the feeling of hate to that of one of basic acceptance of any current situation so that this problem is no longer a problem. A fully proven system for the mother-in-law problem is either to shoot her or to follow the following procedure: You must have a blackboard prepared with the *ten commandments* printed as follows

1. Thou shalt not be rude to your son-in-law.
2. Thou shalt not be miserable unless on your own.
3. Thou shalt not argue with your son-in-law.
4. Thou shalt not be a rotten person.

5. Thou shalt not spread lies asunder.
6. Thou shalt try to smile or fall asleep.
7. Thou shalt not commit suicide without a will.
8. Thou shalt only visit when invited.
9. Thou shalt leave when told to.
10. Thou shalt leave all wealth to your son-in-law.

This blackboard should be the portable type that can be wall mounted opposite dear old mother-in-law wherever she sits. Whenever she breaks a commandment you can walk to the blackboard and say, "Now, now Ma Ma, we must not break the ten commandments." You must always smile, never argue, never raise your voice and always buy her a small present like weed killer or fly spray at Christmas.

You are now in control of the situation, all hate has gone and indeed more than a little amusement has come back into your life. This procedure is just one of several hundred found in my publication entitled *How To Handle Miserable Sods And Succeed* that is ideal for any undergraduates who intend to enter the banking profession.

In 1987 a case was reported back to my literary agent, Howard Duckworth, of a mother-in-law in Inverness who actually had a change of heart towards her son-in-law after he had received details of the Dick Head method of mother-in-law control of hate and applied it to his life and his mother-in-law. She was so pleased at his new respect and dignity that she actually smiled on several occasions in the presence of several witnesses and then made this new sympathetic man her sole heir. Unfortunately she then died in absolute agony after inadvertently mixing a full pound of weed killer with her Dundee cake and cream.

She is now buried alongside her beloved husband Jock, both now overlooking the sea where amazingly their graves require no weeding whatsoever since she was laid to rest. Something good really does evolve from everything bad.

Having fun in our modern world becomes really difficult because nearly everybody is so miserable. Just watch these satans of misery and depressions frown profusely if you dare laugh out loud or enjoy yourself in the restaurant or any other public place.

In the future, ignore these spoilers of fun and relive your childhood dreams of real fun every day of your lives. A really happy fun person does not even need a partner to share his fun with because the greatest art of all is to amuse one's self - try it some time, my miserable readers, it really works a treat.

Let's arrange some fun parties to spend evenings telling jokes and letting our hair down. Switch off the telly, bring out the drinks, get smashed and let's have a bloody good old fashioned laugh. Go and pick up the oldsters - your old aunts and uncles you've ignored for so long, get them all to join in. Fun is not just for the young set who prefer posing than laughing, it's for all the family being together. Anyone visiting Disneyland in Florida will experience the ultimate in giving fun to children and to the majority of adults, although I cannot really believe that many Tory ministers would enjoy Space Mountain.

The people that operate this fantastic commercial operation should be employed by our government to form a new "Department for happy people and clean Streets" and I guarantee you success. With very little make-up added, we already have ideal actors in Parliament to take on the character roles of Mickey and friends - you know whom I mean? We could have a new *Donald Duck's Question time* once per week, because not only would the whole nation get a real howl but we may get something positive done by our wonderful government at the same time.

I will bid for the promotional franchise if this progressive idea ever comes to fruition. I wonder if Donald votes Labour or Conservative, or maybe for a new party? One thing is guaranteed, the weekly *Donald Duck's Question Time* would become the number one programme in the ratings on television. Some bitchy political commentators are under the impression that once this became so popular, then all MPs would be forced to dress up in similar duck clothes to even stand a chance of reselection. The constituency party in Wiggleswash would say: "Bertie, unless you openly reject those bloody communists in Peking and wear that duck uniform in

Parliament then you will not be selected to stand for Wiggleswash at the next election. In future you must call him The Honourable Mr. Donald and not you poxy duck!" Careful attention would have to be given not to take Donald to any Cantonese restaurants in Aylesbury, particularly during the hunting season.

Schools should have one hour per day just to let the kids tell jokes and laugh, thus enabling tensions to be eased and friendships strengthened. Being happy and laughing is not natural to everybody and must be taught and expanded like any other characteristic of the human body. I wonder how many problems would be solved if we just allowed the kids to be naturally happy for a few hours per week?

Qualifying for a post as a happiness teacher could be problematic, and certainly most existing teachers would fail at the first hurdle. "Can't you even smile Mr. Walterby!?" Examinations in happiness would of course all be of an oral nature and it would consist of watching a Billy Connolly concert for two hours after drinking six large gins and tonic. Not only would the lads have a great time, but they would all obtain a grade "A" pass mark, albeit with a thick head in the morning.

No Welsh boys would pass this new exam, because of the basic impossibility for them to even understand our Billy; but that's how it's been planned anyway. For the Welsh we will arrange extra choir lessons and a different end of term exam; details of this exam to be published in a new book entitled *Laugh at the*

Welsh. This book will not be available in the Welsh language. It will be available in English or Italian by mail order only at £13.75 for people living in England, Scotland & N. Ireland, but at £49.99 for addresses in Wales and bordering territories. This higher price is also applicable on all sales made on Irish Ferries originating or terminating in Wales. A special extra front page has been inserted into the books destined for Welsh readers to make sure that the views of the author are made fully clear on page one to save the reader wasting time reading on any more.

I know, I know! "What's that got to do with fun?", all you graduates from the Welsh mountains are shouting at me. I can now explain that 55,879,987 non-Welshmen do not have this question to ask or have any doubt about the answer. Enough of this shepherd bashing, let's look forward to greater things.

During my lifetime, several things stand out in my mind as being extraordinarily funny. In 1985 I visited the town of Stresa in northern Italy, together with another forty-nine pie and ice cream making people on what was described as *An Ice Cream Training Trip*. Then, Saresh Patel my boss was considering the manufacture of Asian ice cream pies, and as in any case the trip was free of charge that appealed to generous Saresh.

We arrived on a Saturday at about midday and checked into the Hotel La Palma, located on the side of Lago Maggiorre - *Lake Majorory* to you non-Italian speaking cretins. We were invited to join everybody for a nice restful luncheon at a small restaurant on Iso La Bella, a small island situated offshore but only a few hundred metres from the hotel. Never before in the history of lunch time eating have so many people been upset by so few, as Winston Churchill used to say.

A resplendent rendering of the song Volare by all of us, encouraged by seventy-three bottles of the house red plonk, convinced our European Common Market brothers that maybe there were some differences between them and these louts from the home of democracy. Several renderings of the *Wall's Cornetto* song were produced, after the Italian brandy had been vastly consumed. This was to guarantee that anyone that had not appreciated the previous rendering of Volare would be overwhelmed with this *Eye Tie canal boat song.*

Finally, concerning our superior singing, the other local diners of non-Inglesi bloodstock left the restaurant muttering *Inglesi Bastardi!* (meaning "what a great bunch of guys") and we then had the place to ourselves. Our Italian hosts from Milan looked rather out of place as we started the *cheers and salutez competition* that consumed another five bottles of brandy.

Like all good British booze-ups, a few people looked very ill, a few blacked out and a few went to the toiletto where they made some deep throated noises. However, they all returned with a renewed thirst for the brandy. We came, we saw, we consumed and we conquered.

At precisely 3.34 p.m., as confirmed on my Korean

made duty free timepiece, the bravest of our Italian hosts stood up and said, "Gentlemeen, it iz zee toime to goz." To this insult came a barrage of singing, *"Eye tilly eye tie tie!"* on a continuous chorus and everyone started throwing the bread sticks (*grissinni*) around the tables to the dismay of Mussolini the head waiter and his friends. "Wee can now go to zee Napoleon's palatzio on zis izland, or if you prefer you may go on the *la funivia* with meester Deek Ed."

When you are smashed on three litres of red wine and a half bottle of brandy, palaces are not so attractive an opportunity as the la funivia restaurant and bar. Fifteen of us shouted, "We want a bit of the old funivia if you don't mind!" To save a lot of wasted time in explaining the next fifteen minutes of confusion and mayhem, I was elected as leader of "zee funivia party" and us fifteen explorers poured ourselves onto a small boat and upon my instructions of "Zee funivia per favorez - boats away!"

Il capitano took us to a large docking point on the mainland, at a slow chugging speed, but not before we experienced considerable sickness and relieving of the previous drinking spree. Zee Deek Ed Gang had arrived, my students of travel! "We want large funivers" was the battle cry of the British battalion of the Republic, as we fell off the boat and followed the signs for "La Funivia".

To our surprise, we reached what looked like a small railway station where a sign said £2,500 per persone that sounded a bit steep to me for a drink in a station bar but we quickly realised it must include a train trip to a luxury hotel bar. In the fighting spirit that has seen our island race resist all oppressors, my band of commandos shouted out *"Rule Britannia"* and rushed up to the ticket desk waving millions of lire in bank notes and I asked for "fifteen returnez vous ticketos per traino thankou."

A strange looking immigrant from some Arab country with malnutrition (and with about one million spots on his face) replied, "kay?". Not to be put off our invasion plans, we wrote the figures of "15 ticketos" on the window of the ticket desk using one of the commando's lipstick (I'll come to that later) and handed over enough lire to buy the Vatican and two Italian postmen. After laughing his head off for several minutes, this advertisement for "why you should not live in Stresa", handed over fifteen tickets together with a handful of coins and a few bank notes.

Who are we to doubt the honesty of a foreign working class man just doing his everyday job and serving fifteen (drunk out of their brains) lunatics from Great Britain with tickets and being offered enough money to retire on? Certainly we did not doubt this gentleman's honesty but his continuous laughing as we headed for the platform did start to annoy Scrappy Ken and he told the guy so. "If you laugh at me once more you wop tossa, I'm gonna stuff a bowl of spaghetti right up your rear end!" Fortunately for the good of Anglo-Italian relationships, he obviously did not fully understand

Scrappy Ken, because he laughed even louder as we walked towards the very tiny train platform.

Having never travelled on an Italian train before, it came as a great surprise to find the train already at the platform, but my God it was so small, capable of taking only twenty-five passengers and having no seats. After a few minutes waiting on board, our laughing idiot from the ticket desk came along, mounted the train with us and closed the door. The train took off and we were swept up in the air at one hell of a rate of knots - we were on a bloody cable car heading for the skies!

British spirit and humour being what it is, meant that we would overcome this slight shock to the system, but Paul the Baptist (real name Paul Washer) had a different problem when he came over very ill and was sick next to the driver. Unaware of this small accident at the time, we sang the traditional song of "those magnificent men in their flying machines" until after about ten minutes we travelled through the clouds and stopped at our destination - now for drinking some of the old funivia.

Stepping out of the cable car still singing, we asked the laughing driver, "Scuso mateo, whereo we gettio drinkio?" He wiped off some sick from his trousers, pointed up the hill that was somewhat fogbound and said through sarcastic lips "drinkio, Ha Ha Ha!". He closed the cable car door and departed for the flatlands below, with his laughter still ringing in our ears.

It was really bloody cold up there, and we were wearing just summer shirts and trousers. "Are we British or are we Italian mice?" came the shout from Joey, who was still having a go at what was now an almost empty bottle of Italian brandy. To this rallying cry, we stepped out in single file, walking up the hill singing, "Hey ho, hey ho, it's off to work we go............"

In the future, if Hollywood ever makes a film of this trip, it would be at this point that you would have a mountain rescue team flying in by helicopter to save our lives. No helicopter was seen and our story was just beginning.

After walking up this hill in thick fog for some ten minutes and giving twenty renderings of Snow White's seven up surprise, yes you've guessed, we came across a BAR located absolutely in the middle of bloody nowhere. Who said there's no God? Frozen to our lower elements we thanked God and entered this Twilight Zone on top of a bloody great mountain.

Inside we met Luigi for the first time, Luigi who has taught me the simple things of life, Luigi who has become my true friend in the sky. "Gotio anyo goodo beerio mateo?" shouts out Peter from Newcastle. Luigi speaks to us in a slow methodical way, "Ello Ingleesh, pleece you ave a drink wiv me." He then lined up sixteen large tumblers and filled them with what is now known to all of us as Luigi's grappa della casa, which he poured from a gallon sized glass jar.

"Salute ay me ay am meetchay!" he shouts and

drinks his large glass of greeny coloured liquid in one healthy gulp. "Salute aye Luigi!" we all shout in response and do likewise with this nectar of life, which has since been adopted by Polycell as a paint stripping fluid. A red hot shell hit me in the stomach, blowing away half of my inside, followed by shooting pains passing through my near dead body.

Before death arrived, I felt that I must say something to my friends, so I croaked out "Jesus Christ, what the Effing Ell was that?" Nobody could answer me because they had all been shot as well. After a few minutes, no blood could be seen and we realised that it was the grappa della casa causing all these abdominal attacks. Being British, it was not possible for us to leave in disgrace, thus admitting to this mountain man that the British were weaklings in the question of drink.

What would Winston Churchill have done? He mentioned various places but he never said anything about fighting drink in bars located on mountain tops in Italy. We came, we saw and we conquered - that's the spirit that our band lived by on this famous day. We pulled ourselves together, gritted our bulldog teeth and drank another glass of this liquor of the mountain. Feeling totally, totally smashed and brain blown, I kissed Luigi, gave him a handful of money and said "We now goeth to the lowlands, us men of the British Isles. Areeve ay derchi Luigi!" To this he pocketed the wad of notes that we had just given him and then all of his family waved us good-bye shouting "La funivia aye kuso!" which obviously was a good luck chant meaning "return soon to drink some more of the old funivia."

Because there existed on this mountain side just one narrow road, we did eventually manage to reach the cable car station. The doors were locked and closed with a notice on the outside saying "La funivia e chuiso". As drunk and as ill as I felt, it registered fairly rapidly with me that we were in deep trouble - two miles in the air, lost in the freezing cold mountains, smashed out of our tiny skulls and no way home. There was nothing for it but to ask my mate Luigi the best way home, so we all walked back to the BAR, a few of the commandos being rather ill on the way.

As we walked into the BAR, we saw on the counter, lined up and waiting for us, sixteen glasses of Luigi's grappa della casa. "Ello ingleesh, la funivia chuiso si? You ave drinko wiv me si?" To cut a very long story short, Luigi's family cooked a full evening meal for all of us and the whole family brought out an assortment of musical instruments and we sang Italian songs until about 3 am the next morning. No money was accepted from us because "per miei amici tutti libri".

We had ordered five taxis from Stresa to drive up to collect us and quite honestly after stepping into the taxi, I don't remember a thing until I awoke at 7.30 am the next morning.

Luigi and his family taught me the true meaning of

kindness as is only possible from simple folk. We were foreigners behaving quite badly in an alien manner to an Italian and his family and he not only understood it for what it was, but he looked after us, like the friend he has become. Whenever I visit Stresa, I take the train up into the skies to see Luigi and his simpatico family and experience real respect and dignity. I have never drunk grappa since that memorable first outing.

Purity of mind is unknown to mankind wherever progressive thought clouds such perfection.

Upon our return from Stresa, I tried to share our experiences with Bandy Barry, the female cashier at *Patels Cheapo Pie Factory*, but to no avail. If ever the United Nations were to organise a *World Ugly Competition*, Bandy Barry would have a reasonable chance of a medal providing the fish gutting community from Hull did not participate.

The finals are to be held in Zanzibar at the Crooked Baron Casino on De Avenue de Champs. Lucky is far too beautiful to consider entering this year, but she should beware of all the worry that can lead to ugliness and pimples. Why do I know so much about Zanzibar? A good question indeed which I have already answered in greater detail in my publication, Great Places To Hold World Competitions. This 32 page booklet is available from all good quiz shops and from the United Nations plastic surgery department.

Don't be confused about the United Nations having a plastic surgery department because this is very easy to explain, without any need of writing another book. Within the United Nations, there are 691 people of the Inner Sanctum who control everything and they don't like sharing with anybody else. Who and what does that remind you of?

To avoid having to democratically share anything they keep all the important jobs at the United Nations that carry any power between themselves. This arrangement was OK in the beginning but because so many new powerful departments were being formed every year, more and more influential positions were being created every year and it was becoming harder and harder to make sure that these positions were held by the Inner Sanctum. Drastic action was required to protect themselves from outside interference.

In a vain attempt to stamp out this type of corruption, the United Nations passed a law that prohibited important members of the United Nations from being transferred from one job to another. In other words, you stayed in the same job until you retired or died. This opened up great dangers to the Inner Sanctum because unless drastic steps were taken immediately, then trespassers would move in and quickly recognise the corruption of the power base that was taking place.

These new people would want to do good for the world and wouldn't realise that this is negative thinking because we need wars, famine, etc. to allow us to continue making so much money on arms and food exports.

At that moment the Inner Sanctum consisted of 691 people, all of white skin and of pure European bloodstock. These new intruders would be of varied race and coloured skin. My God! What is the world coming to, they all thought. At an urgent meeting of the Inner Sanctum on the 1 April 1981 they agreed that it was acceptable to run a United Nations that was totally useless and ineffective at stopping wars, famine, disease, etc., but what had that got to do with power? Absolutely nothing!

A Jewish member from Hamburg, Zacharias Goebels, spoke up boldly as no man has ever spoken up more boldly before him. "Gentlemen, velcomt to zis first meeting oft zee Innertz Sanctum. Vee must zee firstz havetz a nametz andz I propose zee nametz of CokeYouth." So the *CokeYouth Association* was born and this trading name was registered worldwide.

A proposed scheme was put to the *CokeYouth* at their first meeting and it was too simple for words. It was proposed that as each new important job came up, they would decide the type of person that would be acceptable by the committee to hold such a post and the Plastic Surgery Department would exactly create that person by changing an existing member of the CokeYouth. This meant changing every aspect of the chosen person's make up. Not all members of the *CokeYouth* were in support of this drastic scheme.

"I'm not going to be a bloody nigger" shouted out a member from Tennessee. "You're not cutting off my bloody legs to make me into a Chinaman" protested a basketball player from New York. Despite these objections the idea was adopted by the CokeYouth by a huge majority. So my friends, for the past fifteen years all the powerful positions at the United Nations have been held by the same 691 people, although seventeen have died of blood poisoning during a recent skin injection of squid black.

Another poor fellow went crazy and had to be shot just after he had his legs amputated at the knees and had plastic feet screwed into his kneecaps. This drastic operation was essential when the Pigmy minority section demanded to have their own ambassador at the United Nations Assembly. No pain - no gain, but he still shot himself and in his will asked to be buried with his feet sewed back on. This was not possible as these feet had already been transplanted onto a short *CokeYouth* member who was to become ambassador for Uganda next year.

Many of the wives are also complaining because they too have to undergo similar operations if they are to have any married life that is worthwhile. The *CokeYouth* have opened various camps in the Rockies where rebellious wives are sent for re-education into bars of soap and animal feed. The local farmers are complaining that their cattle are becoming erratic and are nagging the bulls twenty-four hours per day when they are not complaining of headaches. When reprimanded, these cows sulk for days on end. Nobody wants to buy the milk because it tastes sour and the meat because it is too tough to eat.

All this trouble has been caused by the re-education of only seventeen wives - God only knows the effect of processing all of them. Now you may wonder what all this has got to do with Bandy Barry, the female cashier at Patels Cheapo Pie Factory. Absolutely nothing my friends but women upset me - back to Bandy Barry.

Bandy Barry was born on the 10 June 1964 as the partially deformed daughter of Jacko and Brenda Bates at the Hammersmith General Hospital. Jacko Bates had turned into a very nasty person ever since he was nicknamed Wanker Bates as a young lad at school when referred to as Master Bates by his masters. Young boys can be so cruel.

At the very moment of Barry's imminent birth, Jacko was completely drunk and singing a gentle rendering of Danny Boy in C flat as he lay across the bottom of Brenda's bed where she was trying her best to bring this child into this world of wonder. With the benefit of some two litres of French cooking brandy inside him, Jacko just managed to finish off his chorus when he heard the cry of a baby. Yessiree, his son had been born to carry on the family name! He half walked and half crawled to where the midwife was holding his son, and then he shouted in terror, "Where's his bloody testicles!?"

The midwife, a woman of considerable prudery, replied, "Mr. Bates, congratulations on the birth of your daughter." Disaster had struck the Bates family because not since 1623 had a Bates wife given birth to a daughter and then the child had been burnt as a witch. They had all since been born as Master Bates, as sons to carry on the noble blood of the Bates family. Jacko rushed to the registry office in confusion and decided to put everything straight as it should be.

His wife Brenda may not be able to do things correctly but he could. "Mr. Bates, you cannot register your daughter as Barry Bernard Beethoven Bates, they're all boy's names." Jacko broke wind out loud and replied to Percy Wallop in a very aggressive tone, "Listen to me you dick, if I want to register my daughter as Poxy Bates I will. If I want to name her Barry Bernard Beethoven Bates then I will and you will please stop your ranting on about what I can and what I can't do; got it?"

As one could have gusessed, his daughter's birth certificate stated that her name was Barry Bernard Beethoven Bates. This was a bad start in life for Barry. Jacko felt pretty smug with himself and caught the No. 9 bus hoping to return to the hospital, but refused to buy a bus ticket as his revenge upon the world for not giving him a real son.

When asked to get off the bus for non-payment, he said, "OK my friend, that seems a fair fare bargain, let me give you a drink for all of your trouble." He proceeded to leave behind most of the French cooking brandy and prawn cocktail that he had consumed earlier in the day. "Have a nice day, my Christian friend" as he fell onto the pavement singing the national anthem.

He had much better luck with the taxi driver who took him to the hospital for which Jacko gave him a five pound note and told him to keep the change. This gentle Greek fellow was very grateful for such a generous tip on just a £2.60 fare. Once he had dropped Jacko off, he pulled away from the hospital and said to himself, "He's a bloody good tipper but what's that bleedin' smell in the back of my cab?" This just goes to show that Greek taxi drivers should never count their chickens before they are hatched.

Jacko returned to Brenda's bedside a little worse for wear and smelling like a man who had just been sick in the back of a taxi, but who cares when you're in love? Poor thick Brenda was found to be in tears as Jacko arrived, saying, "Jacko, it's not fair, why should it happen to me?" Jacko thought hard and replied, "Darlin' I promise to have a good wash and shave tonight to rid myself of this taxi smell." Brenda immediately became aggressive and shouted out in anger, "Jacko, you bloody prat, I'm referring to our dear daughter Barbara who's been born with deformed legs!"

Jacko never did like women shouting at him, even when he was sober and smelling good, so this was not the right time to take this attitude with him. "Brenda, don't blame me for deformed legs because it's from your side of the family. Your mother always did walk around like a constipated donkey! By the way, our daughter's name is not Barbara, it's Barry Bernard Beethoven Bates!"

Jacko left that day and emigrated to Australia where he works for a lager brewery in Sydney during the day and as a taxi driver at night. He almost died of drowning in 1981 whilst under the severe influence of alcohol when he fell into a 50,000 gallon beer fermentation tank. The supervisor pulled him out but not before he had drunk several gallons of the brew. He took his taxi out that evening and drove it off the edge of Sydney bridge where he drowned of natural sea water. He is now in charge of a large brewery in the sky and cleans out the back of taxis.

When Brenda came out of hospital with her daughter Barry Bernard Beethoven Bates, she made a promise to change this name to Barbara. She broke that promise because she spent her life trying to find a doctor to rectify Barry's very bandy legs.

To normal folks it is impossible to understand how bad it is to be really very very bandy. Indeed, doctors and specialist physicians will tell you that there is bandy and there is bandy, from a small deformation to a hoop. Barry Bernard Beethoven Bates was positively the hoopiest example of bandiness ever experienced by the medical profession since Bandy Bill the shark rider who crossed the Atlantic ocean with his bandy legs wrapped around a shark for over three thousand miles.

Bandy Bill died when halfway across but the

rigormortis set in very quickly and locked his legs permanently around the unlucky shark. For over ten years there were many sightings of The Bandy Bill Shark around the Florida Keys, with Bandy Bill's skeleton still on the shark's back. What a guy! Nobody could help Brenda with Barry Bernard Beethoven Bates and her bandy legs, but eventually she was given the choice of several options:

(1) Put her down - upon advice from her vet.

(2) Amputate her legs and fit plastic ones.

(3) Convert her into a self-playing base drum.

(4) Sell her to a circus.

(5) Train her as an astronaut for the one way space shuttle to Saturn.

(6) Send her across the Atlantic on the back of a shark.

(7) Disown her and put her in council care.

What the mind can't take, the mind can't take and Brenda went insane in 1978 and Barry Bernard Beethoven Bates was placed in local council care. Thank God for the welfare state.

She was educated at the local school in Luton where at the age of sixteen she managed to fail every one of her sixteen GCSE exams that she sat. For those in my readership not conversant with our wonderful modern day educational exams, I must point out that even my dog Henry achieved a Grade 5 in Geography and Grade 6 in Biology.

For Barry Bernard Beethoven Bates to fail sixteen exams meant that she had no future except as a trade union officer or member of the government. With greater effort you could even become prime minister. Like me, the educational authorities were confounded by so many failures from one student because it did not fit into any known conventional pattern, and failure is not a word used by authority. An enquiry was carried out which resulted in the publication of a 263 page report that achieved many helpful conclusions:

(1) Exam results were correct if not overstated.

(2) Barry Bernard Beethoven Bates the most ignorant child ever examined.

(3) Work on using her bandy features for future employment prospects.

So it came to pass that Saresh Patel employed Barry Bernard Beethoven Bates as cashier at *Patel's Cheapo Pie Factory* because she would carry out orders without question and then forget about everything within ten seconds. When you are fiddling the tax man and the vat man, you needed a person to be the fall guy in case things went wrong - hence employment for Barry Bernard Beethoven Bates.

All the workers at the pie factory were very confused as to why Saresh employed Barry, because it certainly wasn't for her looks because she was a very ugly person and made a very bad goalkeeper for the staff soccer team. Saresh proceeded to set up a system where Barry apparently was stealing money from the company and conveniently signing documents to prove it.

Saresh was creaming off over £200,000 per year tax free this way and even if the tax authorities found out, it would be Barry going to jail. So for a salary of only £4,500 per year paid to Barry, Saresh saves taxes of over £200,000 per year. That is definitely a bargain of the first order and one that any businessman of ill repute would be proud of. I wonder if Robert Maxwell ate meat pies when he was alive.

How did I find out about Saresh's scam? I thought that you would never ask. I found out purely by accident some years ago when Barry came back from her daily hoop to the bank, carrying a huge sack marked LLOYDS BANK. Barry tried to climb the stairs, but being so bandy this took a huge physical effort and on this occasion the extra weight of the sack was just too much. She fell down the stairs and crashed into a bandy heap at the bottom, just as I was returning from my midday pint of Guinness.

I helped her up and handed her the sack, but unfortunately it fell open, spilling hundreds of fifty pound notes across the floor. "Jesus Barry, what's all this cash for?" I asked in great surprise, knowing Saresh was such a tight and careful Asian businessman and would never himself be so careless. Barry was still very shaken up from her fall as she answered me, "I can't remember Dick, but I've got it all written down in my little book." At this, she proceeded again to climb the stairs, but this time successfully with some help from yours truly

Many times in my life I have been accused of being a nosy sod (or much worse) and sometimes a very nosy sod (or very much worse); and both accusations are true. As I helped Barry negotiate the stairs I was feeling like a very nosy sod. Nosiness is like venereal disease - it doesn't go away unless treated urgently, and my nosiness required such urgent treatment. I waited in the locker room and watched Barry leave the factory and drive away in her bright yellow three wheeled Bond mini-car with racing wheels. The Bond car is the butt of many jokes, and all I will say is that it was originally designed for certain types of people, which probably included bandy ones.

The pie factory offices were now empty of people, so I made my way to Bandy's accounts office on the first floor - but it was locked! Everything comes to him who waits and thinks, or in other words the mind is more powerful than the sword. I went to the gatehouse, borrowed (pinched) the emergency set of keys and returned to my mission. Upon entry into this office of mystery (nobody was ever allowed entry), I fell over a huge box of elastic bands that spilled onto the floor. As I fell, I crashed into a large box of old 78 rpm records, which to my surprise were all of military marching music.

Not being interested in rubber bands or marching around the office, I continued my search for the little white book that I eventually found in the middle drawer of Barry's desk. Upon opening the last page it read: "Collect £8,500 cash from bank - see receipt 7643" I looked at receipt 7643 and it was a bank receipt signed by Barry for £8,500. Funny I thought, why would she be collecting £8,500 cash from the bank on a Monday and where was the money now?

The next morning, I asked Barry about the money. "Hello Barry my friend, what happened to all the cash yesterday? Spent it all on a new car have we?" She looked completely bemused and said, "What the hell are you talking about, whatever your name is?" Then off she went on her bandy ways.

That evening, I saw Saresh walking to his Mercedes 560 SEL carrying the same cash bag from Lloyds Bank. Q.E.D, Dick Barton was on his trail. Oh, by the way, I eventually found out that Barry collected elastic bands of which she has accumulated over one and a half ton to date. She loves military music and has a collection of 23,716 different records of this type. This love of elastic bands and military music held a mystery yet to unfold.

People are cruel to the afflicted and the workers at the pie factory were more cruel than most. Being the bandiest person in history, combined with possibly being the ugliest, is a very heavy burden to carry through life. Barry's one great saviour was that she was just as thick as she was bandy and ugly. This made sure that she did not understand the sarcasm and constant humiliation being poured upon her. As you've already guessed, her nickname became Bandy Bates that she misunderstood with great pleasure. It was this nickname that drove her to collect elastic bands and military band music to show the gang how clever she really was.

Barry's life was changed forever in 1987 when she joined the *BAND-O-DATE* club to find a husband. This had been encouraged by her social worker who was becoming very worried now that the lounge and kitchen were both full of rubber bands and Barry had purchased a commando uniform to wear whilst listening to her music. This kindly social worker helped Barry fill in the club application form, and where it said hobbies, she stopped Barry from writing rubber bands and military music. Also under the heading of "any peculiarities" she wrote "only a person looking for a very bandy and ugly spouse need apply".

One must be cruel to be kind, and I agree with this old saying completely. Anybody meeting Barry would be offered a carrier bag full of elastic bands by a very ugly commando. Quite frankly only someone with serious intentions should have this opportunity. That was what we thought and we quickly found out how wrong one can be.

On the 7 September 1987, hey presto! Barry is invited out for dinner by the one and only Bandy Joseph Peeps, a trickster horse rider with *EDDIES CIRCUS.* Yes my friends, commando Bandy Bates of elastic band fame was having dinner with Bandy

Joseph Peeps the trickster horse rider. God can be so kind to the afflicted.

Little did we know that Bandy Joseph Peeps had naturally assumed that Barry was a man. More is yet to unfold.

So our friendly horse rider Joseph met Barry at the local McDickalds and he was very impressed by the highly polished buttons but annoyed at everything else. He was searching for a homosexual partner and here in front of him was Mrs. Very Ugly. He would ask for a refund immediately after he had eaten his BigDik hamburger (see *The Working Man's Guide To The Galaxy*). There must be something about eating a BigDik that we mere eaters of pizza do not comprehend, because after eating the last morsel, Joseph somehow began to find Barry not quite so objectionable and dressed up in the commando uniform she did at least look like a man.

So the plot continued and eventually Joseph took the plunge and a sperm of an idea was sown. When pregnancy was confirmed, Bandy Joseph Peeps proposed to Bandy Bates and she said YES! without hesitation. She wrote in her diary, "Ate *BigDik*, made love, got pregnant, proposed to and accepted". Few words with a powerful meaning.

We were all invited to the wedding that turned out to be a wonderful affair with Saresh paying all the bills. A nasty little man (me) had informed him that the cash scam was known to us and that in return for our continued silence and return of the little white book he should pay these costs.

The wedding cost Saresh a total amount of £26,879.78 plus the use of his Mercedes. A chauffeur's hat does not suit Saresh. I returned the little white book to Saresh with a receipt inside which simply said, "132 copies of Miss Bates diary @ 60p per set". This was my safeguard against being fired.

After the wedding breakfast, which included two hundred bottles of Dom Perignom champagne, it was agreed that it would be great to play that game of Mr. & Mrs. This is the game where one of the happy couple is sent into exile whilst the other one is asked intimate questions. Then the other partner is brought back and asked the same questions to see if they can give the same answers.

By tossing a coin, it was decided that Barry would go into exile and she was therefore locked in the coal cellar. Joseph was then asked various questions, such as "who does the washing up?" and "what is your favourite television programme?" Snzzzzzzzzz it was so boring, so I decided to enliven the proceedings with my own question of, "Where is the kinkiest place you have ever made love to Barry?"

Guffaws and cheers resounded around the church hall that just goes to prove what a great leader of men I had become. Joseph needed some extra encouragement from the audience before he let the cat out of the bag. "In the back of Barry's Bond three wheeler car!" There was uproar in the church hall as we tried to visualise two bandy people performing in the back of a Bond three wheeler. Impossible we all thought.

Eventually, Barry was let out of the coal shed, which had made a real mess of her wedding dress, and asked the same series of questions. She answered them all differently from Joseph but little did we care because we were awaiting the juicy bit. I couldn't wait and eventually I asked the question that the audience was drooling for, "Barry, where is the kinkiest place you've ever had sex?"

Barry was extremely embarrassed and looked towards Joseph for some support to help her over this very personal question. "It's OK Barry my darling, I've already told them all about it; you can tell them everything!" said Joseph in a drunken carefree manner. I asked her again, "Barry, where is the kinkiest place you've ever had sex?"

"Up me bum" she replied.

Chapter 10

From Carnivores to Larry

We herd them in, We hear them cry, We eat their flesh, And don't even sigh.

Robert Butcher "They Cry For Life" (1990)

Is it morally right to eat the flesh of our fellow beings?

Have you seen our fellow animals slaughtered at the abattoir? Would you kill the beasts that you intend to consume? Would you look into their eyes as you pull the trigger? Would you drain off the blood and gut the beast?

These questions are intended to shame the average carnivores of the human race into reconsidering their moral stand on eating the flesh of another living animal. Shame on you all. These very same questions were recently asked in a national survey carried out by the *Ripon Artistic Pea Eating Society* and the results were staggering. Most of the people questioned became quickly disturbed, but with some monetary persuassion, this resistance was quickly overcome.

Those who answered "no" to all questions amounted to 99.67% . Of the 0.33% answering "yes", the following assessment was further made by a group of doctors and vicars at a secret meeting:

87% - Schizophrenically inclined to murder their mothers.

10% - Nutters who kill for a laugh or a jam doughnut.

1% - Ex SAS soldiers of a disturbed nature and twitches.

1% - Low class butchers with bloodshot crossed eyes.

Statistically speaking (to a level as though I had been educated at Oxford), these very few people analysed as being in the 0.33% group should be protected, just as any minority group should be. This protection should be by extra special rights which are enforced by government decree.

Because I am a famous author, beyond the laws protecting these weirdo minorities, I can safely say that these fools can be totally ignored within the frame of this very important chapter of teaching by me and learning by you.

Therefore, my analysis of these figures obtained from the *R.A.P.E.S* survey is that there is nobody in a modern civilised country wishing to kill the animals that they are going to eat. And why should they indeed?

Just because Tony Hancock hated nut cutlets, this snap judgement by a first class fool shouldn't be taken as a criticism or condemnation of all vegetable foods. I like French onion soup with grilled cheese on the top, and roast parsnips.

So, why do we do it - why do we continue to eat the flesh of the animals that we refuse to kill ourselves, or see killed? This quandary, is of course, answered by understanding the "out of sight, out of mind" philosophy that has taken over many areas of our mundane lives and allows us to believe that the lamb chops were born inside plastic bags.

It's also interesting how our upbringing can teach us that eating a beautiful lamb is OK, but eating a scraggy old dog is not OK. A nation of pet lovers must find it even more difficult to understand their reasoning behind being carnivores without being the killer. Just ask any pet lover in the UK what they think about the Chinese eating dogs, and they will reply with an angry reply such as, "The cruel bloody bastards!", or something of the same ilk.

I recently watched some British housewives in a Hong Kong street market after being told that the meat hanging on hooks outside the shop was that from dogs. These women looked sick and rushed away in real distress, not even commenting on the chicken and beef hanging alongside.

Such reservations were not present at *Patel's Cheapo Pie Factory,* where any kind of meat was used to produce his range of very famous and very cheap meat pies.

Did you know that 83% of the population in the USA under the age of thirty believes that a hamburger is an American designed root crop grown exclusively in Hamburg by a guy called Ronnie

"Big" MacDonald who drives his tractor wearing a clown's suit. Believe me, this tractor looks really strange wearing a clown's suit.

They all are further convinced that Hamburg is in the Bronx. Another 11% of America's finest and younger population believe that a hamburger is the clown's suit itself, and the remaining 6% assume that a hamburger is made inside a Wendy house by a big Cuban chef in Florida. I'm no hamburger expert, but they all taste like burnt animal flesh to me.

Only 67% of the American youth have fallen for the my latest gag put about at last year's Oscar presentation, that "French Fries" are made from deep fried used condoms. You cannot fool all of the people all of the time - but 67% believe they are deep fried used condoms?

I did not win any Oscars last year. In fact, I was told to sod off once they realised that I was not Robert Redford, but Dick Head that anti-American world famous author. "We'll give you a piss-pot gallon in your *Working Man's Guide To The Galaxy*, you *limey* imbecile" shouted a very famous television presenter as he assisted the thugs to eject me from this glittery ceremony.

Such a disturbance shown on international television has increased my book sales by over three hundred percent. There is great method to my madness and you can stuff the awards.

To bring home the obscenity of this philosophy to our kids today, I have spoken to John Major and he is going to put forward a new *Bill of Hamburger Rights* in the next parliamentary session. This would compel every hamburger outlet to install its own abattoir at the back of the shop. Before you could buy your lovely cremated flesh (hamburger), it would be compulsory for you to go and witness the cow being slaughtered.

To prove that you had been a witness to this murder of a fellow living creature, you would be given ten blood coupons for presentation at the cash desk for ten hamburgers.

During a test run of this project, held in Guildford last month, the biggest hamburger chain sold only three real meat hamburgers and the remaining two tons of minced beef from the slaughtered cow has gone rotten and has been thrown away. To obtain blood coupons is now a matter of joining a waiting list. Not until the list contains six hundred will they go to the expense of killing another cow which costs them over £2,600 per animal.

The interesting point is that overall sales have not dropped because the replacement *DikVegiburgers* have overtaken the previous sales of cremated meat burgers.

The *British Carnivore Society* are understandably worried about John Major's proposed new bill and expressed such worries in their *Bloody Good Times* magazine with the headlines, *"By the year 2001 planet overrun with cows"*.

Now my friends, foes and countrymen, don't give

me any of the standard foolishness about how the animals are not aware of their impending demise when being taken into the abattoir. I can assure you all that this thinking is a cart-load of cow's dung because they know that death is but a killing bolt away.

They do not know that they will then be skinned, gutted, minced, formed into hamburgers, frozen, wrapped, boxed, frozen, transported to the shops, cremated, stuffed in a bun, covered in crap and eaten by spotty little kids called educated and caring people who never even knew that she existed. Do not criticise our cows for not being intelligent enough to know what is going to happen after we blow away half of their brains, but it is not a question of intelligence on this occasion. It is because (to date) no cow has survived the killing to being eaten chain and therefore such information has not filtered back to the herds.

It would be bad for the meat quality if posters were placed on the walls of barns advertising the wonderful future we had in store for them. I shall report back to my readers again if any cow does survive the process and returns to disrupt the farmer's easy life.

Believe me, fellow human beings, the animals at the abattoir can smell the death within such an evil place and you can hear them crying in pain and anguish the moment they arrive. Such unnatural howling is a harrowing experience as they enter the *humane killing area.* I can imagine the same *save me from death cries* coming from millions of human beings not such a long time ago.

One day, when aliens from an advanced civilisation will most certainly land on Earth, I wonder how they will interpret our carnivorous tendencies? As they will have totally different features from mankind, doubtless they will consider us as guilty of murder as the mass murderers in human history.

Even worse for us all is if they are an advanced and intelligent form of chicken - I fear that a particular colonel living in Kentucky would be in deep trouble.

In other parts of the world where hunger is rife, it is understandable that the flesh of animals is eaten to ensure the peasants very survival as they know no better or alternative way. Once they are educated and learn the art of crop farming, then they will have a choice which is not present today. Eating crops grown for human consumption is far more efficient than growing crops for animal consumption.

Hunger, combined with the instinctive wish for survival, will even force the most educated and advanced people to eat the flesh of dead colleagues if death is the only alternative. In fact, it can be argued that the more advanced the civilisation, the more drastic will be the actions to support such survival.

Whether my theories are true or not, I have taken

certain precautions to protect me from abuse if ever I crash on top of a remote mountain.

I confirm to you all now in this blockbuster book, that if ever I crash on a mountain and need flesh for human survival, I guarantee without fear of contradiction that it will never (and I mean bloody never!) be that from a Welshman, no matter how far his blood is removed from that of his Welsh forefathers.

Imagine the unbearable hypocrisy that would be thrown down upon me from a great height as I travelled the globe to enjoy the fruits of my literary labours. "There goes that extremely hypocritical Dick Head who says he hates all Welshmen but ended up eating six of them on top of Mount Everest last year. He only took the good morsels and left the cheaper joints for his publisher."

An even worse thought is that I might be dead on landing, up on the mountainside - God forbid that a dickey aero-engine be responsible for me not completing my promise to you all. Being snuffed out by some drunken fool in Derby who didn't check the eibenflugen bolt on the main engine rotor is too terrible a thought to even entertain.

If I ever do end up very dead on the mountain side, I have taken precautions to prevent my soul screaming in terror for the remainder of eternity - this is a very long time indeed even based upon the Post Office's letter delivery time. I have just had a huge tattoo applied across my body (at all the butchers cutting points) saying, “In case of Dick Head’s death on the top of an isolated mountainside, keep all those short arrogant Welshmen away from my body”. A nice concise and easy to understand message. Do you think that they will get it?

The reason why we still eat the flesh of some animals but abhor the thought of eating the flesh of some other animals, is one of culture. This is the culture as passed down by thousands of generations, from the time when Adam started eating ants. Our current culture has been handed down from our own parents and further modified by our contacts with other people and ideas from the current world.

The more we travel, generally the more we understand. The commercial pressure placed upon us by the retail trade to eat meat is ever present and unrelenting. For maximum sales, these flesh salesmen must wash away all the blood down the drain. We can then be presented with pretty looking plastic wrapped meats and camouflaged processed products to tempt our palate.

The reason why I know so much about the feelings of our slaughtered animals is because a friend of mine, Arthur Butterscotch, has the unique gift of being able to speak to the animals. Such a gift has led him into a permanent state of shock as he listens to all the horror stories told by the sheep, cows, chickens, calves, lambs, etc. The stories are so shocking that I refuse to be tempted to write a book on these experiences because I realise that the human guilt factor will come into play and will stop anybody buying the book.

Dick Head only writes successful blockbusters, so the animals must await another day for their champion.

Everybody I spoke to about Arthur Butterscotch's gift looked at me in disbelief and amusement, with more than a small amount of loud guffawing. I won't write a book doomed for failure, but equally I won't accept anybody taking the mickey out of me. Therefore, especially for you minority group of hypocritical fools, I can confirm that you will never be issued with any level of *DikHed* degree and I am now going to give proof to the world of Arthur's gift.

I recently challenged Arthur to give me sufficient proof of his special gift for talking to the animals, explaining that a minority of hypocritical readers, who were obviously envious of my position in society, needed to be corrected in their opinions. Arthur was only too happy to oblige.

We visited *The Merry Months Of May Abattoir* in Kensington, which is situated below ground in an old disused tube line complex. This location is very smart because it is out of sight and sound (and out of mind?), and allows all of the tens of thousands of cattle per year to be transported from Dagenham docks directly off the trucks, boats, and trains, into the old tube line complex and then on to Kensington killing grounds.

The abattoir is situated some six hundred feet

below ground and is a well hidden secret from the local residents. Quite frankly it's none of their bloody business so to speak.

"Dick, my son, you are my best friend and the most wonderful man in the world (correct) and for you I will speak to the animals so that you can record the conversations to show those snotty guys just who you are and that as usual you are correct. Obviously you cannot understand what the animals are saying, so I'll give you the translations as we go along."

The abattoir was having a terrible time with getting a lovely old cow, who went by the name of Daisy Belle, to the killing station. A group of five children about ten years old were hanging onto her and pleading with the man in a bloody red and white apron, "Please mister, we love Daisy Belle so much and we've looked after her for so long, please spare her! We've saved up over sixty pounds from our pocket money and you can have it all, and our combined pocket money of five pounds twenty pence per week forever! Please spare her, please, please, please................"

No chance, my children, because Daisy Belle is worth over one thousand pounds and money is more important than life. The distraught children were thrown out of the abattoir and Daisy was led to the killing point where Arthur Butterscotch was waiting (with a suitably glum look on his face) to demonstrate his lingual skills.

I can now report this conversation exactly as it took place between Arthur and Daisy Belle because I had taken my Sony pocket tape recorder with me. As all Japanese people will confirm; "A Sony tape recorder does not lie". It's really that simple to understand.

Let's get on with the cow saga:

***Arthur**: "Good morning Daisy Belle, my friendly cow, it's a lovely sunny day outside and the birds are announcing the onset of spring. How are you feeling today?"*

***Daisy**: "Hello Arthur Butterscotch, I've heard a lot about you and I think that you are very clever to be able to speak the Cattlish dialects and languages. About how I feel, well my friend, I was feeling great yesterday, but six of my tits hurt today because that bloody milking machine badly requires an overhaul. The rubber suckers have gone hard and are now very abrasive indeed. Now Arthur, why am I here and what do you want?"*

***Arthur:** "Daisy, I've never once lied to my animal friends and I don't intend to start now. I've got some bad news and I've got some good news, which would you like first?"*

***Daisy**: "Stop mucking me around Arthur, I've told you my tits hurt and I'm in no mood for such talk today. Just give me the good news first for God's sake."*

***Arthur**: "Well Daisy Belle, the good news is that your tits will never hurt again."*

Daisy: *"Great news, they're going to fix that rough old milking machine at last!"*

Arthur: *"Daisy Belle, my lovely animal friend, that's not exactly what I'm trying to tell you. The bad news is that you're now inside an underground abattoir and by this time next Tuesday, you'll be on the shelves of Sainsbury's and other supermarkets all over the country. But don't worry Daisy Belle my old friend, you wont feel a thing - just lie back and enjoy it."*

Daisy: *"Oh no! What about my son who is only four months old? Who's going to look after him? He'll miss me so much!"*

Arthur: *"Don't worry Daisy Belle, they'll be here in a minute also. They've sold him to an Italian producer of frozen spaghetti Bolognese. Buono vita!"*

Daisy: *"You bastaaaaaaaaaaaaaards!"*

This recorded conversation shows that it is possible to talk to the animals and that cows facing the impending death with their children can become very abusive. There was her son being offered free overseas travel and she became so aggressive.

Arthur is trying to write an *English/Cattlish* language dictionary, but since Daisy Belle was chopped up, the word has got around the cattle community and Arthur is finding out that he has been sent to Coventry. This non-cooperation pact within the cattle community came to a head recently when Blue Belle told Arthur to "Clear off Arthur. My tits hurt like hell but I'm not saying a word to you because any tit aching cow talking to Arthur Butterscotch is likely to receive a death warrant just like Daisy Belle. I'm not saying another bloody word."

So if anybody else requires additional proof that Arthur can talk to the cattle, this is now an impossibility. Arthur has therefore turned to talking to the lambs which he says is much easier because they don't sulk and are far more trusting. In other words they can easily be conned. The pigs are the most difficult members of the animal kingdom to talk to and they continuously show a negative and aggressive attitude towards Arthur. I warned Arthur not to discuss his favourite foods with them, but would he listen to me? No, he would not and he let it slip that his favourite breakfast was egg and bacon, plus that his favourite dinner was spare ribs from Wo Hu's Chinese takeaway.

When Arthur explained that the chicken also had reason to feel aggrieved over his choice of breakfast, the second little piggy said, "Arthur, sod the chickens, what about us?" So even in the animal kingdom you quickly experience the self-centred attitude and selfishness of the worst kind.

Arthur has at last joined me on the literary path to fame with his first faction novel entitled, *Eating The Ones I Love*. This is now available at a price of £19.99 in all vegetarian bookshops, racecourses, conscientious butchers, and most pet shops.

Arthur could not find a publisher to print this book and he therefore produced it himself under the "self-publishing" theory. He printed 25,000 books at a cost of £63,786.00 which he financed by mortgaging his house. Six months after release, Arthur has sold 163 books, of which 144 were purchased by a sex shop group who misunderstood the title.

The bank have now evicted Arthur from his home for non-payment of the second mortgage and it's up for auction next week. Arthur is attending the auction, just in case the bid price does not exceed £76.50. He would be a cash purchaser.

Arthur's book was produced to raise funds for the RSPAC (Royal Society for the Prevention of Animal Consumption) where a donation is invited on the last page. To date only £16.20 has been received, plus 2000 out of date Esso coupons. If we had 25,000 of these coupons and we had them last year, we could have exchanged them for a plastic picnic set. We've missed the summer and the surrender date of the coupons, so we've written to Esso asking them if they could send us a cash equivalent of the coupons as a donation for the RSPAC. To date we have received no reply but we are confident that we shall succeed.

I was even more angry than Arthur concerning the really poor response to his book, which had been printed in a noble cause. I decided to take some more aggressive action to ensure that the RSPAC was to survive and the people's consciences were to be awakened out of their I'm OK slumber. If I was to sacrifice the eating of flesh (which I love), then everybody else must make a similar sacrifice.

Arthur and I opened up a new ultra-posh restaurant in The Strand in London which we named *The Bloody Freshest Meat Restaurant In The World,* I invested £830,000 in equipping this incredible establishment with all the latest and greatest restaurant equipment and decor. Dick Head never does anything by halves. The £830,000 invested represented about three months royalties on my books and other products, so the risk to me was insignificant and one I was very pleased to take. We were all ready to open and we placed full page advertisements in every national daily newspaper:

The Bloody Freshest Meat
Restaurant In The World

Eat the Freshest or take home £50,000!

We are now open and taking bookings. This incredible establishment will pay any customer the immediate sum of £50,000 if it can be proved that the meat served could be any fresher! We have a fixed price of £250 per person which includes wines of your choice from our extensive wine list. Over 150 choices of Champagne are included on the wine list.

Telephone 081 001 9999 for reservations.

Give a rich and big headed tycoon a challenge which he is sure he can win and he becomes even more big headed in his attempt at humiliating the luckless challenger.

From the first evening, we were overbooked with people of unbelievable wealth who came complete with their lackeys to tell them how great they were. It was apparent from their swagger that they had come not to dine but to win £50,000 they didn't need for attention they did. Many of them bought sample jars and carniscopes to give them instant readings on the freshness of the flesh to be served.

Dick Head in trouble at last? This is a question that my students should never ever put to me. Why not? Because I am one very smart and crafty cookie.

Upon entering *The Bloody Freshest Meat Restaurant In The World* all clients were given a menu card which asked them to select the meat of their choice, from a total choice of: Beef, Lamb, Veal, Turkey, Chicken, Pork, It was carefully explained to our customers that the tables were set out according to the meat chosen ie: all lamb eaters would sit on the lamb table. We had 280 tables, each sitting sixteen people, so you can see that we were one very big operation.

Alongside each "meat table section" were double doors leading to the food preparation areas and kitchens. Each "meat" had its own food preparation area and kitchen. At least one hour was allowed for the clients to soak up the booze included intake, to a point where most of them were becoming boisterous and noisy. At that time we circulated betting forms which gave you odds of 1000 to 1 on the freshest meat syndrome with minimum bets starting at £50 per ticket. For the meagre investment of only £50 you stood to win £50,000 and this was very tempting to a room full of drunken customers who all had their pre-planned way of taking my money away from me.

One must understand that most of these clients were leaders of industry and many from government circles. They considered that taking money from Dick Head was only a matter of using the schemes as taught at Oxford, Cambridge, Harvard, Yale and the like - it was going to be so easy. They had not yet learnt their lesson: Dick Head by name, but not Dick Head by nature.

The getting smashed out of your brains period was over and it was time to get down to the real business of serving fresh meat and making a great deal of money at the same time. All customers were requested to sign a *"get-out"* legal form that released us from any responsibility for physical or psychological (mental) damage or disorders that may result from the evening's dining. We could not be responsible for any reactions after serving the freshest type of meat at *The Bloody Freshest Meat Restaurant In The World* where the meat was fresher, or as fresh, as sold anywhere else in the world.

With much sniggering, all our merry customers

willingly signed the release forms and started chanting in a highbrow way the words of, "We want the bloody fresh meat, we want the bloody fresh meat, we want the bloody fresh meat................" My God, they do become boring after a while. At last their time has come.

"Follow me!" shouted Arthur through a large Victorian megaphone, whilst wearing a beautifully cut white rubber coat with matching Wellington boots. Arthur went to the Lamb Section first and asked the Lambettes to follow him at the slow march. To make the exit from the restaurant and entry into the preparation room more realistic, a recording of the death march at double time by the rock group *Queezie* was played. This record has never been released and I now know why.

Each section was led out of the dining room in the same orchestrated way. The Lambettes arrived into their Lambette preparation room, which was a huge room measuring over six hundred square metres fully fitted out in stainless steel with floor drains. Each client was invited to sit inside his own plastic cubicle which was placed around the outside perimeter of this huge room.

Once inside, the doors automatically locked, and Arthur started to speak through a microphone: "Ladies and gentlemen, welcome to this exciting evening at *The Bloody Freshest Meat Restaurant In The World,* where we intend to show you that we only serve the freshest meat in the world. As you already realise, this is a combined restaurant and gambling club and it is the gambling that brought most of you here this evening. If we fail to prove our point, then we shall pay out over £150,000 to just this Lambette group of sixteen people this evening.

"You are confident of proving us wrong and winning and we are confident of proving our point and winning. Ladies and gentlemen, we are now going to offer you the bet of a lifetime - a no limits bet! You can now write down on the betting slip in front of you the total amount that you wish to bet on the fact that we cannot prove to you our claims.

"No money is required from you and if you win then we shall pay you your bet, but if you lose then you pay us the same amount. Gentlemen you have five minutes to make your decisions and once you have completed your betting forms, please fold and post them into the slot marked, *Slot for posting folded betting forms."*

What would you do? Unbelievably, out of the sixteen "cubicle prisoners" in the lambette section, we had five of them take up this extra betting offer and the total amount staked was an incredible £8,500,000. This is what we stood to lose or win. Taking candies is too simple an answer, because these people didn't understand, or care to understand, the planning that we had put into *The Bloody Freshest Meat Restaurant In The World* scheme (or is it scam?).

Arthur opened a side door to the food processing

area and called out in Lambette lingo, "Hurry up Larry, your visitors are waiting." He then shepherded (sorry!) Larry into the centre of the room and asked him, "Larry, get your woolly backside onto this table." Larry the lamb climbed onto the table and laid down like a tired child going to sleep. Arthur proceeded talking further to Larry:

Arthur: "Now Larry, I've explained that by sacrificing your life tonight you will be helping the future of Lambkind and Dick Head the world famous author. I saved you from being sold in pieces at Finefare last week, so you have had longer on this earth than already planned."

Larry: "Arthur, thank you for that extra week alive, which I estimate as an extra ten percent extension to my life - I am really a lucky little lamb. Indeed, all of my cousins are already eaten and digested and I feel all alone anyhow. Arthur, please thank Dick Head the world famous author for taking up the Lambettes cause and please don't forget me. I know you'll carry out the sacrifice without giving me pain, but before I go I want you to use all my fleece to knit Dick Head a nice jumper."

Arthur: "Larry you hero, I'll make it completely painless and arrange for Dick Head to have a wonderful jumper made from your wool. I know he will be very touched by your kind consideration. I know it's difficult to concentrate at a time like this, but can I have your hide to make myself a nice soft leather jacket?"

Larry: "Jesus Arthur, don't push your luck too far"
Arthur: "Good-bye Larry"
Larry: "Good-bye Arthur"
Arthur then grabbed the huge humane killing gun with its huge metal bolt killing device and held it against Larry's head and pulled the trigger. Nothing happened!
Larry: "For God's sake Arthur, you forgot to put the firing cartridge into the breach you daft idiot! Ohhh! Pleaaaaaaaaaaase! Donnnnnnnnnnnnnnnnnnn't Kiiiiiiiiiill! Meeeeeeeeeeeeeeeeeeeeeee!"

This begging from Larry was terrible to behold as Arthur put the cartridge into the breach, placed the gun against Larry's right ear and thought of pulling the trigger. "Thunk!" The cartridge fired first time at the second time of asking and Larry went to meet (meat?) his cousins in the sky above and we had one less Larry the lamb down here on earth.

By this time, all sixteen of our dinner guests locked in the plastic cubicles were screaming and vomiting all over themselves, and even more seriously over the front plastic windows. You could hear them all shouting, "Stop it! Jesus Christ!, Oh my God!" and many other very rude words that you would not expect to hear from such people of upper class upbringing.

Whilst we left these messy guests generally continuing to puke all over themselves, Arthur proceeded to start skinning, segmenting and gutting

Larry. In less than five minutes all the lamb joints were laid out on the marble preparation table ready for our dinner guests to make their choice. Arthur tried to hide Larry's hide in a spare refuse bag, but I reminded him that I could only turn a blind eye to such thieving from the grave, if he agreed to have this wool washed, spun and knitted into a jumper as requested by recently departed Larry.

I carefully marked this black bag with a white label bearing the words, *Dick's pullover wool and Arthur's coat hide*. This callous act proved beyond reasonable doubt that Arthur gave more thought to his new leather jacket than trying to save Larry's life.

Arthur pushed the red button and all cubicle doors were unlocked albeit covered with dripping vomit of many different colours. All sixteen crawled out, most of them still vomiting across my stainless steel floor.

"Ladies and gentlemen, we have just witnessed the slaughter of a live lamb which was sacrificed to give you only the freshest meat for your dinner this evening. I believe that this proves that *The Bloody Freshest Meat Restaurant In The World* really does serve up the freshest meat in the world. Please now sign your cheques to the value of £8,500,000 to honour your bets and then feel free to select your cut of lamb and our chef, Adrian, will cook it exactly to your taste.

"Please get all the mess hosed off of you by Arthur in the back yard and we can sell you some one-sized plastic suits from Hong Kong at £500 each so that you don't go back to the restaurant smelling like puke."

Probably due to embarrassment, everybody paid up their gambling debts, but nobody felt hungry any more and we sold Larry in little bits at the wholesale market the next morning for £8.50. At the end of the evening, after repeating the same procedure with the other meat sections, we had accumulated bets paid to the total sum of £51,800,004.00.

They paid up but they were not happy. What they forgot was that they thought they had a sure win on a 1000:1 bet. This hardly ever exists in the gambling world and never exists in Dick Head's world.

The next morning, the newspaper headlines screamed, *Dick Head is an animal murderer!* Surprisingly enough the whole front page of the T Newspaper (can't say the name because of libel laws) was dedicated to criticising this practice of killing animals on the premises. They called it barbaric, horrific, unbelievable, a blood lust, etc. This press coverage continued for over a year, and the more we ignored it, the more they pushed it. I now know how the Royal Family feels.

We encouraged this coverage by becoming antagonistic towards the press, because for each page coverage, I sold a further 60,000 copies of my *Working Man's Guide* books. It was like telling the world that a princess was unfaithful; I became even more famous overnight. Due to the world-wide demand to eat in T*he Bloody Freshest Meat Restaurant In The World*, we had to increase the seating to accommodate 5000 people.

We increased the fixed menu price to £500 each and still we couldn't take all the bookings. We then cancelled table reservations and went over to a *first come - first seated* concept. The result was extraordinary because queues were there permanently and normally stretched as far as Trafalgar Square and on Saturday nights as far as Buckingham Palace.

To avoid similar vomiting and breaking of wind fits, we now add an excellent hallucinatory drug called *Bloodlust* which allows the diners to become ecstatic when the killings take place and audience participation is becoming very popular. Sometimes the diners lose control after the animal is slaughtered by eating the raw meat and biting other diners on the neck and leaving huge open gashes, but all in all this is better than everybody being sick and making the place smell.

The newspapers continued their media war upon us and the more they tried, the more customers came in and the more books I sold. Animal rights groups demonstrate outside our premises every night but a cup of tea tainted with the drug *Bloodlust* solves this problem. Three of these long haired liberal minded school teachers driving Volvos have since died of loss of blood, but they cannot identify us as the root cause. We are very smart people.

The clock is striking twelve midnight on the 31st December and within a few seconds we enter a new year which should be a turning point regarding the eating of meat by humans. Since 1993, meat consumption has fallen by 83% and every time the media highlight the activities of *The Bloody Freshest Meat Restaurant In The World,* the consumption figures drop even further.

My woollen jumper fits great and is dyed a beautiful blue to match the colour of my lovely eyes.

Arthur's leather jacket is rather too large for him but this is because he has allowed for the extra weight he expects to put on during his old age drinking sessions. He now runs language courses for conversational talking with the major animal languages.

If Robert Butcher who wrote the little ditty at the beginning of this chapter is still alive, then he will see that we have caused more than just a sigh. Every animal has its own soul and we have no right to destroy this unique piece of God's property on earth simply for the glorification of our stomachs.

In 2001AD, when all my readers have become vegetarians, you will see that nut cutlets are fantastic.

See you in the next world Larry.

Chapter 11

From Big TITS to My Best Chinese Joss

"Today's luxury is tomorrow's poverty."

"You've never had it so good."
Judith Wallingbury (1979)

If you were given the choice of time travel, would you go forwards or backwards in time? This is an interesting question and one that should be decided upon before the new millennium, at which time, such travel will be in everyday use.

Already the secret laboratories in the USA have developed prototypes that are now under full trials. The first one, now known as the *Philadelphia Experiment*, is still being denied by the American government, but people in the *know* have informed me of the truth.

I have a Hispanic gentleman, Pedro San Miguel, living next door to me who was actually a chief cook on board the secret ship involved in the experiment. He is now eighty-eight years old according to his passport, but only looks a young twenty-seven. When he moved into the house next door last year, he immediately told me about his ghastly experience of being shunted back in time, which was nothing like that depicted in the movie. To prove his point for you, doubting readers, he has a huge multicoloured tattoo on his chest that says, *I was born in 1905.* Pedro's house is one of the smaller four bedroom houses with one acre of ground and without a swimming pool that cost him £290,000 on which he still owes the bank £187,000.

How can he afford this type of bank loan on just a cook's wage? Well, my friends, I know the answer to this: he is being paid a pension of £100,000 per year by the American government in exchange for his silence. His silence is guaranteed by the pension cash and the sure knowledge that a CIA hit man will not miss him if he opens his mouth about the experiment. The CIA has given him a new identity of Fidel Castro but I refuse to help him with his identity crisis and always refer to him as Pedro the brewer. He really hates me for this.

Dick Head's house is the huge white marble mansion at the best end of the private park, with a gate house (complete with electric gates), standing in twenty acres of landscaped gardens with a huge swimming pool and six floodlit tennis courts. This mansion cost me £1,890,000 in 1991 and is fully paid for from book and invention royalties. I give you this information on both houses and our financial status to avoid any confusion over the rewards available in this life of ours.

It is clear to you all that it is far more remunerative to be a world famous author of many blockbusters and a famous successful inventor, than being a Hispanic cook from a battleship sent forward in time and living under an assumed name.

I don't particularly like Pedro and his wife Wanda very much, or his twelve really horrible children who are not allowed to use my swimming pool or tennis courts. These children are very rude and call me Da Meestah Dicko Pricko Ed. God, how I hate rude and abusive children.

The Americans now have their T.T.F (*Time Travel Federation*) located at a secret underground facility called Cape Einstein, located under the township of Albertsville, somewhere in one of the southern states. The exact location is, of course, a top secret, known only to a few people with the correct security clearance. Apparently, a large number of these people are always winning huge sums of cash betting on the horses and the bookies are becoming more than a little bit annoyed and want to find out how they always bet on the winners.

The starting date for T.T.F flights is 1 January 2000 AD and a special booking office is being built in Time Square, New York. It makes you wonder just who chose this venue for the booking office - was it chosen by deduction or by a practical joker. Not very adventurous, but who could criticise it? All forms of credit cards will be accepted for payment of tickets purchased from the central booking office. Return tickets for travel into the past are essential and compulsory if you want to return.

It is a proven fact that time travel into the past cannot alter history because it would already be part of our history. When you arrive at your destination you are in a transitional state where you can witness and see events unfold, but you cannot be seen or nor can you alter such events. Some time travellers with special gifts can develop psycho-energy fields and appear as spirits for short periods of time, up to twenty seconds for the really good people.

Dorothy Burton, a dedicated left wing nutcase professor in economics from Durham University went back in time to 1992 and tried to warn Norman Lamont about the ERM currency crisis, wine purchases and the profession of one of his tenants, but was totally ignored. You've got to give it to good old Norman, he got all the answers to all the difficult questions at the right time but in the end he had to resign so that John Major did not have to fire him.

Dorothy has now been banned from all future TTF flights for not complying with the rules and Norman Lamont may be invited to be a guest of the TTF to travel forward into 1996 to witness for himself the results of his labours. The trick is that only a one way ticket will be offered.

Norman may refuse our kind offer and possibly he would prefer to travel back in time to 1 January 1990 when things looked much better. In case this is what he wants, we are reserving fifty return tickets for his continuous use. Each time he reaches 15 May 1993, he can use another ticket and go back to 1 January 1990 again. As we don't expect him to live beyond his 150th birthday, there will be some tickets left over after he passes on to a better place where John Major does not screw and fire him.

It is now thought by the new breed of time travel experts that all the really famous smart guys in history were time travellers who had gone back in time with the sole objective of becoming famous. With this idea in mind, I shall be travelling back in time to China in the year 5517 BC and assume the name of Confucius. I will take with me a philosophy based upon my notion that what you do not want done to yourself you should not do to others.

I shall invite followers to listen to my teachings in classics and I shall hope that my followers will turn my philosophies into a religion based upon mutual duties of the five basic relationships that I shall divide out into:

Ruler and Subject
Father and Son
Husband and Wife
Elder and Younger Brother
Friend and Friend

I realise that for anybody to assume such philosophies, many people will consider that it will all boil down to accepting a pious attitude towards superiors and a respectful attitude towards your elders. This pious attitude is greatly needed today to pull us back from the brink, but will always have more appeal in some quarters than in others.

Maybe I can dream of going back to the year of

5637 BC and being *Siddhartha Gautama*, known today as Buddha. This wonderful Holy Man had the name of Buddha given to him after his death. This name is a Sanskrit word that means to be enlightened. He spent a great deal of his time doing yoga, fasting and meditating.

Buddha told us that we could all find nirvana or painless peace on the Noble Eightfold Path that connsists of:

Right BELIEF
Right ASPIRATION
Right SPEECH
Right ACTION
Right LIVELIHOOD
Right EFFORT
Right THOUGHT
Right MEDITATION

There must be no anger, no passion and no sin. The crowning jewel of the Buddhist's achievement is to love your enemies and turn the other cheek. Unfortunately, I am an insignificant man in the presence of such a Holy Man and can therefore only be him in my dreams. How I wish the Western world would take the trouble of teaching the theories of Buddha and the Noble Eightfold Path. Such teachings need not be for religious conversion, but merely a serious attempt at changing and improving our morality and standards of life.

Once the Noble Eightfold Path is understood, we

can leave it to the individual to choose the name of his religion. If it creates the standards of life, what's in the name of the religion anyway? Chinese astrology is older than Western civilisation and should be treated with deep seriousness to ascertain its value to modern man.

Before Lord Budha departed this world he called all the animals of the to his side but only twelve succeeded in joining him. In gratitude he named the years after them. These Animal Signs for the years go in sequence as follows:

1993 - The year of the Monkey
1994 - The year of the Rooster
1995 - The year of the Dog
1996 - The year of the Boar
1997 - The year of the Rat
1998 - The year of the Ox
1999 - The year of the Tiger
2000 - The year of the Rabbit
2001 - The year of the Dragon
2002- The year of the Snake
2003 - The year of the Horse
2004 - The year of the Sheep

Then the cycle starts all over again. The Chinese also have Five Elements, often referred to as Five Forces of:

Water - Fire - Wood - Metal -Earth

Each element is in both positive and negative and

therefore an elemental cycle takes ten years to complete. In determining your dominant element, there are five factors to be considered:

The element of the year of birth
The element of the animal sign
The element of the hour of birth
The element of the month of birth
The element of the country of birth

There are many very good publications on Chinese Astrology and it is well worth spending some time on this subject and to amaze yourself with the inner truth than can be found within them.

I also give you the Chinese magic square where all columns add up to fifteen:

4 9 2
3 5 7
8 1 6

Apart from the Confucias and Buddhist religions in China, the third great religion is that of Taoism, which is based on the word of Tao - The Way Or The Channel. Taoism tells us that everything in our universe is meant to move in its own ordered and harmonic way. According to Taoism and Dick Head, mankind has lost its way but can find harmony by returning to a life of simplicity and humility. All can be read in the book *Tao Te Ching* that means *The Way And Its Power*. Over a period of time it has turned into a form of magic and superstition.

Why do our schools not teach such basic learning

that has been proven for more than seven thousand years? Are the governments afraid of a bigger truth that could change the built-in partnership that they have with Canterbury and Rome? Are they afraid of the people seeing the truth and taking a variable path? Are they afraid of the people being given a real choice? I know the direction that I would choose.

Just imagine the existence of such an advanced culture in China whilst we lived in mud huts and chewing gum was not even invented. How sad that our Western religions and governments have suppressed such wonderful teachings from our children since modern civilisation began and the people lost control of their own lives. How much better a life and mutual understanding it would be if these feelings could be part of our national heritage.

A major part of my future "Working Man's Guide" theme, from book number 45 onwards, will be to open up the in-depth Chinese culture. By the year 2001 all my students and their children will be able to talk with love and conviction about The Five Basic Relationships of Confucius, The Noble Eightfold Path of Buddha and The Way Of The Channel of Taoism.

Our country is in a violent mess and everybody is pretending to search for urgent ways of solving this garbage can of cancerous growth. We don't need new ideas! They're all here ready to give our people the belief, aspirations, speech, action, livelihood, effort, thought, meditation. People will be able to understand the basic relationships between people developed through thousands of years of evolution, surviving the test of time. All we need is the willpower to enforce this wonderful way of living upon our own corrupt society until it learns this better way and then chooses this way by freedom of choice.

Democracy as we know it today cannot achieve my dream - only the people can. I would like our children to believe in the very basics of understanding that a people's culture is irrevocably linked with the rules by which they conduct their daily lives and how they spend their time. Each one of us will then listen to the Joss of the Chinese Fung Shui (pronounced fung soy) expert to guarantee that we live our life with the best joss to help us on our happy way. Joss is an English-Cantonese word meaning bad luck.

The Fung Shui man can be seen using a special instrument that looks like a compass and has eight positions to indicate:

Heaven - Water - Fire - Thunder
Wind - Rain - Hills - Earth.

These eight further represent:

Horse - Goat - Pheasant - Dragon
Fowl - Swine - Dog - Ox.

Fung Shui is based upon the principles of Ch'i, the spirit that animates yin (female-passive) and Yang (Male-active). Chinese people can often be seen pasting a Fung Shui paper onto their doors to keep the evil spirits away and thus guarantee them peace, health and a happy family (joy).

We can then move onto Pao Kung, the God of Justice, to show mercy upon our rotten Western souls and help us out of our wilderness of corruption. Maybe Mo, the God of Martial Arts, will also give us his protection from the deprivations of war, which will surely be soon upon us all. If all this fails then every one of you should rush out and find yourself a soothsayer to read you your number that hopefully will fall into a lucky field, such as:

3 - Life
6 - Longevity
8 - Prosperity
9 - Eternity
162 - Easy all the way
168 - Prosperity all the way
222 - Easy, easy, easy
913 - Everlasting life

Enough of Chinese Joss!

Pedro told me that the development programme at the TITS (*Time in Time Ships*) facility in Albertsville, USA is moving ahead fast but there is bickering whether to build little TITS or big TITS as the main production time travel ship. Indeed, for cost reasons, it has even been suggested that a jumbo TIT should be built first to handle a thousand passengers at a time. A little TITS domestic version is planned for selling at Harrods in London for rich Arabs and the Royal Family.

Imagine the difficult choice of going on a

PISSOFF (see *The Working Man's Guide To The Galaxy*) or on a TIT, whether it be jumbo, big or little. So you can choose whatever size of TIT you prefer.

Randy Rowbottom, the chief engineering officer at the Albertsville facility, was fired last month for abusive language to his superiors during a production meeting. There had been over two years of dispute concerning the size of ship to build and Randy just blew up, "For Christ sake, why don't we just build standard TITS and forget jumbo TITS, big TITS and little TITS! After all what has the size of our TITS got to do with this meeting anyway you idiots!"

Now I must say that Randy does have a good point. Despite Randy being fired, they have now standardised on just six various sizes of big TITS and everybody appears to agree with this choice.

Huge new storage buildings have been built to house these huge time travelling ships and these buildings are named BRAS, standing for Big Range Accommodation. They have been numbered relating to the size of the big TITS they house; 34c, 36b, 38d, 40c, 42d and 44d. Somebody has a real good sense of humour.

My God, my mind does roam away from my questions once I start talking about TITS. Back to the original question, my boy!

If you were given the choice of time travel, would you go forwards or backwards in time?

Your choice should be tempered by the fact that return is not a guarantee and if you don't reach your destination you'll never know. In all truth, the BIG TITS can almost certainly get you there but only long term production line trials with actual humans will show if return is also guaranteed. Like all other subjects covered by Dick Head, I recently arranged to have a time travel survey carried out at The Puke and Bucket pub in Dartford and the results were very interesting, if not disturbing.

By taking 1000 people at random we came up with the following answers to our questions:

1. Where would you go on big TITS?

(1a) Into the future.................................. 11%
(1b) Into the past.................................. 6%
(1c) Stay at home.................................. 3%
(1d) Told us to sod off.............................70%

2. How would you pay for the big TIT trip?

(2a) Credit card.................................. 9%
(2b) Petrol coupons.................................. 91%

3. Would you take your wife/spouse?

(3a) No.................................. 100%
(3b) Yes.................................0%
(3c) Send on a different TIT from me..... 94%

4. What items would you take with you?

(4a) Television.................................. 100%
(4b) Credit cards.................................98%
(4c) Condoms (throwaway).................. 0%
(4c) Condoms (Dishwashable)............... 100%
(4d) Bible.................................. 2%
(4e) Carling Black Label beer.......... 100%

(4f) Portable phone.............................99%
(4g) Computer.................................. 87%
(4h) Sun cream................................. 100%
(4i) Duty free booze & fags............. 100%

5. What name would you use for your travels?

(5a) Dick Head................................. 72%
(5b) Nero.. 1%
(5c) Jesus..5%
(5d) Hitler... 1%
(5e) Stalin...2%
(5f) Wally..3%
(5g) Robin Hood.............................. 2%
(5h) Bugs Bunny............................. 1%
(5i) Prince Charles...........................0.01%
(5j) Biggles..1%
(5k) Ronnie MacDonald..................3%
(5l) Elvis Presley............................. 3%
(5m) Misc...4.99%

You can see from the survey results that, as usual, the people interviewed didn't understand the repercussions of some of the decisions they had made. With 70% of the people telling us to piss off, clearly they did not comprehend the real meaning of travelling on the big TITS and were not prepared to have a serious discussion.

All market research surveys have a margin of error, normally in the +/- 3% bracket when one thousand people are interviewed. The margin of error could be somewhat greater for this particular survey, because on the Saturday night in question when the survey was taken, we had a full view strip show going on and the beer was free. Maybe our questions were not considered as seriously as we had hoped.

I am deeply concerned about the fact that 100% of the 16% of the 1000 people (160 people) who chose to go back in time wanted to take a television set with them. But this is less disturbing than having thousands of counterfeit Dick Heads floating through time to confuse the people at large over just how good I really am.

Prince Charles has chosen to go forward in time to see Lucky on her seventieth birthday before he eventually committed suicide.

Any student wishing to complete the same questionnaire may do so and send their answers to my publisher. The sender of the most original answers will win two first class big TITS tickets to go anywhere they please, but they cannot use the name of Dick Head.

I have given a great deal of thought to the question of time travel and believe that the worlds of the past, present and future can be greatly improved by adopting a real common sense policy for big TITS. You are now leaning forward in your chairs in nervous anticipation of this latest Dick Head masterpiece - and you would be doing the right thing.

How do we achieve such a stroke of genius? Very simply indeed, my friends.

Only fully satisfied people should be allowed to

stay with us in the present. To qualify for this present group you must have no gripes or complaints about anything linked with your life or standard of living. You must be immune from making comments such as "I'm living in poverty or I'm paying too much tax." You are happy with your lot and want things to stay as they are.

The living in poverty group will be shipped back to the East End of London in the year 1810 where they will learn what real poverty really is. They will understand what Judith Wallingbury meant with her quotation at the beginning of this chapter:

"Today's luxury is tomorrow's poverty."
(You've never had it so good.)
Judith Wallingbury (1979)

For these moaning people sent back to 1810, we could just as well quote the very opposite for them to consider in their new horrible home to make them really feel fed up. I think I will do this now, just to prove to you all that even Dick Head can be clever at this sort of thing:

"Yesterday's luxury becomes today's poverty"
(You've never had it quite so bad..)
Richard Head (1993)

Pretty good stuff, Huh? Now I continue. The paying too much taxes group will be sent into the future to the year 3500 AD where they will find that individual wealth is a thing of the past and everybody lives the same mundane life completely dominated by the state. The Labour Party has been in power for the past 1476 years so that everything is nationalised and all the public services are absolute crap. Our travellers into the future will soon realise that:

"Tomorrow's poverty is today's luxury."
(You'll never have it quite so good again..)
Richard Head (1993)

I'm getting quite good at creating original quotations, don't you think?

One other option is that we take the whole population of the earth and all go to hell as one unhappy family.

On a more serious note, let's look at travelling back in time to see if for once the human race could do something right for themselves. Can you imagine 250 people (all carrying Japanese television sets) boarding a big TIT from the 38b BRA storage building, heading for 0 AD to meet the three wise men.

I personally cannot say that I agree with the olde time experts who try to convince me that the three men seen following a star in the sky should be described as wise. If I was to see three men in Hyde Park following a star, I would consider them as three daft idiots. However, the three wise men are in the Bible and I am not.

I dream of my first famous meeting and saying, "Hello Jesus, my name's Dick Head and I'm from a world that is in the future, 2000 years after you get crucified oops! I'm sorry me Lord, I forgot that you probably don't know about this yet. Now I want to talk to you about how you fed all those people on such a few fishes and loaves. If the fish were six hundred pound sharks and the loaves were two hundred metres long, I could understand, but................? Now about your mother being a virgin........."

We would all be there with our Sony video cameras, waiting with anticipation to record all the miracles and the crucifixion in full glorious colour. For once we could forget the *Charlie and Lucky* fiasco once this film was made available to all the world's television stations when we return to our present time aboard the big TIT.

Upon our return, out would come all the experts on television chat shows to explain why the miracles were not miracles and the guy nailed up on the wooden cross was positively dead and would not be rising up again. The Churches would be stammering to explain the many discrepancies between the live filming and the storybook edition. These holy people have no choice if they wish to keep a well paid job with free accommodation, clothes, food and wine.

With the wrong explanations, there could be a huge amount of redundant holy real estate without central heating; all with graveyards in the back garden. Some of the very large churches could never be sold because of the bodies buried below where the kitchen should be.

The more inquisitive amongst us may want to go back and witness (with video records) Moses talking to God and being given the Ten Commandments. If it turns out to be true, what a great way of turning everybody into religious fanatics. Gone will be all modern degradation of society and back will come solid values - for a few months at least. If it turns out that Moses was a con man writer then I want to be his agent!

The more intelligent people amongst us will, of course, choose to go back to the creation of Man, just before Adam and Eve arrived. We shall be able to confirm and record how the earth was created and check out conclusively whether Adam was an ant, or if both Adam and Eve were Darwin's monkeys or man and woman. We can even check out whether they were Chinese, White European, Negro or any other nationality, but my bet is that they will both be short little people from Ireland.

Whatever the result, somebody is going to be proved wrong. One theory is that Adam and Eve liked pork sausages and if this is proven, then eating fashions will change overnight and fatty pork sausages would increase in price to £26 per pound - now that is really very expensive. An average sized pig would now sell for more than £3,000. The Chancellor of the Exchequer is working out a new pig tax and all MPs have taken personal offence.

Even more dramatic would be if we found out that Eve had no teeth, flabby breasts and big feet. Dentists would be overworked forever removing teeth, plastic surgeons would need to develop a flabby breast technique and shoe shops would need to supply male hormone injections to develop huge women's feet to suit the latest jumbo shoes.

An even worse scenario is if Eve turns out to have no breasts, a fat backside and a big hairy chest, then I'm going to go out and get drunk on Guinness. One thing that is sure, Adam is unlikely to be a homosexual and Eve will not be a lesbian.

As usual, some eccentric bright spark will cause a nightmare situation by travelling back in time aboard a chartered big TIT to the day before Adam and Eve are created. They will take with them a picnic set with barbecue feast to await the great creation of mankind.

"Hello Adam, Hello Eve, my name's Bert Plunkett. It's nice to see you but I would ask you to sod off as we arrived here first!"

For me, I think that I would just like to go back to when I was ten years old so that I could live my life again, but this time taking care to live my life by the good Joss of Confucias, Buddha and Taoism. I may not have the guidance of my own Fung Shui man, but by all the Gods, I promise to live a real life of total fulfilment. big TITS will take me back to this new life where I shall dedicate my life ready for man's destiny in the years beyond 2000.

Thank you my best Chinese Joss.

Chapter 12

From Waste Not to Want Not

"Waste for some means life to others."

"Plastic Cycles" United Nations (1978)

After seven years of extreme hard labour and terrestrial brain exertion, I have at last completed the design of my DikMobile!

During my many happy and productive years whilst employed at *Patel's Cheapo Pie Factory*, I had became slowly fascinated with the business activities that were located near to us. These could be viewed during the tea breaks with my good friends Fingers, Boiler Bill, Scrappy Ken, Pastry Pete, Watcher Will and all the other guys of meat pie endeavour.

Whilst I drank my free allocation of Patel's factory brewed "tea", I often gazed through the filthy factory windows, across the road to *Wally Flashman's Best Buy Car Mart*. This garage establishment included a neon lit car showroom of gigantic proportions that made Blackpool illuminations look positively second class. Making such a comparison between an illuminated car showroom and a town like Blackpool may seem rather pointless and confusing to some of you readers of the Dick Head word. Have faith my hero worshippers, because by further concentration and study the reasoning behind this clever comparison will become apparent to you all.

You will very soon obtain similar skills and will practise them by making your own comparisons with towns to highlight an important point that would otherwise go amiss and consequently lack the approval from your envious friends that it fully deserved. For example, you may decide to say, "It stinks like Grimsby" or "It's as crappy as Cardiff" or indeed quote the ultimate of *"It's wonderful and has a world famous author like Rochester"*. There's nothing like comparison.

I simply needed to describe in this book just how bright the lights were at Wally Flashman's Best Buy Car Mart and hey presto, the name of Blackpool automatically came to mind to achieve this aim. During our tea break discussions, Pastry Pete thought this comparison was being far too generous to Blackpool and suggested that we should put an overrider at the end of this chapter to cover ourselves. This overrider could be something like "our comparison of *Wally Flashman's Best Buy Car Mart* with Blackpool illuminations is in no way intended to improve the overall image of Blackpool as one real crappy town". That should do it.

Turner Tom didn't understand what all the fuss was about and loved Blackpool because it brought back memories of funny hats and his weekends spent there with his Japanese girlfriend in 1947. Boiler Bill cared little for any of this conversation but he did manage to make one important statement that was destined to become reality. "Dick my son, I don't give a toss about the bleedin' car showroom or that bleedin' Blackpool, but I do care that this bleedin' Patel's tea tastes like rotten bleedin' liver. You talk so much rubbish that I'm sure you'll be famous one day." History was to show just what a clever man of foresight was our Boiler Bill, but unfortunately he was made redundant last month after Patel's installed a fully automatic gas fired boiler at the pie factory. This was perhaps poetic justice, because Boiler Bill had hated the miners and Arthur Scargill but loved Margaret Thatcher.

Margaret and Arthur are doing fine but Bill (the "Boiler" bit must now be dropped to give an accurate new description) and most miners are on the dole. Bill had to sell his car and is forced to live on boiled turnips, which he steals from the canal path allotments, and meat pies that are smuggled out of the factory for him every Friday night. Bill says that turnips are OK when mixed with Oxo gravy, but stooping so low as to having to eat Patel's meat pies is the final disgrace. How the mighty do fall.

At the back of the chilled pie store (from where they nick Bill's pies on a Friday), located alongside the rat infested canal, we have *Gypsy Jack's Scrap Yard*, which is like a real crappy war zone. Combined with *Wally Flashman's Best Buy Car Mart*, we have two complete industries involved in the well tuned process of screwing the working class man in the name of capitalism. Sell the working class man a glittery piece of trash (crap), make sure that it will fall apart within seven years, and then crush it up and start the conning process all over again.

This real gem of the ultimate confidence trick from our car manufacturers is arranged to maintain this endless cycle of car sales to cars falling apart to cars being smashed apart. Otherwise, how can they grow and make even more money than last year? I wonder why we don't build passenger airliners with the same philosophy?

A great con that is all based upon the notion (fully proven) that the human ego begs to be dressed up inside the latest designer clothes to express superiority. These clothes are sent to the Oxfam shop immediately some Aids infected designer from Paris or Milan launches his latest collection that is so much more twee and with it than the ones he designed last month. How can women be so stupid as to believe this cranky idea that clothes designers designed awful looking clothes last month but next month's clothes are so fan-tast-ic!!? Have I misunderstood the real truth?

Is it possibly that by wearing last month's clothes you are showing the world that you don't have enough of the dosh or style as the woman next door or your colleagues at work? No, I must be wrong to think of such stupid ideas. Let's buy a new latest outfit and then put fifty pence in the collection box for the third world starving people. Life is a bitch, ain't it? God forbid that clothes designers survive because of the inbred female catty jealousy that drives us all nuts all the time.

Before we continue along this delicate avenue, let it not be said that I, Dick Head the world famous author, ever described women as being obnoxious, nasty, beastly, horrid, horrific, horrible, gruesome, ghastly, awful, foul, rotten, lousy, putrid, putrefying, loathsome or horrendous.

Also, let it not be said that I, Dick Head the world famous author, ever described woman as being always jealous, jaundiced, green-eyed, distrusting, envious, yellow-eyed, consumed with jealousy and plainly a pain in the arse at all times. No, my friends, let it never be said that I made such accusations.

Cars are like clothes and car designers design cars that are different from last year's models for the same reasons, as otherwise why would you bother to change your car? No new car means no car factory that means no job for the car designer. Car designer wants job..................

Even our infantile government of incredibly stupid politicians complicates this conning game even more because they have arranged for our car number plates to be identified with a year letter that shows the world which year the vehicle was manufactured. Now why on earth would any sane government put into place such a stupid regulation? The result is to allow rich people (and/or company car drivers) to drive around with smug looks upon their faces every August, leaving the rest of us feeling really upset because we don't have this new registration plate.

To emphasise the lunacy of this number plate law, we have a black market and an official market in personalised number plates which are outside normal government control because with these number plates you cannot tell the age of the car. Whoopee! You're allowed to pay several thousand pounds to buy a number plate that doesn't show the age of the car - you are so lucky to have such liberties in this land of the free.

These special number plates are purchased by either rich people who wish to be seen as rich, or by poor people who want people to think they are rich even though they are very poor and are driving a real crappy old car that they hope people will think is not a real crappy old car. Life can get so complicated.

My own real crappy old car carries a number plate with the registration of **DIK 1** that is not a legal one, but as I have never been stopped once in twenty-seven years for having these false number plates fitted, then why should I change such long held habits now?

Being the most honest world famous author can sometimes lead to unexpected problems and I now envisage having every police car in the South of England chasing me in the future when they see that famous DIK 1 number plate. "Get that false number plated car and that cocky Dick Head at any cost - no Dick Head can flout the law in my precinct!"

Have no fear, my redoubtable friends, I have carefully laid plans to counteract this official victimisation. I have prepared a complete set of new number plates - one for each day of the year, including my favourite new one of **UPR 1K** that is not exactly perfect English, but it is surely near enough for them to get the point.

We also now have the government joining in the privatisation of the personalised number plate game by selling you numbers of your own choice, providing it still informs the world of the age of your car. Why not let everybody drive whatever age of car they desire without the humiliation of other people in the street or in the family (the family are the worst) saying, "Old Dick's got a real old banger there."

We all surely know somebody who changes his car on the 1 August every year to be the first person in the road to have the latest registration letter. They take deliver of this gleaming chariot at 12.01 that first possible day and park it in their driveway so that everybody can see it as they pass by to go to work. When they do drive this new vehicle, they wear their best clothes to rub in the humiliation even more. God, it really hacks me off.

If we were all being totally honest, this one-upmanship annoys us all, leaving a strange taste of envy inside our mouths, tasting something like "you cocky little smug-faced twit, I'd like to scratch all your paintwork and then see you smile!" You may have a slightly different type of taste than this, but I have no objections to such independent thought patterns - after all is said and done, that's what The Working Man's series is all about. We are all guilty of looking at a car's number plate to identify its age before we even pass comment on how nice the car is or looks.

Ask your business friend what car he is driving and the answer will be something like, "Dick, you nosy bloody world famous author of endless crappy blockbusters, I drive an S registered Ford Scorpio with all the extras, a fitted car phone of the new micro design, condom warmer, satellite navigation system and a bail of straw for the old horse, ha, ha, ha." What your friend is really telling you is that he's a real clever fellow who has conned his company into giving him a modern chariot to drive about in whilst you drive that horrible vehicle you call a car.

If, on the other hand, you see a friend of yours driving a ten year old car then you make suppositions about his lifestyle purely based upon this car information. Before these new identification "letters" were brought into our complicated world, the car trade had a very easy life in offering you a second-hand car of a certain year; simple and to the point.

Since the change in government policy on number plates, you are now offered a "J registered (1992)" vehicle that is far more descriptive than before? It cannot be described as only a "J registered" vehicle because it could be a 1991 one. It cannot be described as a "1992" vehicle because it may be a "K" registered one. In the good old days before the year letter had been introduced into our already complicated lives, the buyer of a new car at least had to wait in the freezing cold at 12.01 on the 1 January instead of waiting in the summer's warmth at 12.01 on the 1 August.

Yet again, the law has been changed so that the rich inherit the earth and don't freeze off their privates. All this complication just because a stupid government made a wrong decision and decided to separate the rich from the poor. If you can give me any other logical reason, then I shall be very happy to listen. You will be wrong, but I promise to listen.

I've heard the argument from many quarters (up to four) that the year letter number plates makes it easier for the police to identify cars over three years old that may not have a current M.O.T certificate. As most people can buy their M.O.T certificates cheaper and easier on the black market than going through all the expensive official rigmarole at an authorised M.O.T garage, then this cannot be a valid reason. As the police cannot, and are not interested in, pursuing these vendors of the illegal sacred certificate of car incompetence, then how far can we take this useless argument anyway?

Furthermore, if identification was called for to protect us from over aged items that are below operating condition, then special numbering is most certainly required on most council houses, pavements, prisons, courts, judges, English cricketers and all women in Chelmsford and Southend on Sea. How nice it would be for me to hear anyone telling me one day, "Dick, you super world famous author of blockbusting novels, my company has just issued me with a really cheap and awful Japanese car which is a bunch of Nippon junk". Such realism is just not going to happen. Back to my DikMobile story.

The car manufacturers have a real interest in making sure that this cycle of car uselessness is maintained, so that after a seven year cycle the beautiful model of 1993 is entering Gypsy Jack's Scrap Yard for crushing into a giant matchbox cube. Try imagining the total waste of natural resources involved in maintaining this endless cycle of utter waste.

Building crappy cars with a skin deep facade to deceive is like breeding whores. We pay more money for cars in our lifetime than we do for our houses and yet we fall for this master con. Now all this is about to change, because the present automobile will soon be replaced by the *DikMobile*. What is the *DikMobile*? I thought that you would never ask such an incredibly sensible question.

Quite simply put, the *DikMobile* is the Dick Head designed automobile that will last for several lifetimes or more, and will be treasured and passed down from father to son, or stolen by some bright lawyer in an acrimonious divorce settlement. "You can keep the bloody house, the BMW, the jewellery, the stocks and shares and the luxury apartment in Florida - but you're not having the bloody *DikMobile* because that's mine!"

The *DikMobile* is built entirely of top grade stainless steel and other materials guaranteed for a life span of several hundred years. It is built on a DikBlok system that allows any component to be replaced easily by the owner himself within a very short time and at a low cost.

Power is from a combined electric and solar drive unit with a diesel back-up power unit. Only the electric drive will be allowed to be used within our cities, thus the *DikMobile* will eliminate pollution where other efforts have failed to reach.

Governments of the world will assist my transport revolution by installing plug-in points for the DikMobile power pack on every parking meter, lamp post, castle railing, police station, town hall, traffic light, level crossing and sex shop.

By the year 2001, traffic jams will be so bad that the *DikMobile* power pack can be fully recharged during the time it will take to travel to the extreme reach of the DikCharger cable. You may die of boredom in the traffic but at least you can die of something different from lung cancer.

My newly designed and patented (world-wide excluding Peru) wheel & tyre combination, the *DikWeel,* is a fantastic advance over conventional wheels with separate tyres. By carrying out over four years of research at both the *German Skin Institute* and *Noddy's Plastic Factory*, I came up with a new mixture of skin from the Fatherland mixed with the best of Noddy's plastic nuts, to which I have given the name of *Polynoddydeutcholene*. I agree that this is a long name for the hardest wearing synthetic plastic ever known to mankind and I could have called it *DikPlastik* but this would have shown some considerable conceit. After all, just how famous does one wish to become?

Polynoddydeutcholene is a plastic that has wearing characteristics beyond the belief of non-teutonic class citizens but has a toughness that is fully expected by all citizens of Hamburg, Munich, Dusseldorf and Frankfurt between the ages of five and sixty-two. After the age of sixty-two the beer sausage takes over the brain and then you can hear the same words in all the beeren-hauses, "Sod the *Polynoddydeutcholene*."

In a laboratory controlled test carried out in 1989 by a secret atomic energy plant in Cumbria, a rubbish bag manufactured from *Polynoddydeutcholene* was filled with atomic waste weighing 130 kilograms and it was found that this bag lasted 6,780 trips between Cumbria and Tokyo before splitting due to wear. Unfortunately the *Polynoddydeutcholene* bag with the atomic waste inside split on the back of a truck in the centre of Wigan and Wigan therefore exists no more. Shame about the rugby team.

As I was saying, the *DikWeel* is an all-in-one wheel and tyre manufactured by a blow moulding process using the new *Polynoddydeutcholene.* Actual road tests (avoiding the Wigan area) of the *DikWeel* fitted to a *DikMobile* have given us over three million miles, and so far we have worn down only 5.6% of the tyre tread and no nuclear fall out. These *DikWeels* are sold for just £11.67 at any good garden centre and can be found alongside the hosepipes and barbecues. My local garden centre, Greenfingers is not impressed with the business experienced during his first six years of selling *DikWeels* because he bought fifty for stock and has sold just one. This was sold to a retired gardener who fitted it to his wheelbarrow because it was less expensive than the metal and rubber replacement ones.

Since then, all manufacturers of wheelbarrows fit *DikWeels* as standard and the *Bristol Wheelbarrow Wheel Company* has been forced into liquidation. Their ex-managing director, Ernest Gifford, telephoned me in anger on the day the receivers were called in and shouted down the phone line, "Shame on you, Dick Head!" Never react to aggressive language; just reply, "Shame on you too but have a nice day!" and then put the phone down.

The *DikWeel* is so light that it requires no wheel balancing when fitted to the DikMobile and it has one central locking nut to secure it to the axle - just as in formula one racing cars. In the almost impossible situation of getting a puncture in your *DikWeel*, you simply buy a new one from your garden centre for £11.67 and throw the punctured one away.

If you are one of the worrying kind and are obsessed about the number of miles that you can drive before replacing tyres - forget it! You would need to live over four thousand years driving an average of 100,000 miles per year to stand any chance of wearing out a *DikWeel*. No more of the old crocodile tears such as, "Sorry guv, your new GXT 77 low profile racing tyre was split and beyond repair and we had to fit a new one. Here's your bill for £254.88."

The complete engine department slides out from the chassis by simply releasing four locking screws and this operation is simpler than opening the bonnet of a 1993 model car. A new all replacement all-plastic engine lasts 750,000 miles, costs only £270 and can be replaced in less than ten minutes.

The complete specification of the *DikMobile* can be found in my new 1634 page full colour publication of *DikMobile* and Noddy's Plastic Nuts that is available at all toy shops at £27.00. I mention this because I have no intention of boring you any more in this book by discussing the brilliant inventions installed within the *DikMobile*. Just let it be said that it is the car transport of the future and full patent coverage has now been granted world-wide, excluding Peru.

Designing the *DikMobile* has proved to be a much easier task than getting it into production but you can't expect everything to fall into your lap. Please read the following note carefully before continuing with this chapter. The following text originally identified the car manufacturers by name, but my Irish friend and libel lawyer, Paddy Filpatrick (of merry from Derry fame) told me, "Dicko me boy, I tink you should not be a mentioning dees dare names. "I am renowned for taking advice from clever people and ignoring advice from stupid people - this is one of my advanced traits that has made me what I am today. Paddy is a clever man.

So, I set out on my commercial travels to make my multi-BILLION pound fortune with my *DikMobile*. I first visited the F motor Company located in D in the county of E to offer them a first refusal on this revolution in mass transport and pollution elimination. My business plan ran to 2,675 pages and I had used a real computer model upon which this planet revolves around today. I think they look ugly.

I had calculated that my eight seater *DikMobile* with ALL THE EXTRAS could be sold for £4,500 as an "on the road" price. Naturally, to achieve such an attractive and low price there were certain cost and other elements to be clarified:

Development costs of £3 billion.

Tooling costs of £6.5 billion.

A break-even sales figure of 1.3 billion cars per year. Convince all governments to install electric plugs everywhere.

Scrap all other models of cars.

Pay Dick Head £50 million up front and thereafter £5 per car plus 50 pence per car for use of my DikMobile trademark.

Change the company's name to the F-DikMobile Motor Company.

Fire all Welsh workers and burn down Welsh car plants.

To my surprise, I received no reply to my first letter sent to The F Motor Company in D in the county of E, even after six weeks of waiting. I did not even receive an acknowledgement that they had received my letter. Working at *Patel's Cheapo Pie Factory* showed me that the decision making people are often kept in the dark concerning the ways and means of revolutionising the business, thus not allowing them to be at the forefront of technology. I witnessed this very point at the pie factory in 1981.

Following the consumer's initial enthusiasm for pies at the right size and price during the 1970s, the sales of these disgusting items dropped dramatically during the last two years of this decade and Saresh the owner became a very worried man. I had already carried out my own in-depth study of this worrying drop in the company's profitability because after having bought a black coloured Capri 2.8i car in 1979 on hire purchase, I required an income of exactly £52.34 per week to cover the loan and insurance premiums.

If made redundant, I felt sure that Pastry Pete or Scrappy Ken would supply me with free meat pies to live on. Dick Head was not going to be seen walking anywhere - so I had to keep the car - therefore I had to halt the slide in sales of meat pies. I really do have an incredibly analytical mind once my lifestyle is under threat and so I set to work.

The problem became very apparent during my first day on the streets carrying out a meat pie survey next to Randolf's Pie Stall that is located halfway across Lambeth Bridge. Randolf Schickler has operated this pie stall for over twenty years and makes most of his money by selling pies to tourists (63%), itinerants (28%) and pub drunks (6%). This meant that only 3% of his turnover is made from anybody who has any real influence upon his business future, "So Dick Head, why should I give a toss if I do sell crappy pies?"

I tried to explain to Randolf that this self-centred attitude would do nothing to increase his business and he told me to "sod off!" He is not a very nice man but he does drive a new Bentley Turbo and lives in a huge mansion in Wimbledon.

On the 21 November 1981, I carried out a survey at Randolf's Pie Stall on 1,780 people to isolate the real problem with our meat pies. I had to dress up looking like William Shakespeare because if Randolf was to have recognised me, he would have realised that something untoward was going on. I asked the consumers one simple question of "What does your pie taste of?" and the results were staggering.

Because of so many rude answers, I am ignoring such abuse and informing you of the central opinion of the masses. We had 74% say "rotten fish", 13% say "crap" and another 6% say "Jesus Christ!" The remaining 7% gave an assortment of verbal abuse. We had now isolated the real reason for not selling the pies - nobody liked them!

I set to work to solve this problem - to make everybody like them. Firstly, I must see where the costings allowed such an improvement. By bribing the cost accountant, Larry Loot, I came up with the following figures for the pie costing but without the meat:

Pastry.. 1p
Gas for baking.. 0.2p
Wrapping paper.. 0.5p
Shipping box... 1p
Distribution costs...................................... 1.8p
Shop profit.. 12p
Patel's profit... 25p
TOTAL COST **WITHOUT** THE MEAT......... 41.5p

The selling price of the pie was 42p so this only left half a penny for the meat! No wonder the pies tasted like rotten fish, crap or "Jesus Christ".

In my previous book, *The Working Man's Guide To The Galaxy,* you probably found it utterly disgusting for me to describe the events where carcasses of animals were delivered at night to the pie factory by Andreas, the dog catcher. I can now throw back this criticism upon ye, the criticisers, "How else can you get 100 grams of meat for half a penny? Meat at five pence per kilogram is very cheap indeed and therefore one must expect the quality to suffer.

To get rid of the highly disgusting smell that arose from these dark red cheap cuts of meat, it was found necessary to steam for two hours and then camouflage the remaining gunge as best as you can with a good healthy dose of *Wong's Tenderising Compound.* Patel's sold three flavours of meat pies, but it was a closely held secret that all flavours used the same meat. Nobody could distinguish the difference, but everybody was left feeling sick after eating the pie. Good system for minimum production costs but a very bad system for market response.

Thousands of complaints were received and sales fell to disastrous levels - da de da! Dick Head came to the rescue with his new *DikTaste* meat flavouring system. Clever it was not - but effective it most certainly was.

When allowed to study the overall problem, it was clear that Saresh would not reduce his profit per pie and therefore we had to try to solve this problem bearing this greed and intransigence in mind. I always thought that it was better to make half the profit on a hundred times the sales - but what do I know about economics? It was obvious that as nobody could detect the difference between the flavours of the meat pies, then why keep up the pretence of running three separate pie production lines? Saresh was excited about this possibility of making more profit and he could be seen reading the new Mercedes brochures during his lunch break on the day it was first suggested to him.

Eventually, sales dropped to such a disastrous level and Saresh became so desperate that he was prepared and willing to discuss my *DikTaste* device. Did you know that you can reconstruct the exact taste of virtually anything by using a range of synthetically created elements? I can inform you that this is now a fact of our everyday lives and that the item you are eating may be a by-product from rotten seaweed.

I approached *The Geordie Meat in Pie Flavouring Company Limited,* who are based in Hartlepool, requesting their assistance in developing a full range of flavouring liquids to solve Patel's problem. As their name suggests, *Geordie's* are the world's leading producers of flavourings for meat used in meat pies and had a solution within a few days. They delivered four 100 kilogram drums of flavouring for Steak & Kidney, Steak & Onion, Beef & Potato and Lamb.

I had already informed them that the cost should not exceed 0.156p per dose/pie as this was the saving that had been made by combining the three production lines into one. After the results obtained by using Geordie's flavourings, I can highly recommend these people to any other crooked meat pie producer who wishes to use doubtful and crappy meat in his pies.

My *DikTaste* system consisted of a row of four stolen bicycle pumps mounted above the PERFEKT PYENFABRIK MACHINEN and four second-hand fibre glass central heating water storage tanks for holding the various flavourings from *Geordie's*. A flexible pipe connected the tanks to the bicycle pumps. Saresh then employed four illegal immigrants from Chile and connected an electric wire to their large toes.

When a dose of *Geordie's* flavouring is required (which is 47 times per minute), an electric shock is sent to each bicycle pump operator and hey presto the job becomes automatic. As the day goes on, these operators become tired from the continual electric shocks, so the power is gradually increased to offset this drop in efficiency. Nothing must affect our pie making procedures.

Constant electric shocks have had a few side effects upon these operators, but they never fall asleep on the job.

Patel's pies are now on the best seller list and Saresh did not have to sacrifice any of his 25p profit. What did I get in return for my *DikTaste* invention that saved Saresh's pants? Saresh gives me twelve meat pies of my own choice every week and buys me a turkey at Christmas. This year's turkey was thrown away before cooking as it had Use before 1 June 1972 printed on the label. Saresh had tried to change the 1972 into 1992 but the ink had washed off during defrosting. They now manufacture turkey pies at the factory.

Sorry about this little tangential wandering, but I needed to highlight that when the going gets tough then the tough get going. i.e: You must persevere if you are to succeed in life. With this in mind, we can get back to the DikMobile story.

After receiving no reply to my business proposal from the F Motor Company Limited in D in the county of E, I decided to make a personal appearance at the head office upon a very sunny day in 1992 to discuss it with Henry F himself. He would understand even though I could not allow my DikMobile to be painted black. "Excuse me sir, but do you have an appointment?" shouted out a burly ex-docker security man at the main gate. I replied with the greatest confidence, "Good morning my man, I have an appointment with Mr. Henry F. himself. I am Richard Head, the world famous author and automobile designer."

Docker Jock was so taken back that he sent me across to the main reception area where a really attractive 1955 model plastic blonde dummy was acting as receptionist. As she spoke, some of the eggshell cracked on her lips but she continued smiling. "Good morning Mr. Head, I understand that you have an appointment with Mr. Henry F, but I'm afraid he died many years ago."

"Quick thinking starts with a slow response."
Janet Bloomsbury (1991)
"How Soon Is Tomorrow."

"Oh dear, that's terrible news, I must send some flowers to the funeral. I told my secretary that the appointment should have been made earlier. Never mind, when you're dead, you're dead. Please inform your chief executive that a friend of Henry F needs to see him urgently to discuss a revolutionary new car that Henry was interested in." Not bad, ha?

The cracked paint stand looked at me very strangely and said, "Mr. Head, are you really serious?"

"My dear girl, stop staring and wasting my time and get on with my request - I don't have all day as I must also visit the V motor Company in L before close of business today." Believe it or not, it really worked. Within ten minutes, a secretary from the cod family came out of a nearby lift and said, "Mr. Head, good morning my name is Jean Haddock, will you follow me please."

I proceeded to follow her into the lift and we then sped up to the top floor executive suite. I was so sure she was from the cod family. I was shown into a mahogany panelled executive boardroom where no fewer than nine dark suited executives were seated. They all rose in unison as I walked in and I noticed that they were all over six feet tall and I felt humiliated in their presence - but not for long.

"When facing disaster, kick them in the balls."

Richard Head (1993)

I sat down without being invited and spoke out boldly. "Gentleman, bad news about Henry. However, I have brought with me today the design and patent details of the revolutionary *DikMobile*, the vehicle to make other vehicles redundant. Please feel free to read through the plans which include our licensing contract. I'll have black coffee with biscuits please." Not bad for an ex-pie maker!

I proceeded to hand out copies of my business

proposal that had a Japanese version at the back. Because I had no intention of spending £25,000 on Japanese translation services, I had pasted in cut-out material from the Tokyo Times that I had purloined from a Japanese traveller at Heathrow Airport whilst he was checking in. The resultant translation looked better and more professional than the English version.

While I drank their cold black coffee with non-dairy creamer, but without any biscuits, I slyly watched their reactions to the *DikMobile* proposal out of the corner of my left eye. Looking out of the corner of one's eye is not a natural gift afforded at birth and is considered a great art form in many Eastern countries.

Millenniums have been spent developing this skill to perfection which by the natural selection process has given these Eastern races much wider and narrower eyes so that looking through the corner of such stretched eyes becomes second nature. When Adam and Eve's descendants first moved to the Far Eastern areas of the globe some three million years after Adam died, these colonialists travelled to these far off lands because of their love for rice. Then they had normal bulging eyes with no corners to them.

I recently went on a package tour to Hong Kong that had promised to show me the mysteries of China and the Far East, and I believed that this would include helping me perfect this business technique of looking out of the corner of my eyes in a more efficient way. My skill in this area is now greatly increased, but after corner of the eye viewing for more that a few hours, I experience tremendous cramp spasms that can only be eased by consuming quantities of Guinness and Champagne within a short period of time.

My books are today already translated and printed in all Chinese dialects and they are now in the best selling lists of Hong Kong, Taiwan and mainland China. This unforeseen interest in the Far East has forced me to develop a new wider version of the DikSpeks that are manufactured in rice paper for followers of the corner of the eye viewing technique. The *DikWissal* has been withdrawn from sale in China following the riots during the launch, when they expected a free dog with every whistle. Back to the DikMobile story.

After reading through my business plan for some ten minutes, our super executives from The F. Motor Company in D in the county of E all started to shuffle their feet, scratch their faces, avoid any personal eye contact and looked positively very confused.

After reading through my business plan for some ten minutes, our super executives from The F Motor Company in D in the county of E all started to shuffle their feet, scratch their faces, avoid any personal eye contact and looked positively very confused.

Any business school will tell you that groups make group decisions that the separate individuals would consider stupid decisions. I was relying heavily upon this principle to see me through this oncoming crisis, but I was to find out very quickly that my faith in such business school theories was heavily misplaced.

The leader of the pack, who was referred to as Gabe, looked up with a devilish grin on his face and spoke out in a deep American accent. "Richard Head, Dick Head, *DikMobile,* Henry F, three billion dollars development costs, six and a half billion tooling costs, one and a half billion vehicles per year to break even, pay you fifty million up front, pay you fifty pence trade name royalty per car, scrap all existing car models, change our company's name to The F DikMobile Company, fire all Welsh workers and simply ask all governments in the world to fit DikPlugs everywhere! You are of course **PISSING ME, DICK HEAD OR WHATEVER YOUR BLOODY NAME IS!"**

Whilst Gabe was fuming and frothing, a short man of Japanese heritage also spoke up to me in a very confused voice. "Mitter Head, can you hees exhain the sectshun in Japarnhees on the subhect off tooing whish shays Mad cow disease is becoming an epihemdic in Hingland." So much for fooling the people all of the time. I pretended not to understand him and refused to reply, despite verbal threats spoken in Japanese that were backed up by hand signals of intended violence.

Whatever your opinions may be about Americans with the name of Gabe, an independent observer would have a justified reason to say that Gabe had a point. I later found out that his grandfather had been born Welsh and was a miner just outside Cardiff.

After checking with the Trademarks Office, I found out that I could use the name of *DikPlug* if ever I found a suitable use. I registered the name but have found no suitable use to date and invite suggestions from my readers.

In response to Gabe's outburst of temper, I replied, "Gabe, my friend, am I correct in assuming that what you are really saying is that you need more time to consider these exciting proposals?" I shall not relate the remainder of this sad story because Gabe, within a few minutes after seeing my proposal, had made a decision that was destined to put The F Motor Company on D in the county of E out of business.

I received similar responses and very rude reactions from every other motor car company in the world and their reactions varied from "piss off" to "get the hell out of here" to "get that nut case out of here" to "what the fu......." and many more. Little did they all know that each one was signing their own death warrants.

When adversity is unjust then join the freedom fighters.

After carrying out a rapid self-analysis to find out why I had failed in my attempt to revolutionise the people's transportation stakes, I quickly found out the answer. We didn't need a car company because they had too much self-interest - we needed a government who needed a system upon which they could improve the lot of their people. I sold out to the Russians!

With my help, they had the *DikMobile* production car ready by June 1999 and by the 1 January 2001 had sold over ten billion world-wide. The *DikMobile-Ruski Motor Company Inc* has since taken over every car manufacturer that existed in 1993 and I personally went to The F Motor Company of D in the county of E to see our old friend Gabe.

"Gabe, my friend, my name really is Dick Head and I was not pissing you before and I am not pissing you now - you're fired."

It has been estimated that until the 1 January 2000, the *DikMobile* has eliminated pollution in all cities of the world and as a consequence has saved the lives of over six million people. Our two postmen are still going strong.

Health costs world-wide have decreased by $2,450 TRILLION per year and the Russian people are now the most affluent in the world. Arab countries are all bankrupt.

I recently delivered a single seater gold plated *DikMobile* sports version to *Lucky,* complete with telephone and make-up department. Look out for the registration number **D1 HARD**.

So, because Dick Head persevered with his *DikMobile*, the world is a much better and healthier place.

Waste not - Want not.

Chapter 13

From Eternity to Diana Head

We search afar in foreign lands,
Different folk and timescale bands,
Our boys and girls left home alone,
Whilst we pursue our dreams half grown,
Then we grow old with no repose,
Dreams dried out in all the throes,
The world has fully passed me by,
Nothing left but to cry and now die.
"The Sun Sets On The Empire." Sir Peter Kitchener (1897)

This penultimate chapter before your M.Sc. (DikHed) exam is the continuing story of the rise and fall of the human race that first began in my previous book *The Working Man's Guide To The Galaxy*, in chapter 4 entitled FROM UNCLE TO ETERNITY.

The PISSOFF (People's Interstellar Solar System Official Fleet Flights) space ships had left the earth some 34,877,564,315 years before and were now lost in space heading for eternity. Nobody was getting any older and marriages were breaking up so fast that a new law allowed you to marry the same person only thirty-six times every thousand years. This made the Royal Family very happy.

Each time the fleet came upon a Frogomat's gate house, they blew off the gateman's head and sailed on towards eternity, without a care that they were trespassing upon another race's property.

The Prime Minister had just fired the Home Secretary by saying: "What bloody use are you in finding us a home" and the Home Secretary was very grateful and relieved because finding a home was proving difficult.

The Royal Family were all divorced but were still not talking to each other. Lucky had run out of batteries for her mobile telephone and was in a constant sulk because no photographs of her had appeared in the *PISSOFF TIMES* for over thirty thousand billion years. Charles could now speak fluently to the royal daffodils and had bought an imitation plastic crown that he wore in private in hope for the future. The Queen's crown polisher and her shoe polisher KIWI were the first to really understood the meaning of eternity, whereas the rest of the travellers still believed in miracles.

The story continues!...................

Boredom was leading to daily arguments at the highest level of authority and eventually the Queen called John Major to her study. She made a fateful speech that should have been made whilst back on earth all those years ago when Norman Lamont was still looking after the country's money: "John, you're fired! I'm dissolving Parliament today and taking full personal control. The first thing I want you to do is repay me all the income tax I've paid over the years!

Please return your orange box to me in the morning and get your wife to dress less glamorous again as before."

I must say that I'm not a royalist, but she had my support at the time. I didn't find out about this firing of the whole government until a few light years later, because I was engrossed in writing my book number 23,786 entitled *Homeward Bound, My Beauties.*

During the first few weeks of direct rule by the Queen, she was more interested in counting up all the money than worrying about the dire straits we were all in. It has been said that a very miserable person cannot be any more miserable than she already is but I can now inform you that this statement is untrue. Maybe this is one theory for me to look into if ever this period of the human fight for survival ever comes under close scrutiny.

Once we return to free speech, I shall write a book entitled *Happy Cows & Miserable Queens.*

The Queen found out many disturbing things concerning the country's finances and called in the Ex-Chancellor of the Exchequer to give a full explanation. "Kenneth, I see that you were gullible enough to accept bank drafts to the value of £600 trillion as payment for this trip on the PISSOFFs by many of the wealthy travellers. I told you before we left that the only payment worth taking was that of gold bullion, to be used as funds for our life on a new planet. Indeed, I gave you explicit instructions to take only gold, or at the very least to take the same value in condoms or toilet paper. Now tell me why you accepted these stupid paper bank drafts?"

"Your Majesty, you did indeed instruct me to take gold bars with me, but unfortunately the government had made such a mess of the economy during the previous twenty-five years that all of our gold had been used up to pay our debts in Switzerland and Japan. However, even if we had the gold Ma'am, we could not have taken it with us because such an amount of gold would have weighed about three trillion tons. This would have necessitated building a PISSOFF fleet three thousand times the present size to carry such extra weight.

"To build these extra ships would have taken an extra six hundred years and we would all have been dead or living under six metres of polluted crap by then. Already the Crapper Tax (thought up by Dick Head the famous author), meant that most of the people could not afford to pay this tax, so that they openly fouled the streets to avoid paying, thus increasing the pollution level and reducing the remaining time of Earth's survival.

"Therefore, Ma'am, I assumed that you did not wish to die under a pile of crap and took it upon myself to allow the PISSOFFs to take off before we were all dead. I can keep all of the bank drafts in a biscuit tin under my bed for safekeeping. The presidents of all the world's banks are on board and have guaranteed to pay these bank drafts on demand at any time.

"Your second idea of taking the ticket values in condoms is also something that I looked into in great detail, Ma'am. The Minister of Sport, Reginald Love, calculated that the value of the bank drafts equated to twenty trillion condoms of the average size. To produce such a number of condoms required the rubber production from the world's entire stock of rubber trees for over nine hundred years, providing people stopped using condoms during that period to preserve the rubber stock.

"So, for nine hundred years we would have been living under an even bigger pile of crap and would have no condoms, rubber bands, car tyres or Wellington boots. In addition, your knickers would have fallen down.

"The Minister of Transport also informs me that such a volume of condoms would mean an extra three trillion cubic metres of cargo space required for the PISSOFF fleet. Such extra baggage space equates to trying to ship Russia and China with us on our voyage. This, of course, would have been impracticable.

"Ma'am, I took it upon myself to bring with us two million of the *Johnies* dishwashable condoms, two hundred *Wallywash* dishwashers and six hundred tons of recyclable *Zappaz* dish washing powder with automatic sperm remover which I saw advertised in *The Working Man's Guide To The Galaxy*. A government condom company now hires these out on a nightly basis and is making a healthy profit.

So, Ma'am, I believe I have executed my responsibility to the best of my ability."

"Kenneth! Don't you be cheeky with me - now go away and bring me the biscuit tin as I shall store it under my bed!"

Because nobody aged on board the ships, the only deaths experienced were from unfortunate accidents. A few days after the government had been fired, we had a terrible tragedy on board the library ship when Joseph Pepper died of suffocation during one of his stuttering fits. There was a suspicion that he died whilst making passionate love to Agatha Angela Abagail Antwerpen, a lovely young nurse who needed constant reassurance that Joseph loved her madly. She always insisted on being referred to by her full name during their passionate moments.

We buried Joseph Pepper in space and sent him towards eternity with a poem attached to the plastic handles of his blow moulded plastic coffin made from recycled toothpaste tubes and soap powder cartons. Polluting the Earth is one thing, but who wants a crappy eternity? The Joseph Pepper poems went like this:

Joseph Pepper is now dead,

Joseph Pepper was once alive,

Joseph Pepper was a saint,

Joseph Pepper was never in the army.

Joseph Pepper was born in Bedford on 1 April 1952 as the only son of Ruth and Jack Pepper, who were both from Galway in Ireland. It became apparent after a year or so, that Joseph had a serious speech impediment and was going to be a stutterer of vast proportions.

Indeed, Mr. Coffey, the throat specialist at Bedford Hospital stated that Joseph was the worst stutterer he had ever treated during his forty years of treating stutterers. Joseph was at one time recorded as saying sssssssssssssss sssssss sssss sssssssssss ssssssssss s s s s s s s s s h h h h h h h h h h h h h h h h h h hhhhhhhhhhhhhhhhhhhhhhhhhhhhhhhhhhhiiiiiiiiiiiiiiiiii iiiiiiiiiiiiiiiiiiiiiiiiiiiiittttttttttttttttttttttttttttttttttttttt ttttttttttttttttttttttttttttttttttt! and taking over three minutes saying it.

The point was lost on all the audience by the time he had finished. Joseph became a very intelligent lad and when he grew up, he developed a new system for understanding and recording the words of stutterers. This is what today is called *PepperPower*, a system to alleviate the stutterer's nightmare of taking so long to write anything down. To explain PepperPower, the stuttering word above would be written down as:

$$\mathbf{S^{57}H^{53}I^{49}T^{66}}$$

Now this may seem a simple development to the casual observer but we must remember that no system had ever been previously devised to solve this huge stutterer's problem. *The Stutterer's Handbook* has been reduced from 2,567 pages down to only 32 pages by printing it all in *PepperPower*. Whereas it used to sell for £345.50, it now sells for £3.99 as a paperback version. Unfortunately, the Institute of Stutterers are very unhappy at this reduced income, but all is fair in love and choking.

Joseph also developed the *PepperKode*, a system by which a stutterer is identified based upon the intensity of his stuttering. If you are classified as having a *PepperKode* of 54, this simply means that over your speaking of one thousand words, each syllable would be stuttered an average of 54 times each.

This information is extremely important when you are planning a prepared speech on television for a known stutterer. Imagine giving a one thousand word speech to a stutterer having a PepperKode of 3500; my God, he would take sixty-three hours to complete the message. Without hesitation, we shall all remember Joseph Pepper with gratitude and love.

At last! Lucky approached me last week and complimented me on my Working Man's Guide series of books. "Richard, or may I call you Dick? I have just finished reading your book *The Working Man's Guide To Being A Queen* and must say how wonderful this was." I was flabbergasted and started to worry about this new book that failed to describe her by name.

Notwithstanding these worries, I filled my mouth with marbles and replied as best I could. "Your Royal Highness,...." She interrupted my speech with, "Dick, my subject, please call me *Lucky* because I feel as though I've known you for a long time. Do you have a portable phone?"

I was in heaven and almost thought of joining the pro-Lucky set but my absolute integrity held me back. How could I sell my ethics and friendship for just a few compliments from a young woman who was trying to separate from our next King?

Of course she could charm me because I am such a real nice guy and she has had these many light years of experience, including posing for over seven million photographs during that period. If they hadn't run out of film last year, the photographs would have continued forever.

"Lucky, were you serious when you suggested that I should shoot the Queen and Prince Philip with Charles's shotgun and them put the blame on him?" Lucky was very embarrassed and replied, "Well, yes Dick, I thought that this would be the best solution for me, my sons and the rest of us who want to go back home to Earth. How else can we get the old dear to change her mind?"

I became rather disturbed as I replied, "But Lucky, you need to find a much more permanent and safe solution." "Great thinking Dick, but I might shoot Charles with Prince Philip's gun and blame it on him and the Queen. Or maybe I'll take the plunge and arrange for a hit-man to shoot all of them and we'll blame it on Fergie and that boyfriend of hers. Yes, that's the answer!"

"But Lucky, I have no reason to arrange for a hit-man to shoot the Royal Family. Why do you think that I would even entertain the idea?" Lucky started sulking and rushed off in tears whilst screaming out at me in a furious temper, "Damn you Dick Head, you're as bad as the rest of them. I'll go and find myself somebody else who thinks I'm the greatest and will do the shooting for me. Just wait until I'm the Queen Mother with all the influence, you'll never be Sir Richard Head!"

My God, my dreams of palace recognition were being endangered by a frustrated princess who is planning to shoot the Royal Family. Would she go as far as eradicating the evidence and shoot me as well? The next day, an insane ex-North Sea oil driller was caught in the Queen's cockpit with a loaded machine pistol and he was shot for treason after a trial that lasted three minutes. Just before being shot, he screamed out, "I want to be King; where's my Queen Lucky!" Lucky went bright red in the face before she pulled the trigger and said, "Rest in peace."

So the days continued, with more and more frustration creeping in, until the 4 February last year. A man named Cromwell Benn led a group of frustrated SAS special forces, captured the Royal Family and declared himself as the new President. As he was sworn in by the Royal Family, he demanded that Captain Kirk turn the PISSOFF fleet around and that we return to Earth.

During Cromwell's first day in charge on the Palace PISSOFF ship, the Queen became very annoyed and said to him, "Stop kissing me, young man, and I'll abdicate immediately, providing you don't make that fool Charles the new King. Please get a shave and clean your teeth before you see me again." Cromwell was quite adamant and explained gently to the Queen, "Liz, your days of power and living in splendour are now gone forever, so it is better that you learn very quickly how to converse and be happy with ordinary folk.

"Phil must try to be less of a misery-guts and your children should join in the spirit of things. By the way, shaving is difficult, because my razor blade is over 32,000 years old and my last toothpaste tube was commandeered to help produce Joseph Pepper's plastic coffin.

"To help you understand the lot of the working class people, I am going to present you with a signed copy of a very special book entitled *The Working Man's Guide To The Galaxy*, written by that extraordinarily brilliant writer Richard Head. You will see that he has signed it especially for you." The inscription read:

To Lizzie who's not so busy,

All good things must come to an end,
Have a nice day

Best regards to Phil and the kids,

Richard Head Ph.D. (DikHed)

PS: I feel obliged to inform you that being dethroned was a good thing and saved you from assassination by Lucky. Lucky knows who the Royal Bugger is!

The new PISSOFF constitution has recently been finalised by a full and free referendum and amongst the points of freedom was included a new system for electing a new monarch once we found a new home. The new King or Queen would be elected by the people every ten years with princes and princesses voted on every three months. Candidates had to return their application forms within six months of this referendum to be considered for selection by the International Selection Committee For New Kings And Queens.

My readers may consider it presumptuous of me, but I filled in and returned one of these application forms for myself as a candidate. Under the question of, "What name would you prefer" my reply read, ***King DikHed I***, which I think sounded very regal indeed, showing respect and recognition for my millions of graduates studying the Working Man's Guide series. If you vote for me, I promise not to wear a crown or become distant from my people who are the life blood of any country. When you need me, I'll always be there!

So it came to pass that God decided that the PISSOFF fleet should return to Earth. The fleet tried to retrack its steps through eternity, a huge task greatly helped by following the dead Frogomat carcasses and stream of pollution that had been left behind during our outward journey. "Star date 546,543,533,565,437,676 Captain's log reports that the PISSOFFs are now............................." During our return, some amazing things started to occur. Ex-Queen Liz started to enjoy living in the Merseyside ship and fell in love with an Irish sailor whom she will soon marry. Ex-Prince Philip met a beautiful Italian girl on the Wops ship and they now have two wonderful dark haired children. Prince Charles married a tall pansy and Lucky is preparing herself for the television cameras when we eventually land back on Earth. My election campaign is working well and I am becoming optimistic that my next book, entitled The Working Man's Guide To Being A King will be by King DikHed I.

Apart from the honour of serving you as your monarch, I am really excited about the tremendous sales potential and income from this publication. We are now just seven million miles from earth, but the expected radio contact is not available, so we cannot arrange our homecoming celebrations just yet.

To guarantee a fair vote for the new monarchy, the committee decided to hold the election now, rather than during the euphoria of our reception at home on

Earth. By a massive vote of 73.88% in favour, I was elected as King DikHed I and was crowned during a very touching coronation ceremony in the Palace ship. The old Royal Family refused to attend, all of course except Lucky who posed alongside me in several photographs using film from the Royal Reserves that had been hidden away from Lucky.

We had chicken for lunch.

I bear no grudges and feel quite happy to let Lucky keep her false images.

Still no contact from Earth and we are now only sixteen thousand miles away, our arrival scheduled for next Saturday morning in time for the soccer scores. We launch our unmanned space probe which orbits only two hundred miles above earth and relays television pictures back to us of the Earth's surface. Everything looked so blue, green and clear of pollution that we all became excited at the prospect of returning to live in a land where man had at last conquered pollution and protected the environment. Inexplicably, we could detect no sign of human life.

"Gentlemen, as your King I have decided to land on Earth alone to ensure that all is safe and secure for my subjects to join me for the start of our new life. The fleet committee has voted and put into place, the self-destruct system on board all of the PISSOFF ships so that in the event that Earth is uninhabitable then I shall push the red button on the console I will take with me.

"We have all voted for this, not wishing to spend our lives lost in Eternity as before. I agree that death must have a better future than this. However, my people, King DikHed is not going to Earth for this reason; I am going to see our new home!"

"Your Royal Highness, I beg of you to take me with you! If I also confirm that all is well on Earth then the people will have no hesitation in believing me." My God, doesn't she ever stop? It was, of course, Lucky speaking and she obviously had the support of the entire audience who were all saying "Great idea!" or "That's my girl!" or "Take Fergie as well!" or even "By golly she's got guts!"

So, ***King DikHed and Lucky*** landed our Earth capsule along The Embankment in London, just a few metres from Albert Bridge. Lucky searched around for the hordes of press men who didn't turn up. In fact, nobody turned up.

We witnessed a completely dilapidated London, with everything in disrepair. Rusting bridges, crumbling buildings, no MacDonalds, no Coca Cola, No cars, no people and nothing created by man. It was wonderful! Lucky started crying on my shoulder as we sat on the riverside, watching the salmon jumping and the butterflies floating serenely through the wild flowers that had burst into glorious bloom as far as the eye could see.

We saw deer in their thousands feeding on the far river bank where a group of several hundred swans with their offspring was having fun. There were birds by the million from countless species thronging around us, chirping their stories to the wind and beyond. The air was so clean that we became intoxicated by its strength. Above all, there was no noise of mankind, only the beautiful sounds from Mother Nature.

"Hello, we are calling King DikHed and Lucky, are you receiving us? Is it safe for us to bring down the PISSOFF fleet?" I switched off the receiver. Lucky looked at me with sparkling loving eyes and spoke the words I was feeling, "Your Highness, how can we let mankind destroy Earth a second time?" I picked up the transmitter console and moved my finger towards the red self destruct button and.....................

Welcome to this new Earth World

Diana Head.

Chapter 14

Further Quotations from The Masters

The following are famous quotations selected to give my post graduates a feeling of conscience and obligation to make the world a better place.

Criticism increases geometrically in proportion with the time lapse after the event. Silence is the golden rule before this hindsight takes over.

Father Dunstable of the Stable (1267)

Honesty is a gift purchased by an expensive education and a handsome inheritance, used to buy the tool by which dishonesty is no longer required. No rich man can be dishonest; only guilty of creating envy which must be punished by a democratic government representing the wishes of the envious electorate.

Piento Gwynest (1974)

Charity is run by thieves looking for a quick buck for themselves and a dime for the poor.

Arthur Crookshank (1962)

If you live by the sword then you will die by the sword. The people of this democratic land believe in this holy command but the homosexuals in Westminster know better than God.

Boston Chute M.P. (1973)

A few men of generosity experience real satisfaction in life. All fully satisfied men know how to be mean.

Calvert Twist (1894)

We need a world war to bring back the understanding of love and kindness between all men. Between wars the blackness of greed and evil is far too powerful to be held in check.

Roger Constantine (1936)

Investing just part of our national wealth in the compulsory education of all children until the age of twenty five up to graduate standard in the subject in which they excel, would solve our country's problems within twenty years. Unfortunately, this new era of educated people could then never suffer our governmental system run by dimwits. Oh, well we can still dream.

"Polly puts the kettle on" Polly Randall (1978)

It is not the poverty in our society that is divisive, it is the different levels of affluence that lead to self pity and guilt.

Buckingham Palace (1991) Unidentified princess

Given the chance of a transplant operation, I would choose a brain from Einstein, Jagger's prick, Coe's feet, Hercules' chest and the Queen's bank balance.

Arthur Newfitt (1987)
(died of broken neck after wing transplant)

Where there's a bill, there's a way.

William Rhodes (1976)

If killing was no longer a crime, then murderers would be brought to justice without delay.

Lord Justice Eiforan (1964)

They work unsociable hours serving piggy rude men under dangerous working conditions for lousy pay - such is the life of an air stewardess in search of screwing all the pilots within the shortest period of time.

Protect Our Pilots Institute P.O.P.I. (1986)

A hypocrite is a combination of genius, sarcasm and wit bonded together to ensnare the easily offended man in a violent posture of self-defence seeking revenge.

Ernest Frederick Bacon (1865)

Pretending to laugh has become an accepted pattern of behaviour within the egotistic fool, presented to the rest of us to tolerate in silence. Life without laughing is more enjoyable for the individual but portrays you as an egotistic fool who should not be tolerated.

B.B.C. - "Drains of laughter" (1963)

The taller you are, the more likelihood of succeeding in business and losing sight of your balls.

"Tall Stories" Klaus Towers (1990)

Artificial stimulation of the human brain by modern marketing techniques creates a euphoric need that exploits our basic human instincts for a better way of life as perceived by our subconscious greed. The subsequent post euphoric depression requires constant feeding by further addictive marketing delicacies. Without this constant fix, the post euphoric depressive becomes yet another modern day aggressive individual living in isolation in his own hidden world. This steak and ale consumer now shuns mere bread and water, whilst whole nations in famine beg for the same.

Advor Teising (1987)
Helsinki Media Advertising Standards Institute

A government is elected to serve the needs and wishes of the people, but the people end up serving the needs and wishes of the government. The two are incompatible but the people are otherwise engaged with greed to have any time to object.

"Sutch is life" Lord Sutchcliffe (1861)

Conversion of our inner goodness into positive help for those in real need has no natural direction in which to move without working through an organisation. Once organised, this goodness is blinded by outside influences and dogma, too busy looking after its own self interest to give real help.

"Help Not Pity Please" Wilhelm Givanbitten (1959)

The modern world is far too busy making war, money and starving its peoples to witness today's miracles.

Cardinal Stalin (1976)

Being famous is easy and a thankful task; just shoot the Labour Party leader during live transmission time. This is described as justifiable homicide and a reward will be paid.

"Guns & More Guns" magazine (1990)

Lawyers project an air of silence and mystique during their introduction and an astronomic bill after you are dissatisfied. A close resemblance to being with a whore, except that the lawyer screws more professionally and you can offset the charges against company expenses.

"Old Bailey My Ass" Percival Pernot (1969)

Oh, I dream to be lying on a beach,
Cold rum and Cokes within my reach,
Loneliness lost in this world of sun,
Old and retired, my life just begun,
Memories so bright as a child and a man,
All now destroyed by God's fair hand,
Dearest son and daughter leave me in grief,
With two BMWs and a house in Tenerife,
Grandchildren unknown to a downtrodden chap,
Who is dying all alone in a poverty trap,
Please excuse my dreams of lying on a beach,
Love and luxury are now beyond my reach

"An ode to our heroes of war"
Anthony Witheringbury (1957)

I was born a working class buffoon,
Without even a magic silver spoon,
Attended the local cowboy school,
Left at sixteen, a communist fool,
Spent two years bumming on the dole,
Joined the army as my final goal,
Killed little kids for our Queen,
My God, how loud in death they screamed,
Left this slaughter as soon as I could,
Praying now for justice and for good,
If I can help just a small way to see,
Further hope for the needy and me.

Unnamed A Soldier of Salvation (1957)

Education elevates superiority but degrades sensitivity.

"Heated Arguments" Wilber Anthrocite (1867)

Manners are for the well mannered but rudeness is for the poverty stricken.

Chief Akbo Tepolermas (1990)

We'll decide about the war after I finish my round of golf - God help the enemy if I lose!

President Arthur (1903)

Laughing one's head off is a fate reserved for humorous traitors ahead of their time. A headless traitor is better than no traitor at all.

"The mint eating lamb" Pierre Mouton (1972)

A hole in one is preferable to castrating Hitler.

General Green (1943)

By talking with myself I am guaranteed to receive an intelligent answer. By talking to others I am ensured a headache and diarrhoea.

Wilberforce Hanworthy Edwards (1875)

I am a high class business executive,
Taking the best that money can give,
My importance must always be seen,
Including my suitcases glossy and clean,
First class tickets being part of the scene,
I am a high class business executive,
My suits must show a classy flair,
A few grey streaks improve my hair,
Pin striped suit with a real silk tie,
Electronic organiser with me when I fly,
I am a high class business executive,
Talking louder than the pleb rubber neck,
To be envied as a senior business exec,
Except by that bloody author Dick Head,
Who ridicules me from morning till bed,
I am a high class business executive.

"Executive Fears" Noddy Napps (1967)

Willy Wonker went to Mars in a beautiful pea green boat.

Clarence Cadbury (1987)

My name is Freddy the fox,
I live in an underground box,
Growing up was really good fun,
Until the hunting season had begun,
Red men with hounds chased us about,
My young fleeting legs avoided a rout,
Dear mum was less fortunate than me,
The pack chewed her up for their tea,
The red men cheered and blew the horns,
Left me in distress and my heart mourns,
Freddy's now an orphan at the age of one,
For what? So those red men have some fun!

Freddy Fox (1986)

Give me a country without race hatred and our world problems will evaporate. Here lies the fermenting nub of our crisis.

Jericho Vandervelt (1956)

Humpty Dumpty bought his wall from MFI.

"The truth about heroes" David Donovan (1963)

If I was planning ahead, I would choose brown hair, blue eyes, fifty sets of solid gold teeth and the Pope's hat.

"Carrots Galore" Janet Redhead (1956)

Some like it hot, the rest of us read The Times.

"Quaintly Done" Peter Duckworth (1959)

Dead heroes are remembered, live ones are plain lucky.

Major Pugwash (1946)

If the Queen shook hands every five seconds during daylight hours she could meet all of her subjects twice during her lifetime, have arm muscles like coconuts and sleep like a log with dirty hands.

"Say Hallo" Rapsody Randerson (1975)

If Super Brand X washed as badly as advertised then most shoppers must be arseholes.

Dazzoli Persillonini (1989)

Pansies look great in the springtime but look pathetic when playing mum.

John Smith XXI (1965)

Glasgow is a cultural paradise for one million drunks and eleven catholic football players.

"Glasgee iss Greeeeet!" Willie Tennents (1990)

An unskilled man is skilled at neglecting the skill of becoming skilled and he doesn't give a shite.

Ronnie Bucket (1935)

A shy German is arrogant; and apart from this one exception the remainder are unbearably arrogant.

Name and address supplied
(withheld for fear of retribution)

Our scientists will soon visit other planets where a virgin birth and magical tricks will lead another world into a history of bloody conflict.

Bjorn Sundell (1990)

Sulking is a deep thinking skill not afforded to happy folk or the mentally insane.

Ernstine Pithall (1957)

A bad penny is the one you've spent.

"From Riches to a Fortune" Randy Smith (1991)

A parrot should be stuffed and not heard.

"Polly put the kettle on" Jane Fontana (1929)

If laughing and happiness were to become a habit, habits would become a very rare commodity

"Give us a break" Warren Mitchelmore (1954)

An honest politician has the ability to solve the world's problems. A successful politician knows better.

"Truth is but a small sacrifice"
Ronald George Thatcher (1961)

The bitter truth is hard to swallow but preferable to choking on lies.

"The Citrus Grove" Larnica Liverus (1929)

Accounting for money's sake is a greedy occupation.

Count Proffeato Legia II (1843)

A good bribe reaches places where moral persuasion cannot reach.

Sonia Summerfield (1918)

Style breeds arrogance and is therefore the ruination of mankind.

Sir Allen Smartfit (1745)

Arseholism is an addiction reserved for the human race.

Crappy Stories" Ernie Bogface (1958)

Oh dear God, please help me to control myself,
Protect this shrunken body from any further abuse,
Such drinking, all day and over half of the night,
And yet, I'm only four years from my mother's sight,
With a shiny new car and so much money to spend,
I conquered all of this glittery world from end to end,
Total abuse destroyed all dignity and self control,
Encouraged by friends living out a similar role,
My dying is now with me, this day or very soon,
Oh dear God, please help me to control myself,
Protect this eternal soul from further abuse.
Amen.

Ruston Whitaker (1954)

Constipation is a hard thing to swallow.

Professor Suppositoria (1953)

Due consideration should be paid but not heard.

Lloyd Moneygun (1986)

Fishing is just angling for position.

Captain Hook (1856)

If I was a man on the moon,
I'd eat cheese with a bloody great spoon,
Made from milk from those flying cows,
Matured for ages in large square towers,
This poem may not be better than this,
But it's better than you taking the piss.

Benjamin Prikstead (1974)

Hope is a foolish conception.

Oliver Cromwell (1756)

Being a hangman gave me the chance of working with the underprivileged at close quarters.

Jack "The Rope" Crooper (1946)

One should never worry about relaxing but should relax when worrying.

Ostel Backwith (1756)

Waiting is a long-winded game not suited to the impatient.

Othello Zacharias Cambiaso (1534)

Peace of mind is a small price to pay

President Kennedy (1966)

Without a word of a lie, I'd like to save my head and piss on the queen.

"Royal revenge" Sir Alfred Pontwhistle (1983)

So far I've only been to New York; Christ only knows how bad the old one was.

Anthony Bramble (1964)

Nelson's column could never have been that big.

"Jealousy gets you everywhere"
Torbet Scheindigger (1937)

Frankly speaking, barracudas are preferable to my mother-in-law

Mervyn Crosby (1966)

Success for one individual is detrimental to several other folk.

Gabriele Mozzart (1876)

Plastic destroyed credibility.

Derek U Pont (1968)

A brain surgeon who breaks wind in public is a disgrace.

"A Cut Above The Rest"
Ronald Arthur Windermere (1967)

Arrogance leading to disgrace is like being a headless chicken with egg on your face.

"Cock & Bull Stories" Jimmy Bucktar (1961)

Business ethics have made me forget who my real friends are. By the time I remember, they no longer exist and I am alone.

Richard Kennedy (1931)

If malt vinegar was alcoholic, I would eat lots of fish and chips.

"Fast Food For The Masses"
Fred Andrew Gummer (1993)

Best friends are the first to be hurt by the truth.

Andy Jacks (1959)

A man in debt leads an interesting life.

"Life's Mortgage" Sammy Winters (1978)

Banks are the whores of modern society - they take all your money, screw you and leave you needing medical help.

Rodney Franks (1993)

Obligation is a personal honour; a natural gift available to all mankind and yet spurned by the majority.

Much Obliged" William Yu (1991)

Modern business has moved the line of truth to where lies look the same. This has the benefit of allowing ethical business to make profitable decisions with a clear conscience.

"The Power Game" Steven Wartburg (1986)

We are what we eat, and we eat crap.

Jack Witherspoon (1975)

German measles are far stronger than our own.

Doctor Humphrey Dawson (1989)

Every Labour party I've ever attended has served up stale sandwiches and cheap beer. Every Tory party I've attended has served up delicious food and expensive wines. For this reason I vote Conservative.

Sir Wilfred McVitie (1964)

Compassion grows stronger as the bones grow weaker.

"Home Made Glue" Rolland R Roberts (1957)

Logical thought is illogical to a man of dreams.

Ilia Positano (345 AD)

I sit and watch the people walk by,
So rich, so poor, no thought of the sky,
Deeply involved with both worry and love,
No time to consider the powers up above,
Tomorrow I see the green hills of Rome,
All love, just God and my very new home.

Cardinal Augustus (1834)

Two faced is not enough in American business.

"I Swam With The Sharks"
Rich D'Archangelo (1989)

Morality is obstructive in business.

John Peterson (1966)

I pour the wine,
In a glass that shines,
I sip the wine,
Whilst relaxing my mind,
I taste the wine,
Floating through time,
I swallow the wine,
Life is really divine.

Wayne Kerr (1992)

Today's loss is greater than my being. Today's gain is my reason for being. Both are destined to meet in paradise.

"Family Lost" Joseph Johnson (1912)

Author's Thanks

I hope you enjoyed these few masterful quotations which I created whilst away on my travels. Life is full of both humorous and sad things that bring you to the very edge of wonderment and despair. We should all try our best to help one another to help others.

Thank you for reading this second book of my *Working Man's Guide* series.

Richard Head

Chapter 15

DikHed Masters Exam

Verification of one's own academic success is when you are sure that you know what you know and not after you are sure that others know that you know what you know, so to speak, so help me God.

"If You've Got It Don't Flaunt It"
Barrington Edward Dewsbury (1933)

We've reached the stage in this book where I feel a little bit sad because I shall now be losing so many students who have risen up from their lowly and downtrodden lives to take up the DikHed challenge. It takes real guts and character to have come with me so far and I compliment every one of you, whether you pass the M.Sc. (DikHed) exam or not.

Barrington Edward Dewsbury was born in Bradford on 1 April 1706 as the son of Bertie and Anne Dewsbury. He was destined to change the way millions live today. His parents both died of small-pox when he was only twelve years old and he was forced to steal food where he could to survive in these hard times. Upon attempting to steal a freshly baked loaf from the local bakery, he was caught by the Jonathan Wetherby, a kind and understanding gent. Rather than cast him into the poor house, Jonathan offered Barrington the opportunity of learning the trade and become a Master Baker. With only two choices on offer, it was not surprising that he chose the dough.

With just this small sign of kindness, Barrington quickly took to his new trade and qualified as a Master Baker within five years of crossing paths with his mentor, Jonathan Wetherby. By the age of 29, Barrington became renowned throughout Yorkshire as a man who really knew his loaves.

When Jonathan Wetherby died, on Barrington's thirty-first birthday, all his worldly goods were left to him in Jonathan's will with the note, saying:

Dear Barrington,

You're a bloody thief, but a damn good baker!
Go out and help others as I helped you.
Deepest Regards

Jonathan

The rest is engraved into folklore, with the opening of over three hundred **Dewsbury Bakers Training Schools**, based all over England. Many of these schools have survived to this day. Within these establishments, boys and girls were taken in from the streets and given a new life and future.

Barrington cultivated that small seed that was originally sown by Jonathan. Over 90,000 people were given this new chance, which subsequently gave a better life to over **six million** people all told.

So much good from one little act.

Thanks for listening and good luck in your exam!

M.Sc. (DikHed) Exam Paper

Name:.. Date ....

Address: ....

Date of birth: ....

Sex: (**M**ale or **F**emale): ....

Marital Status: ....

Political Party you vote for (optional): ....

Why do you vote this way (compulsory)? ....

....

....

Support DikHed Club

Most of our graduates and post graduates are proud to belong to the DikHed club and due to popular demand, we offer you the following promotional items. All profits will go to a charity chosen by Richard Head.

The **EXAM FEE** must be paid in advance if you require your M.Sc. (DikHed) personalised exam certificate.

Order Details

Qty

........M.Sc. (DikHed) EXAM FEES & Certificate.............£15.00

........M.Sc. (DikHed) special one size tee shirt..................£10.00

Return all exam papers(with exam fees) and tee shirt orders to:

Londinium Press Limited, DikHed M.Sc., P.O. Box 102, Rochester, Kent, ME1 1NS.

DikHed 20 Questions

M.Sc. (DikHed) Multiple Choice Exam

All questions must be answered. Where appropriate tick the answer you think is correct. All students have ten DikHours to complete this exam paper.

1. Should we hang Lucky for treason? ....yes/no/maybe
2. Should we retain the monarchy? ....yes/no/maybe
3. Will you vote for Sir Dick Head?......................yes/no/maybe
4. What is your PepperKode (mark nearest) 5/25/9999999
5. Can you remember the longest swear word ......yes/no/maybe
6. Do you respect the EL-BIB Church?.................yes/no/maybe
7. Are you an expert on anything?.........................yes/no/maybe
8. Was Alexis the fisherman a fool?......................yes/no/maybe
9. Would you marry a penguin? ....yes/no/maybe
10. Are CHOCKER BLOCKS the answer? ....yes/no/maybe
11. Would you have a Tahl-Tan as a pet? ....yes/no/maybe
12. Would you like to be stuffed when dead? ....yes/no/maybe
13. Do you respect Humphrey Bogart? ....yes/no/maybe
14. Would you buy SOUP discs? ....yes/no/maybe
15. Do you think Luigi was simpatico?...................yes/no/maybe
16. Was Bandy Bill a shark? ....yes/no/maybe
17. Would you ride on a Big TIT? ....yes/no/maybe
18. Do you feel guilty for Larry?.............................yes/no/maybe
19. Are you using Polynoddydeutcholene? ....yes/no/maybe
20. Should I press that button? ....yes/no/maybe

See Also

THE WORKING MAN'S GUIDE TO THE GALAXY

ISBN 0-906264-09-x

Richard Head's first book in the ***Working Man's Guide*** series.

An absolute *must* for those DikHed students wishing to fully understand the mind explosion that has set Richard Head apart from other writers.

"A stunning novel that rips apart today's conventional thinking and has opened my eyes to a better world for all of mankind. My fellow passengers on a recent flight to New York looked at me sympathetically as I laughed like a hyena all the way across the Atlantic whilst experiencing Richard Head at his funniest, The Working Man's Guide To The Galaxy is truly the funniest and yet most serious book I have ever had the privilege of reading. A masterpiece not to be missed!

Reginald Jeffries

Editor's addition

Richard Head introduced *The Working Man's Guide To The Galaxy* with the following profound words. Although unusual, I find it appropriate to include these thoughts as a finale to his second book.

Writing a book is a personal achievement that involves great anguish and suffering which only the most foolhardy and dedicated should attempt to achieve. During the writing of this book I have been infected with an incurable mental virus that has led me onto a fool's paradise of disillusionment; a dark place better left alone by the silent majority.

This planet of sadness is full of disturbing conclusions relating to the endless cruelty of the human race upon itself. Cruelty as a physical activity of the barbaric mind is horrific enough, but is a mere slap on the wrist when compared with the mental cruelty dealt out by nations upon their citizens as a matter of policy.

If we don't stand up to be counted then where is the future for mankind?

Richard Head